THE RAILWAYMAN'S WIFE

THE RAILWAYMAN'S WIFE

a novel

ASHLEY HAY

ATRIA BOOKS

New York   London   Toronto   Sydney   New Delhi

ATRIA BOOKS

An Imprint of Simon & Schuster, Inc.
1230 Avenue of the Americas
New York, NY 10020

First Atria Books hardcover edition April 2016

ATRIA B O O K S and colophon are trademarks of Simon & Schuster, Inc.

The epigraph on p. ix includes two lines from "Poem of the Gifts" ("Poema de los Dones") by Jorge Luis Borges and English translation by Alastair Reid, quoted from *Selected Poems* by Jorge Luis Borges (New York: Viking Penguin, 1999, pp. 94–7) edited by Alexander Coleman. Translation copyright © 1971, 1999 by Alastair Reid.

The poem "Lost World" (pp. 183–86) was written for this novel by Stephen Edgar: © Stephen Edgar 2013.

For information about special discounts for bulk purchases, please contact Simon & Schuster Special Sales at 1-866-506-1949 or business@simonandschuster.com

The Simon & Schuster Speakers Bureau can bring authors to your live event. For more information or to book an event, contact the Simon & Schuster Speakers Bureau at 1-866-248-3049 or visit our website at www.simonspeakers.com.

Interior design by Kyoko Watanabe

Manufactured in the United States of America

10 9 8 7 6 5 4 3 2 1

Library of Congress Cataloging-in-Publication Data

Names: Hay, Ashley, author.
Title: The railwayman's wife : a novel / Ashley Hay.
Description: First Atria hardcover edition. | New York : Atria Books, 2016. | 2013
Subjects: LCSH: Widows—Fiction. | Loss (Psychology—Fiction. | Triangles (Interpersonal relations)—Fiction. | Thirroul (N.S.W.) —Social life and customs—20th century—Fiction. |
BISAC: FICTION / Literary. | FICTION / Historical. | FICTION / War & Military. | GSAFD: Historical fiction. | Love stories.
Classification: LCC PR9619.4.H38 R35 2016 | DDC 823/.92—dc23
LC record available at http://lccn.loc.gov/2015042234

ISBN: 978-1-5011-1217-1
ISBN: 978-1-5011-1218-8 (ebook)

For Les Hay

It's not what we forget
But what was never known we most regret
Discovery of.

—STEPHEN EDGAR

I, who had always thought of Paradise
In form and image as a library

—JORGE LUIS BORGES
(TRANSLATED BY ALASTAIR REID)

THE RAILWAYMAN'S WIFE

1

SHE SITS, her legs folded beneath her. The fingers of one hand trace the upholstery's pattern while the other hand holds the pages of the book.

It could be any day, any year: call it 1935, 1938, 1945, or somewhere decades away in her future. Perhaps it's the day after her wedding, the day after her daughter's birth, the last day of the war, the last day of her life. Whenever it is, Anikka Lachlan is reading, swallowed by the shapes and spaces made by rows of dark letters on pale paper. She wets one finger, not slowly, but absently, and moves it to turn the next page.

From outside, across the roofs of this small town, comes a sharp line of noise—a train's brakes and the squeal of wheel on rail, metal on metal. Ani looks up from the page but at nothing, and at nowhere, as if the room she's sitting in and the rest of this whole cacophonous world do not, at this moment, quite exist.

The sound fades. The silence holds. She looks down, and finds the next word.

2

THESE ARE the sort of people they are, Ani Lachlan and her husband, Mac. They are people who make a fuss of birthdays, people for whom no effort is too great in search of the perfect present, the perfect tribute, the perfect experience. Even during the war, when their daughter, Isabel, had asked—impossibly—for a bicycle, Mac found the bits and pieces to craft a tiny ornamental one, to see her through until a proper one could be sourced, and saved for, and procured.

And so in late 1948, on the weekend before Isabel's tenth birthday, Ani and Mac take the train up the coast to Sydney to find her next birthday present—she's asked for something magical. All morning they rummage in dusty shops near Central, until they find—in the last quarter hour before their train—a dull cylinder with an eyehole at one end and a round dome of glass at the other.

Mac holds it up to one eye, the other eye closed, and the kaleidoscope transforms the overfull shop into a series of mosaics. Now it's a stained-glass window; now a fan of Arabic tiles. Now it flares into brightness as he angles the tube towards the shop's open door. He hands it to his wife, smiling. "You'll love it," he says, watching her turn the tube, watching her transform the busy mess of the shop. Its drab brass looks heavy against the glow of her skin.

"Yes," she says, turning the tube to make another image. "Yes, she'll want this. She can make everything she looks at into something beautiful with this." No better present for their Bella. Mac pushes the coins across the counter to the old lady who stands there, wrapping the gift in a thick sheet of paper the color of a pale-yellow dawn.

"For a present?" the shopkeeper asks, tucking the parcel's ends neatly into themselves.

"For our daughter," says Mac.

"Turning ten," says Ani.

The old lady smiles. "So many ways of seeing things," she says, patting the paper. "I hope they are all beautiful, the things your little girl sees." And she wraps the tube again in heavy brown paper, tying its ends with string, like a bonbon.

Ani smiles in return. "You should see where we live," she says, touching Mac's arm while he packs the parcel into his bag. "Most beautiful place in the world."

Mac blushes, partly at the extremity of his wife's words, and partly because he loves it when she says this. Because he was the person who took her there, the person responsible for delivering her to this beauty. In a scratched and spotted mirror behind the counter, he sees them standing together, Ani a little taller, and fine, like the saplings that grow down by the beach. The paleness of her hair is so uniform that she looks as if she's been lit from above. And there he is, Mackenzie Lachlan, solid next to her, his head thick with hair that looks blond next to any but hers. Her reflection smiles, and he turns to catch the end of the real thing. That's what illuminates him, that right there.

In the shop's darkness, a clock chimes, and he grabs her hand again. "Train, love."

The shopkeeper comes around the counter, bows her head with her hands pressed together like a prayer. "Then a safe journey back to your home and your little girl," she says, standing by the door. They fly out to the street, past shop fronts, across roads, around corners, up stairs, and onto their platform. As they swing into an empty compartment, the engine gathers steam and lets out one perfect cloud of white, one perfect trumpet of sound, and begins to move off.

"We've got a good loco in front of us," says Mac, leaning over to watch the big green engine take a curve. "Home in no time—it's a thirty-six; nice run down the line."

Most beautiful place in the world. He feels Ani tuck herself between his body and the angular edge of the train's wooden window frame. The warmth of her arm brushes his own as he turns the pages of his newspaper and mutters the names of the countries in the news—Burma, Ceylon, Israel, South Africa, two new Germanys. By the end of the second page, he feels her heavy against him and knows she's going to sleep through this patchwork of suburban backyards, their clotheslines, their veggie patches, their hemorrhaging sheds. She'll sleep through to the slice of the journey she loves best, when the train surges through one long black tunnel and delivers her onto the coast, the northern tip of Ani Lachlan's most beautiful place in the world.

"I'll wake you up when we get there," says Mac. And she nods, squeezing his hand. She sleeps quickly, deeply, on trains, as if their rhythms and noise were a lullaby. He watches her breathing, feels the air from her mouth on his shoulder.

They cross the Cooks River, then the Georges, pushing south. Through the window now, thick bush rushes by, transformed into fragments and segments of trees, palms, grasses, birds, and sky as if they'd been poured through the kaleidoscope too. His eyes flicker and dart, trying to isolate a single eucalypt, the fan of a palm, and then they close. His newspaper drops to the floor as the landscape changes from eucalypt forest to something more like a meadow—almost at Otford; almost at the head of the tunnel—and her fingers, light, begin to pat his arm.

"Not often I get to wake you." She smiles.

"Almost there," he says. The engine is puffing and blowing, pulling hard, and the train presses on towards the archway that's been carved to open up the mountain. "Now," says Mac, taking his wife's hand. "Now," his mouth so close to her ear. They're in darkness, the sound monumental, the speed somehow faster when there's only blackness beyond the windows. And then they're out, in the light, in the space, in the relative quiet.

And there's the ocean, the sand, the beginnings of this tiny plain that has insinuated itself, tenuous, between the wet and the dry.

It's a still and sunny day, the water flat and inky, the escarpment colored golden and orange, pink and brown. As the train takes the curves and bends of its line, the mountain's rock faces become great stone monoliths that might have come from Easter Island, and then the geometric edges of some desert temple. Here are the hellish-red gashes of coke ovens; here is the thin space where there's only room, it seems, for a narrow road, a narrow track, between the demands of sea and stone. And here is the disparate medley of place-names—simple description, fancy foreign, and older, more original words: Coalcliff, Scarborough, Wombarra, Austinmer. And then Thirroul.

They pass the big glass-and-wooden roundhouse in Thirroul's railway yards—*Ani's favorite building* is how he thinks of it, although it's where his every working day begins. As the train slows, they're almost home.

The engine lets out a long whistle and pulls into Thirroul's station, its low waiting rooms set back from the platform's edge and the Railway Institute and its library on the opposite side of the tracks. Ani reaches for Mac's hand, and steps out of the carriage.

The air is thick with salt and ozone from the unseen ocean nearby. Arranging their bags, they begin their slow walk home, east towards the water, south up the hill, east towards the water again, and halfway along Surfers Parade. From the steps to the front door, the view is all mountain and water, while behind the back fence, and maybe a mile farther south, a headland rules off the space she's told him she regards as the edge of their world.

"A mile south of that pine tree, sitting in our yard like a pin in a map for X marks the spot."

"Then I leave the world on any train run to Wollongong," he protested once. "I go out of your world in the course of every day."

"Out of our world, yes, but you're very good about coming home."

When they first came, newly married and more than twelve years ago now, they'd climbed the mountain too, straight up the cliff face to the summit of the scarp, where they turned and stood, gazing east over the limitless blue.

"Nothing there," said Mac quietly, "nothing at all—until you hit Chile." The tops of the trees below looked like crazy paving, and among the grey-green of the gums were the odd cabbage-tree palm, the odd cedar, the odd tree fern an almost luminous green among the eucalypts, the turpentines. In late spring came extra punctuation—the fiery scarlet of the native flame tree; the incandescent purple of the exotic jacaranda.

They'd watched a storm come up the coast that day, clambering down the track in its noisy wetness, and arriving wild and muddy at the bottom. "I've got you." Mac had laughed, wrapping his wet arms around her. Then closer, quieter—"I've got you now"—and he held her fast with a kiss. She'd squirmed then, anxious at the embrace in the open air, and he'd laughed at her for it, hanging on. Hanging on.

Now, as Ani makes a pot of tea and hides the precious present,

Mac watches the sun set, remembering that kiss, that discomfort, and the messy embraces that came next. The shapes of the shadows, the colors of the world begin to shift and change towards nightfall and he longs for the gloaming, for one more walk in the wide dusk of a Scottish summer and an unexpected kiss in the braw open air. But it's too far away, the other side of the world, and too many years since he left. Kisses now tend towards the perfunctory, the habitual, with the occasional moment of surprise, spontaneous or remembered. It's just life, he knows, rather than anything particular or sinister. Still, he's glad for recollections, and the privacy of imagination.

From the corner of his eye, he sees a flash of color against the growing dark, and it's Isabel coming home from a friend's house by the shore. He whistles three times, twice low and once high and long, so that the sound slides back to the pitch of the first two notes. Even through the gloom, he sees her stop and steady herself before she whistles in reply. *It's power, to whistle your girl home,* he thinks, opening the gate and feeling her hug hard against his body.

The next weekend, on Isabel's birthday, after breakfast and the present, Ani slides the birthday cake into the oven and the family walks to the beach with the kaleidoscope. It's a clear morning, the sky very high and light, with a band of clouds, thin and white, tucked in beyond the ridge of the mountain. Isabel stands with the brass tube of her gift, changing the world with the smallest movement of her hand. "Like magic," she says, and Ani and Mac smile. She loves birthdays; the present, the cake, and always an excursion—a milkshake in Wollongong, she wants, and they've promised to take her after school, one day in the coming week.

"Maybe chocolate," she calls now, "or maybe chocolate malted. Or would it be more grown-up, now I'm ten, after all, to have caramel?" She dances circles in the sand around her parents, looking at this, at that, with her precious new spyglass while they head towards the silvery smooth pylons, the fractured segments of joists, that are all that remain of the old jetty, pushing inland above the line of the low tide and out to sea the other way.

"We should've given you a telescope, love," Mac calls to his daughter. Then: "Looks like there's someone sitting up there on one of the poles." And the three of them pause, peering ahead, the sun warm on their backs as they separate the shape of a man from the shape of the weathered wood.

"You know, I reckon that's Iris McKinnon's brother," says Mac at last. "One of the drivers said he was home. You remember, love—he's the one published the poem during the war. We took it round for Iris, do you remember?" He shades his eyes, more a salute than anything to do with glare. "Wonder what he'll do now he's back here? Not much call for a poet in the pits or on the trains."

Offshore, a pod of dolphins appears in the face of a wave, curling and diving as the smooth wall of water curls, and breaks, and surges in to the shore. Isabel laughs, and the dolphins rise up and jump and dive again.

"They look like they're on a loop," says Mac, "like something at a carnival, spinning round and round. And another!" he cries, as a dolphin leaps clear of the sea. "Always there's dolphins for you, my girl, but still no sign of my great white bird." Mac's fantasy, on every coast he'd been on: to look out towards the horizon and see an albatross, bobbing gently and at rest.

"Maybe for *your* next birthday, Dad," Isabel calls, whooping as another dolphin somersaults from a wave's sheer face.

On the top of his pylon, the poet has seen the creatures too, leaning forward towards their movement, leaning back as they plunge down into the blue.

"There's got to be a poem in that," says Ani. "If I was going to write a poem, I'd write about dolphins. They always look so happy—and it's always such a surprise to see them."

Mac laughs, grabbing her hand with one of his, Isabel's with the other, and skipping them all along the sand. "It's a grand omen for Bella's tenth birthday—that's what it is. Now, I want to pop home and try a slice of that lovely cake." And he starts to run, his two girls—as he calls to them through the wind—hanging on to him and flying across the sand like his coattails.

But as they reach the rocks and begin to climb up to the street, he pauses, looking back along the stretch of sand. What does a poet look like, up close? he wonders. Would he look different to how he looked before the war? Would you be able to see some trace of his occupation about him somewhere, like loose words tucked into his coat pocket? Mac strains to pick out the shape of the man's hat, his head, his body way off down the beach. *And how will he get down?* The incoming tide is roiling around the bottom of the uprights, white flecks of spray bursting as the water breaks.

"Do you not want your cake then?" Ani teases from the top of the cliff, hurrying him up. And Mac takes the stairs two at a time, breathless when he reaches the grass.

3

HE'D REMEMBERED as soon as he reached the beach. Way down at the southern end, tucked under the line of Sandon Point, there was the old jetty, its boardwalk fractured here, disappeared there, and its pylons polished to smooth silver wood by the coming and going of the sea. He remembered, too, that when he and Iris were kids there were trains running along it, across the ocean's waves, ferrying loads of coal to waiting ships. They would watch from the northern end of the sand, the distance reducing the engines and their carriages to tiny, shiny toys. That was years ago; by the time he went to the war, nine years back, the jetty was already heading towards the piecemeal forest of trunks and planes that he sees now. By the time he went to war, it was already a relic, a ruin.

This morning, it had come to him all of a sudden, the urge to shinny up the trunk of one of those pylons along the waterline and watch the tide ebb and flow from above. Back then, he'd never tried, but he's lighter now, for sure, and sprier too. He's seen the calligraphic dash of his own shadow as it runs alongside him and its narrow elongation across the sand seems dangerously accurate.

All right, he'd thought, *come on*—pelting along so that the hard sand reverberated with his footsteps. *St. Simeon of Thirroul, will you be, Roy McKinnon? Perch yourself on your pole and wait for inspiration?* And he'd set his foot against the vertical surface and pulled himself up, light as a feather.

"But there's nothing of you," Iris had said again and again over the first meal she made for him. And he explained how little eating he found he did now, how little eating, and how little sleeping. People used to tell him he looked like Fred Astaire, slender, and kind—although it was his friend Frank Draper who could dance like a dream. Now they used words like "scrawny" and "gaunt." And no one hummed "Top Hat, White Tie and Tails" when they saw him.

"We'll soon have you sorted now you're here," Iris had said, plying him with potatoes and gravy, which he arranged on his plate, and then left.

Balancing now on the pole's narrow top, he wishes he could believe her. Or, better yet, that the midday sun might somehow transform him into an extension of this tall, thin trunk, taller and thinner and subsumed into its top. And if he never came down? Surely that would be no less daft, in his sister's opinion, than opting into a war in the first place, or fancying yourself a poet in the middle of it, or taking three years after discharge to come home.

Where he sits now, up in the air, hoping to disappear into the clear light of noon.

From the top of the pylon, Roy McKinnon watches dolphins surface and dive like wooden cutouts in a carnival shooting gallery. Up and down; above, then below. He raises his right arm, steadies it, and points his finger. He could take a clear shot from up here.

How many men did you kill, Roy? How many times did you raise that gun and fire?

Out on the horizon, he sees a ship making for Melbourne, retracing the route that brought him to Sydney and here, at last, just the week before. For the better part of three years, since the war's end, he'd mooched around the farthest parts of the country, staying out of the way of people he knew, staying out of the way of his sister, her questions. There was a strange consolation in his parents' dying while he'd been overseas—if his father had faced him down and asked about numbers, he could never have refused to answer.

Coming back in '45, he'd bounced from Sydney out west to the unknown emptiness of a sheep farm, then down to Melbourne for a disastrous spell back working as a teacher. He'd known from the first day that he'd lost his place in any classroom. Everything he'd loved about the children—their optimism, their noise, and their unbridled curiosity—now rankled and pinched at his skin and his nerves, poking him into impatience and frustration and a final, awful fury. *The things I could tell you*, he wanted to shout above their perceived uninterest, or disrespect. *The things I have seen*. He'd walked out of that school yard and never gone back.

In Adelaide, then, he'd worked peaceably with a bunch of Germans making wine, thinking about the oddness of history. Then he went farther west, across the whole body of the continent, until he landed in the Western Australian wheat fields as a harvest was coming in.

He'd carried a notebook in his left breast pocket, the exact size and shape of the metal-plated New Testament Iris had made him carry through the war. But for all the things he saw, all the people he met, all the places he visited and the things that he did, he could never tease out a single line or observation to write down.

Messed up then, aren't you, buster, he thinks now, taking another shot at a dolphin with his cocked fingers, *if you can come up with poetry in the middle of some muddy bridgehead and not find a single sentence here?* He'd almost put his name down for one of the farm schemes for soldiers—it would be something, he'd thought, to have someone else etch out a plot of land somewhere and tell you

you had to make do with it. But in the end, he'd traced the edge of Australia from Fremantle around to Sydney, and caught the train down here, to Thirroul, to his sister's place—the closest thing to a home he had now, he supposed.

Back along the beach, on a verge thick with lantana, D. H. Lawrence once sat still awhile and wrote a book—Roy nods to the low bungalow every time he passes it. If Lawrence could write here, he figures, maybe he can too. *If it's not fancying yourself to put yourself with* Lady Chatterley, *mate.*

A wave surges up around the pylon, drenching his feet, his shins, his knees—it'll be a wet dismount, if he's going to make it home for lunch. He shades his eyes and looks north along the beach, past the place where Lawrence worked, past a sculptural outcrop of rocks, and beyond to where his sister lives, across from the council pool's pump house. He can almost see her, worrying along the edge of the sand, wondering what silly place he's walked to now. There are dozens more pylons stretching away from him and out to sea, some still topped with wide, wooden girders and the last of the railway line's rails; others bare and uncapped, pointing straight to the sky. *One day*, he thinks, *one day I'll run along here and dive out through the horizon.*

"And will you go for a job with the trains, then, Roy? Or will you try for a job in the mines? Though I suppose there's the ice works, or the ice cream factory, if you wanted something"—she had pawed at the air, perhaps looking for a kind word—"sweeter." That was with his dinner too, the first night he arrived. The anxiety stretched across her elfin face, making it sharper, more judgmental. He'd forgotten how inappropriate his sister could make him feel— so short, she made him loom large; so fine, his own thinness did slip towards scraggy; so dark, his own brown hair looked mottled. He'd forgotten how different they were.

"I don't know, Iris, I don't know what I'm doing. That's why I came home—here. That's what I want to find out." His fingers fiddled with the salt cellar until she reached across to settle it, perfect, in the middle of the table again.

"I just always think it's best to be busy."

Another wave surges up and he looks at his watch—midday, which he should have known, of course, from the sun. *Perhaps I don't pay enough attention anymore.* And perhaps that's the problem with trying to write, if he's walking around with his eyes shut.

He snorts: *In for a penny.* He's sure his sister thinks him mad—a seawater suit is only going to confirm it.

And it feels so good, so good to plunge down into the foamy surf—it's only just lapping his neck when he touches the bottom. The way his suit, his shirt, his underclothes press in around him as if he could feel the edges of himself more clearly.

Back on the shore, he's laughing with exhilaration, feeling in his coat pockets for the miracle of a shell or a barnacle to take home as a souvenir. If he were a cartoon, he thinks, he'd have a seahorse poking through his lapel like a boutonniere and wreaths of seaweed looping around his waist for a belt. And he laughs again, this tall, lean man made taller and leaner again by the tight wet fit of his clothes.

4

THE NEXT week, on the afternoon set for Isabel's milkshake, Ani walks up through the village towards the station—past the grocer's, the co-op, the haberdasher's and the hairdresser's, the café that sells fancy china, the two rival shoe shops. She glances along the side street towards the railways' roundhouse, her view of its windows—glittering like a rich chandelier—cut by a passing engine, 3621: she registers its number, its pedigree, as Mac would say, and takes a deep breath of the thick cokey air.

This place. Down the coast from Sydney, there's a point where the border of Australia's sheer sandstone cliffs pulls inland a little, and a tiny sliver of plain opens up. This is the bluff at Stanwell Tops where the trains' tunnel emerges. This is the bluff where Hargrave flew his famous box kites, more than fifty years ago now. Ani's always wished she could have seen one, soaring high and free.

The ridge heads inland, forming a line that sometimes mirrors, sometimes offsets and counteracts, the shape of the coast. And between these two lines, the water on one hand, the vast spread of the rest of the country on the other, a web of streets and avenues, groves and drives lace across the available land, held firm by the one road that feeds in from the north and out to the south.

And then there's the air, the nor'easters that play along the shoreline; the westerlies that dump fractious moods over the edge of the escarpment; the smoky drafts in late spring and summer that telegraph bushfires and then spur them on. There are soft sea breezes that tease and tickle with the lightest scent of salty water. There are southerly busters, powerful fronts that push up the coast to break open the heat of the day—they smell clean and crisp, and Ani pushes her nose hungrily into hot afternoons in search of their coming.

Reaching the bridge over the railway line, she pulls up short. A hearse is carrying a coffin up to the Anglican church, and Ani ducks her head quickly, her eyes down as the funeral procession passes. Don't turn to look at a hearse; don't count the number of cars following in its wake; touch a button after the hearse has gone by: her father trained her in these superstitions in the wake of her mother's early death—Ani was only four. Now, she touches her finger to the button of her dress, and runs across the road towards the station, where Isabel stands with her nose in a book.

My lovely little thing, thinks Ani fiercely, pulling her into a hug. She's quiet, Isabel, and careful—when she bounds along the beach with Mac, her blond hair flying, or follows his leap from a high board down into the pool, Ani can see the way she works at this playfulness, this exuberance, because she knows her father loves it. With Ani, just the two of them, Isabel has a stillness that Ani knows is not usual in a ten-year-old. And she knows this because she remembers it in herself.

Isabel smiles up at her, then down at the page, as Ani scans the width of the sky, the line of the escarpment against its blue. It's a happy thing to stand and to gaze—she reaches out without looking and pats down Isabel's end-of-the-day hair, and her daughter catches her hand and squeezes it without looking up.

The train is late.

"What flavor milkshake today, Bella?"

"Chocolate malted"—without a glance.

"Chocolate malted," Ani repeats, smiling—it's the full stretch of her daughter's available luxury.

Across the tracks a pane of glass rattles. Ani glances towards the sound and sees a window open in the Railway Institute's library. Such fascinating things, libraries. She closes her eyes. She could walk inside and step into a murder, a love story, a complete account of somebody else's life, or mutiny on the high seas. Such potential; such adventure—there's a shimmer of malfeasance in trying other ways of being.

She loves their trips to the library, loves the sight of their three separate piles stacked on Miss Fadden's desk—the family's collection of daydreams and instruction. Isabel always arrives with a list, filling it as best she can and asking for the librarian's assurances of happily ever after. But Mac loves to graze, weighing up the attractions and merits of different books as if he had really to choose between fighting off Mormons with Zane Grey's spry heroine or undertaking a secret mission with Hornblower in Central America. She loves watching him make his selection, as if it might open up new ways into his curiosity, his imagination.

"What if I kept some books at work, well away from your eyes," he teased her once in a while, "for a little bit of privacy?" Yet whenever she went to the library with him, she couldn't resist watching his hand move along the shelves, choosing an adventure with airplanes and jungles, dismissing another with cowboys and wagons. She'd seen him pause at *Gone with the Wind,* and move on to *Sons and Lovers.*

"What you looking at, Ani?" he'd asked, without turning towards her. "You know where my loyalties lie."

Next to the railway was a field, with men and youths playing football for their lives. When Mac brought her to the coast, she'd carried *Kangaroo* like a literary Baedeker, trawling its pages for identifiable spots, even recognizable people—against Mac's protestations that it was a novel, "a novel, love, that's made up, you know, made up, and years ago to boot." But even now, she shrugs. Here is the railway; behind her is the football—just like the book. This place belongs to Lawrence; she is living the next chapter of a famous story.

From the football field now comes a surge of chants and cheers, and Ani turns towards the noise. It makes her shiver sometimes, that open stretch of grass: effigies were burned there in the war—Hitler first, and then rough approximations of the nameless Japanese men who were thought to be coming to invade. A high whistle rises up and Ani remembers the air-raid sirens, the dark stuffiness of the shelter Mac dug in the backyard.

"Like being buried alive while you're waiting to be bombed," he always said, insisting on sitting aboveground, in the garden, so he could see if any planes came close. He'd been so certain of his own survival—his immortality—that she'd worked hard not to be anxious for him, out there and exposed.

Now, a short, sharp siren comes from the north—*Probably the roundhouse,* thinks Ani—and she turns away from remembering the war, and football, and Mr. Lawrence. Above the ridge, the clouds are inching towards sunset, morphing from puffy, fluffy white shapes that Isabel might place at the top of a drawing to something longer and more elegant. It will be a glorious show, firing the clouds with color while the greens and browns in the scarp and its trees drain towards darkness.

"You're for town, Mrs. Lachlan?" Luddy, the young stationmaster, is at her elbow. But as Ani nods, he shakes his head. "Sounds like there's a problem with the trains coming through—an accident along the line and they're not letting anything pass. Do you want to wait a while, or will I try to get a message to Mac, let him know you're not coming?"

Isabel looks up, her finger marking her place on the page: "My birthday treat, my milkshake . . ."

Ani frowns, tucking Isabel's hair back into its bunches again. She's been looking forward to it too—walking down Crown Street, looking at the shops, sipping her own tall, cold drink. She hates problems she can't solve, but: "I suppose you'd better, Luddy. Tell Mac we'll see him at home?"

And he smiles at her, nodding and tweaking Isabel's neater hair.

"Can we go to the beach then, Mum? Can we go to the beach on the way home?"

"We can, Bella. Still a bit of a treat. We'll go down to the rock pool, see if we can find a pretty shell." She holds her hand out to her daughter, who makes a great show of smiling and waving to Luddy.

The sun has almost left the sand by the time they reach its edge, Isabel flying towards the water while Ani bundles up shoes, socks, and bags and picks her way across to the rock shelf. Almost every day, she comes down to the beach, but nothing has ever taken away the surprise of seeing it. A country girl, grown up on the Hay Plains in the far west of New South Wales, the first time she saw the ocean was the first time she'd seen anything so big and so blue that wasn't a vast, dry sky. When she was married; when she'd moved to the coast.

Leaning against Mac, back then, on her first day in Thirroul, she'd had no sense that the sea would be so enormous. She could hear it; she could smell it. And she could taste it—it was salty, which she had expected, but it was sticky too, which she hadn't. And all of this had seemed so much bigger, so much more impressive than the wide stretch of its color, the vast stretch of its space.

"I didn't think," she'd said softly to her new husband, "I didn't think it would be so many things all at once."

He'd squeezed her hand, kissed her shoulder. "At home," he said, "it's mostly grey, but I like this color, this thick and briny blue." A wave roared at the edge of the rocks, and Ani had jumped back, startled at how high, how near, it reared. "It just wants to meet you," said Mac, laughing, "just wants to see who you are."

Now, in this late afternoon, Ani watches Isabel run across the rocks to the very lip of the land. A surging wave would no longer make her jump, and the tide is a long way out in any case, pushing a low burst of white water against the rocks once in a while. A crab scurries beneath a heap of seaweed that smells of pure salt; another scuttles under a rock at the bottom of a shallow pool. There are purple barnacles and tiny orange conches, striped shells and smooth rocks.

Overhead, two seagulls swoop against the blue sky, making their barking calls. Isabel barks back from the shore and the birds settle on the sand at a safe distance as Ani laughs, leaning forward at the edge of one deep rock pool. There's a clamshell down there, a beautiful thing, pearly silver inside and gold and rose-pink outside—colors that belong to pretty dresses, rich taffeta, and swirling dances. She pushes up her sleeve, dips in her arm, shivering. It will feel warm in just a moment. The strange tricks of distance and perspective—her fingers feel for the shell as deep as she thinks it is, but still wave uselessly above it. She inches forward and grasps the pretty shape.

The number of rocks she's taken from this beach in those twelve years; the number of days she's combed along its shore; the number of nights she's come down here with Mac. She closes her eyes and sees the two of them dancing along the sand in the weeks after the war, their eyes closed to the barbed wire that still looped its indecipherable script along the waterline. On those nights, if there'd been enough moon, she was sure they could have danced out across the ocean's marbled surface, and said so.

"You make me romantical," her husband had said then, and she'd laughed at the frolic of his words. He was many things, Mackenzie Lachlan, strong, and true, and hers. But he was purpose, and he was pragmatism—the moments of sentiment, of soft sweetness or high emotion, were exceptions, and she treasured them for that.

"What about this, Isabel?" she calls across to her daughter. "Treasure enough?"

She loves her daughter's careful attention—the paragraphs in her book; the shell cupped in the palm of her hand; completely considered.

"It looks like something precious," says Isabel.

"Like an evening dress?"

"Maybe, but a listening-to-music one, not a dancing one."

"I thought dancing and swirling," says Ani gravely, "but you might be right." She rubs at the colors, brushing the tiniest specks of sand from the shell's dents and pocks. "Home then?" And her daughter surges back again, butting in at her side.

"How long will it take Dad, if the trains are stopped?"

Ani shakes her head, the opalescent shell heavy in her pocket.

"Let's see," she says. "You finish your book, and we'll see how long it is before he's coming along the street." She holds out her hand to her daughter and they climb the stairs cut into the cliff two at a time.

The house is quiet and Ani, cutting vegetables in the kitchen, can hear the drumming of Isabel's fingers on the windowsill in the next room as she sits and waits for her father. She smiles, singing a soft lullaby in her father's old language in time to the gentle beat, its angular syllables studded with *t*'s and *k*'s and *n*'s. There are still no trains, and the silence is starting to ring.

Then: "Mum?" There's a tightness in her daughter's voice.

"There's a car at the gate." Ani hears her daughter shift, can sense her stiffen.

"Mum?" Isabel's voice is less certain again. "There's a big black car."

In the kitchen, Ani tries to stop the movement of the knife but the end of the blade nicks her thumb. She stares at the skin; just dented, she thinks at first, but then the blood comes and she hears Isabel say again, "Mum?"—and feels her pressing in at her side, against the table.

There's a black car at the gate. She's almost thirty-seven years old. Here is her daughter. Where is her husband? Her thumb is starting to bleed. The kitchen is very quiet and very bright, and Ani hears herself say: "Now, Bella, run next door to Mrs. May and I'll get you when it—when I—"

"But I want to wait for Da—" Isabel begins, and Ani hears her own voice, uncharacteristically harsh: "Isabel—so help me—I will not tell you again." The words scrape the walls like sharpness against glass and she squeezes her eyes tight as her daughter throws the shell hard against the linoleum floor—it shatters into five sharp pieces—and slams the door.

So this is what happens, thinks Ani as the front gate unlatches, the footfalls hit the stairs, a knuckle taps the wooden frame of the screen door, and the minister calls, "Mrs. Lachlan?"

She closes her eyes and sees herself lying next to Mac, nine years ago now, the day Australia's war was declared. "But what does it mean, 'Australia is also at war'? What does that mean for us?"

"Needn't mean anything," Mac had said. "They'll need the railways to keep running, so I should be all right."

"But would you want to go? Would you rather?" She remembered her father's friends trading stories from the Great War, teasing him for missing the fun, the adventure, and being stuck behind the ramshackle fence of some internment camp instead.

"Don't be daft, Ani love; leave you and Isabel and go off to be killed? They'll need the trains, so they'll be after us to stay—and I'm not the heroic type, now, am I?" He tickled above her hip bone so that she giggled and squirmed. "I intend to go on living—always have, and always will."

She'd grabbed his fingers, pushing them away. "But if Australia's at war, then we're at war, aren't we, you and me? Our melancholy duty, like Mr. Menzies said? We'd have to fight, if the war came here. We'd have to be able to kill an enemy. And there'll be dying, so much dying."

Keep us safe, she'd thought, over and over, *keep us safe*, through the next six years. As she watched women becoming wives without husbands, mothers without sons, Ani had an image of a searchlight sweeping around, illuminating this woman: widowed; that one: her son on a drowned ship.

Now that searchlight has found her, catching her in its sweep and pinning her, arbitrary and irrevocable.

So this is what happens, she thinks again—so distinctly that she wonders if she says it aloud. She presses a tea towel onto her thumb and walks towards the front door, the men, the news that the car has brought. The house has never seemed so long and at each step she thinks, *This is how I will remember this.*

The door at the end of the hall is her last hope: Ani on one side and the men, and the night, and the news on the other. *If I keep my eyes closed*, she thinks, shutting them fast, *perhaps I'll open them and find I've been asleep this whole time. Fast asleep and dreaming.*

"Mrs. Lachlan?" says the minister again. "Can we come in?"

5

FIRST CAME the knock on the window, and then the boy's voice: "Mr. Lachlan? Mackenzie Lachlan? Early shift."

Ani opened her eyes as Mac replied, "I'm here, I'm coming," and felt the bed pitch a little as he stood up. "Go back to sleep, love," he said then, without turning towards her. He always knew when her eyes had opened.

She smiled and rolled onto his side of the bed, feeling its warmth and reaching out to touch him as he pulled on his trousers, his undershirt, his shirt, and his coat.

"I'll stay awake till I hear your train, you know that," she said, her palm resting against his back as he sat to tie his boots. "And I'll see you at the end of your day."

And he leaned back then, turning so that she could feel his weight pressed down on her as he kissed her mouth, her forehead, the top of her bright, light hair. "The end of my day is when I come back to you," he said, kissing her with the last word. "Now go back to sleep—there's not even a bird awake out there."

She listened as he opened the front door and closed it again gently, listened as his boots made the front stairs creak, as he stepped over the last one, which was loudest of all. She listened as he went out through the gate and onto the road. And she tried to picture how far he walked before his footsteps faded.

It was early spring, 1945, and the war was over. The war was finally done. The night before, at the movies, they'd seen a newsreel of the celebrations in Sydney—images of a man dancing through Martin Place, spinning round and round. When the film had ended, and the lights came up, Mac had grabbed her waist and danced her out into the street—past everyone, past their smiles and their laughter. And on they'd spun, twirling and laughing, in and out of the puddles of streetlight, and all the way back home.

Now, in the darkness, she heard the train's whistle—there he was; off he went. And as she settled into sleep again, she reached out towards the place where he'd slept not a half hour before and sensed the sure shape of Mac's body against her own as clearly as if he were still there. Bright against her closed eyes, she saw that dancing man, spinning and leaping, an evocation of happiness, spinning into a line of light.

6

SLOWLY, CAREFULLY, Ani opens her eyes, but the men are still there, their hats in front of them like shields: Reverend Forrest, the minister; Luddy Oliver, the stationmaster; and a pale man in a dark suit who she knows, without asking, will be from the railways. She unlatches the door and holds it open, nodding at all three as they walk into her house.

"I'm sorry," she says, gesturing towards the shell, "I haven't had a chance to sweep that up. I'm just trying to get a meal ready for Mac." His name falls hard in the quiet room, and the men smile; three small, uneasy smiles. She says, "Of course you should sit down," sitting down herself. The brightness of that searchlight is unbearable.

"My dear," says Reverend Forrest, disconcertingly familiar. "I'm so sorry, but there's been an accident."

She says, "Of course." She says, "Do you need to tell me what happened?" Because whatever has happened, Mac clearly isn't coming home.

The room stretches as if her armchair has pushed itself miles back—a suburb, a desert, a continent away—so that she can barely hear the men's voices. An accident, an engine shunting—she concentrates on the shorthand of "engine"; Mac would have told her its full number, its every particular, rivet, and plate.

An engine shunting, and Mac had jumped down and gone round to check the coupling. They think. They're not sure yet—no one is sure. But there'll be an inquiry later, and the coroner, they say. The coroner.

What they are sure of is that an engine coupling with something—well, an engine coupling with *anything*—it exerts a powerful lot of force. And.

Their voices fall away to nothing. Ani doesn't move. She thinks, *How dare they bring this into my house? Mac would never have allowed this sort of thing to be said, out of the blue, all of a sudden, and at dinnertime.* She thinks, *If we'd arranged to meet him earlier, this would never have happened. We'd have had our milkshakes and come home together.* She thinks, *I did not keep him alive through six years of war for this.* She thinks, *There's been a mistake—it's someone else's man, someone else's husband, anyone's.* She thinks, *This throbbing in my thumb, I can feel it in my throat, in my forehead, in my stomach.* She thinks, *I yelled at Isabel, I said "so help me." I don't say things like that.*

She says, "I should make you some tea," and the minister stands up, touching her shoulder lightly, and saying, "No, no, let me—the kitchen through here? And what's this blood?" He peels the towel away from her thumb and stares at it a moment as if this might stem the flow. And it works. "You have to be brave, Anikka," he says.

Her Christian name—she's surprised he even knows it. *But perhaps*, she thinks, *you can no longer be called Mrs. Something when there is no Mr. Something. Perhaps you stop being Mrs. Someone when Mr. Someone stops being.*

The man from the railways is talking again. About the accident, about the injuries sustained, he doesn't want her to think of these, of course, but under the circumstances they will arrange for a cremation as soon as possible—it can be arranged for tomorrow, and he tells her this as if the arrangement is already in train. And, "You do not need to see the body, Mrs. Lachlan. You do not need to see the body."

From the kitchen, she hears the kettle clatter against the edge of the sink, its bottom sizzling a moment later as the minister puts it onto the stove. She hears the scrape of it sliding in towards the middle of the hot plate, hears the stove door creak as the minister opens it to add a little more kindling, a little more coal. She closes her eyes and sees the leap of the flames, and their lick.

"What a strange thing," she says at last, "when my husband can walk down to work one morning and be taken for cremation the next. It seems very—" She shakes her head. The rush of it; the rank implausibility.

"This is what we do, Mrs. Lachlan." The railways man leans forward a little, reaching out to stop her words. "The inquiry will happen later, but we organize the cremation as quickly as possible. I'll be there, and Reverend Forrest. But you do not need to see the body." And as he says this again, Ani finds that she cannot disagree with him, is not sure if she wants to, or even if she should. There is something hypnotic about the phrase.

"I'll be with him, Mrs. Lachlan." The minister is passing her tea in a chipped cup she would never offer a guest, very milky and, when she puts it up to her lips, very sweet. "I'll say his prayers." And she swallows, wondering about the pale-black tea, no sugar, which she usually drinks. Perhaps she isn't supposed to drink that anymore either. And this tastes surprisingly good.

Through the wall behind her, Ani hears the kitchen fire spit again in its box and closes her eyes against the image of her husband's body—muscular, burly, familiar—set among its flames.

"Tomorrow, then," she says. "Yes, I see. Tomorrow."

Of course they will organize the notices, the railways man goes on, and the minister will be ready to talk with her, whenever she is ready, about a memorial service in the place of a funeral. "Whenever you're ready, Mrs. Lachlan, just whenever you're ready."

And as they sit and watch her drink her tea, she tries to remember Mac's voice and fails. *Is that it? Has it gone?* And how long will these three men now sit here, watching the rise and the fall of her cup?

"We don't want you to feel that things will be hard now," the railways man says then, patting his hands against the air as if he is trying to soften his own words. "You won't be on your own with this."

"Of course I won't be on my own. My daughter will be with me." Ani wonders that the words can fit through her tightly clenched teeth. "Thank you for the tea." It's peculiar to be sitting in her own armchair, staring, wondering what she's supposed to do, wondering if there's anything she can say that will make it all a mistake that can be swept away, and Mac just home late for his supper.

Now Luddy is crouching in front of her, balancing himself with one hand on the arm of her chair—so close she can smell the sooty steam on him. She draws in a huge breath and the room rushes in across the continents, the deserts, the suburbs, and back to its normal size.

"This afternoon," Luddy begins. "I'm sorry, Mrs. Lachlan, I had no idea this afternoon. I did call through the message that you'd gone home. But of course he wasn't, of course he didn't . . ." He means to comfort her, to say something big and warm—she can see that. But his tears drip onto the carpet while she stares at her thumb, and then her hand's solidity dissolves somehow so she sees only the wet drops he's leaving on the ground.

"Thank you," she says. There are a thousand alternatives, a thousand other possibilities for what else might be happening in the world this night. And Mac is at the center of them all, walking along the street, whistling to Isabel, coming through the gate, food on the table, calling her name—"Ani." She smiles: *There's his voice.*

A sweetness, then, and she sniffs the air. "I've left the chops," she says. The smell of burning flesh is close and enormous; the stationmaster on his feet, the minister into the kitchen to pull the meat away from the heat almost before she's finished the sentence.

The railways man looks into the middle distance, his hands fiddling with the hat in his lap.

As long as I keep them here, thinks Ani wildly, *they can't tell anyone else what's happened. As long as I keep them here, as far as anybody knows, my husband is safely alive.* And so she sits, and she waits, until she can bear the waiting no longer.

"I'm sorry," she says then, "I'm sure there are all sorts of things that I should be asking and you should be telling me, but I think I need you to leave."

"Mrs. Lachlan." The railways man stands up, extends his hand—it's formal, like a presentation, or an introduction. "I'm so sorry to have been the bearer of this news. If there's anything we can do . . ."

But she shakes her head, follows them all to the door, and even thinks to send her wishes to the minister's wife, and the station-master's. From the corner of her eye, she sees Mrs. May framed in her own doorway, imagines Isabel pressed in behind her, wanting to look but not sure if she wants to see.

But where is his body now—right now? Anikka thinks suddenly. *And who will drive it up the mountain to be burned tomorrow?* Her mouth almost opens to call this last, terrible question across her front yard but then she sees the shape its words would make against the quiet night.

Impossible.

The noise of the car, its engine idling, is too round and warm to have brought such cold, hard news. Next door, Mrs. May's screen door opens slowly and Ani hears her call softly, "Are you there, love? Are you there, Ani?" But Ani's voice has gone and she doesn't know if she could have cried out, or stopped herself from falling, if Mrs. May hadn't come through the gate then to put her arms around her and hold her up. Saying, "Shhh," saying, "There," saying, "It's all right—Bella's inside."

"Shhhh, love. Shhhhh."

Across the rooftops, across the backyards, across the grass and the sand and the shoreline, the sound of the ocean is rolling and turning; for the first time in as long as she can remember—as long as she's been on the coast—Ani can't think whether the tide is coming in or going out. She feels a saltiness in her mouth, like a great gulp of the sea, and realizes she's crying. Quiet and awful crying in the dark, as regular as breathing.

This is how it will be, she thinks.

In the darkness, then, she sees something move against the flowers on Mrs. May's side of the fence, and she calls out, "Bella?" The girl is so thin against the night, slipping around, slipping through the gate, wedging herself in between her mother and the wall of the house. "I'm sorry I yelled before, Bella, but . . ." She shudders, appalled that she doesn't even know what to say to her own little girl, and can only let her head nod slightly as her daughter pushes close and asks one small, scared question.

"My dadda? My dad?"

The ocean rolls and turns, and there are stars above now, and a mopoke somewhere close in a tree, calling its own name. *I don't know what to say*, Ani thinks again. And then, *I've got to get the smell of that meat out of the house.* The awfulness of wasted food.

She stands up, Mrs. May holding her left hand, Isabel holding her right. "All right, let's go in then," says Ani. "Let's go in and see what happens next."

And as she pulls the wire door out towards herself, she hears the rumble, the growl of a train moving along its tracks.

~~

At the end of it all, she stands awhile in her daughter's room, watching her quiet oblivion. Every night for ten years, she's done this. *All those years,* she thinks now, *all those benedictions I made for your safety and your health, I was concentrating on the wrong person. I was protecting the wrong one.*

It's a nasty thought. She pushes hard at the side of her head to dislodge it.

"Beautiful Bella," she whispers, leaning down to kiss her shoulder. *You and me. You and me. You and me.*

From some deep crevasse in her mind, she retrieves her father's story about a rainbow bridge that spans the world of the mortals and the world of the gods. If she could find the right rainbow, her father had told her when she was young, she might skip along it to see her mother. But even in the wide space of the southwest, the beginnings of rainbows had been hard to catch.

"You only need one dream to slip along, Ani," her father had said, "one moment, and you're up one side of the rainbow and sliding down the other for the briefest visit, the shortest glimpse—but it's enough. It can be enough."

She smoothes Isabel's blanket, the next thought so strong, so vehement, that her hand shakes and her daughter stirs against the movement. *How could I not have known, not have felt it when it happened? I was on the platform. I was at the beach. I was slicing stupid carrots.*

"Mac?" she says at last, climbing into her own bed. "Where are you?" Outside, a few crickets are calling, and the waves are turning, gently and lengthily, below the staccato beat of the insects' sound. A world with no Mac.

The worst of it is how normal, how usual, how familiar the house feels—*But perhaps this is shock*, she thinks, *and some pummeling comes later*. It would be easier if some part of the house had collapsed, if there was some destruction to see.

In the corner of the room, she sees his socks, an undershirt, crumpled on top of the laundry basket, and is puzzled by the idea of washing them. His feet will never fill out that wool again; his torso will never stretch that cotton to capacity. She makes herself think these things, wondering how she should feel. She recites his name over and over in her mind, wondering how she might manage to close her eyes—or open them again in the morning.

"Mackenzie Lachlan," she says aloud at last, "I can't sleep; can you tell me a story?" The way she used to say it, when he was home, when he was here.

It's the darkest, coldest time of night, and her only answer is three dogs passing mournful barks between them as the night's breezes drop away. Aching with tiredness, her hands rub at her arms, creep across to her belly, up to her breasts, and she is thinking about the last time her husband touched her. Against any other memory she might find, here is this thing that was only the two of them—and she hadn't realized it was happening for the very last time.

She stills her hands, her body uninterested in their cold, tiny touch. *Never again*, she thinks. *Never again*. Somewhere deep in the center of herself, she senses that the decisions she will make tonight, tomorrow, in the world's next days, will govern and dictate what happens in what is left of her own life—she's never thought of that as a finite stretch before.

"No matter," she says, too loud and reckless. As if she will ever care what anything is or isn't again.

A car turns into the street and crawls past the window, its lights stirring up another dog and then the dog's owner, who yells, harshly, for the little bugger to shut up. Ani flinches, as if the command was a response to her noise, her words.

Rolling fast into the empty space in the bed, she presses herself—facedown and hard—into the space where Mac should be and can almost feel his firm, strong shape. A mattress spring twists unexpectedly beneath her sudden movement, poking so sharply into the softness of her belly that she recoils fast onto the other side of the bed, her tears distracting her from the urgent surge of desire she feels and doesn't want to.

The car's headlights move back along the street, the dog silent this time, and as they turn and head down the hill it's as if a little of their shine stays on, stuck in the tongue and groove of Ani's bedroom walls. There are birds then, here and there, and then one massed and raucous outburst.

The dawn is coming, a new day; the next day. She sighs, turns her pillow over, and is suddenly asleep.

Ani Lachlan sleeps through the washes of the morning's colors and the warm brilliance of sunrise. She sleeps in a world where she remembers, perfectly, every detail about her husband, this day, that sentence, another touch. She will remember it all in the deepest sleep, and lose it again the moment her eyes open and she wonders how late it must be for the sun to already be so high and then remembers, in the next instant, what happened the day before.

7

ON THE nights when he can't sleep, which is most nights, Roy McKinnon breaks out of his sister's shut-up house, silent as a thief, and continues the walks with which he fills his days. He's used to the tiredness by now—years without proper sleep will do that for you, and he can't remember having had a decent rest since he shipped out in 1940. He's used to the strange pliability of the time when most people sleep—the way nocturnal minutes can drag out like hours; the way nocturnal hours can collapse into seconds. If war was good for anything, it was good training for boredom; God, the waiting—the noise and the waiting. These things were never what you expected them to be.

He slides the bolt in the lower half of the back door—the half that creaks less—and pushes open its panel, ducking underneath and shushing the hens as they stir and mutter in their coop. It's too quiet tonight; he hasn't heard a train for hours, and as he thinks this, he hears an engine puffing up the line. What is it—nine o'clock? Maybe ten? Iris has been in bed an hour or more already, and most of the lights in the village's houses are already switched off. Roy shakes his head: do people really need so much time to dream?

Stretching up towards the stars, he leaps the fence and pads over to the council baths. He'll stay close tonight, he thinks; his legs don't have the power to stride for miles.

The surface of the pool rocks a little as if it's trying to level itself. It was beautiful here, before the war; its glorious underwater lighting turned the water into a pond of gold. No way they'd put that back—such extravagance, such luxury.

A cormorant raises its head from its perch on the lamppost, but nothing else stirs, and Roy settles himself cross-legged by the water's edge, trailing his fingers through the cool, salty water, and letting them hang, dripping, above the concrete beside him. Once, a couple of nights ago, he was certain he saw the letter *A* in one of these wet splodges on the pavement, and he'd walked through the hours till sunrise calling out every word he could think of that began with *A*, in case one of them sparked some inspiration. On the top of the hill in Austinmer, someone's window had rattled open and a man called, "For pity's sake, mate." Farther down, in the hollow below the station, he called, "Ascendant. Anastrophe. Atlantes"—and a cat called back in reply.

"Adumbrate. Aurora." Those two were particularly beautiful, he'd thought, shouting them as he passed the Presbyterian manse and imagined the minister and his wife sleeping peacefully inside. "Abatis. Ablation. Abulia." It was like the dictionary game he'd played in his classrooms, declaiming words, suggesting meanings, watching the younger kids struggle with the spellings, the older ones puzzle at the definitions. "Abulia: I think it's a flower, sir." And, "I don't. I think it's a country." In the dark night of some battle somewhere, he'd remembered a classroom of voices learning how to spell "accommodation," the way the letters came out naturally as a sweet and lilting song. A-double-c, o-double-m, o-d-a-t-i-o-n. He'd felt the beat, the rhythm, at the center of himself, and he'd sung the phrase out, over and over like a salve, until the firing

36

stopped at last and his world settled into another temporary peace.

He'd known that night, known that he'd never be able to teach a child a thing again, the weight of too many terrible stories pressing against his teeth, wanting to spill out across some innocent imagination, and too much fury and shock stored up in the muscles that used to guide children's pens across their first pages, or kick balls as far as a lunchtime field allowed.

Now, he brushes his fingers across the pool's surface and lets the water fall. Nothing. He stands, puffing out a mouthful of air as he looks across Thirroul's scattered houses. Maybe he will walk a little after all, and he sets off past the pump house and up the hill; he'll just nip round to Lawrence's place, he thinks, and then head home. But every light in the usually dark bungalow is blazing and Roy scoots away from the illumination. What could the matter be? Something wrong? Someone ill?

Why do you always suspect the worst, Roy McKinnon? There must be other people who don't sleep too—or maybe they're having a party. People must still have parties, he expects, although he can't recall having been to one since 1939.

He'd like to set up a fraternity for his fellow insomniacs. There were doctors in the war who said that the worst cases of shock and hysteria could be cured by nothing more than a good night's sleep. He remembers reading about it—it sounded so improbable. Exhausted air-raid and fire wardens were hypnotized into a restful sleep, he'd read, from which they awoke the next day *refreshed and able to carry on.*

He'd spent the next dozen nights or so swinging his own watch in front of his eyes.

He turns along Surfers Parade and a gust of wind buffets him from behind; he imagines himself for a moment surfing along this aptly named street, carried forward over its topography, floating and free. He always meant to try surfing when he was a kid—there must be such freedom, such poetry in gliding across the water's surface on a big, wooden board. But the boys who surfed all knew what they were doing—there were competitions and carnivals—and Roy could never get up the courage to walk into the water and fail in front of their experience.

He surges forward, running now, with his arms out like he remembers a surfer's stance to be. Maybe his missing words are etched farther out on the deeper water—he'll hunt around for a board to borrow tomorrow, old enough now not to care how he looks.

The wind pushes him again and he leaps, stumbling as he hears a woman's voice, low and dreadful, coming out of one of the darkened houses. He stops, counts along. Was this the Mays' place or the Lachlans' place? He remembers Mackenzie Lachlan from the railways, from the football. Must ask Iris if they still live there—or if his counting, like his memory, is out.

Standing in the shadow of an oleander, he leans in towards the noise, its despair, its totality. *If it is the Lachlans', is that Mrs. Lachlan?* He has a faint memory of someone tall and slender, standing very still beyond the rush of a game, with blond hair, he thinks, that lit up under the sun. Someone quiet, contained; it's not an image he can match to this terrific noise.

The sobbing breaks off; there's a cough, then the rattle of a window sash. Roy sees the backlit shape of someone for an instant and senses a pair of hands tearing at hair, perhaps even at skin, it seems, before he darts on past the front of the house and along the street. Not wanting to be caught spying on whatever enormity is playing out inside.

Glancing up at the stars as he turns down the hill, he sees one shoot straight from the west towards the ocean. And he watches it fade, wishing that whoever is crying like a demon in the weatherboard house behind him might sleep long, and sleep well, and sleep soon.

8

"MUM?" ISABEL'S voice sounds far away, but urgent. "Mum? The car's back—those men have come again. Reverend Forrest and the man from the railways. Mum?"

It's three days, maybe four, beyond the accident—Ani has trouble distinguishing them—and as she pushes herself up out of sleep, the memory of Mac hauling himself over the edge of the swimming pool comes to her through her own movement. All the strength, all the push of his arms as he levered himself out of the water, back into his body's weight, and up onto the concrete ledge of the wall; her own wrists feel thin enough to snap.

"Bella? Are you all right? I'm sorry, darling, I must have been sleeping." She takes Isabel's hand and pulls herself up, surprised to find she's been asleep, surprised to find herself outside, in the backyard, on the grass.

"Reverend Forrest's here again, Mum, and I think it must be that railways man. They're on the porch—I didn't know if I should ask them in. But I can make some tea, if you like, if you wanted."

Ani nods, rubbing the grass from her hair. "You do the tea,

Bella, that would be lovely. And I'll see what they want this time."
She leans down to kiss the top of her daughter's head.

But it's strange, sitting in the dim space of the living room—
Ani wonders if she's awake at all, or still dreaming outside, as she
catches at fragments of her visitors' words. As the minister talks
about a memorial service, how many people would like to pay
their respects, she hears her own voice ask if it might be better not
to have one, if she'd rather not be able to remember what her husband's memorial was like.

"Just a hymn or two, Mrs. Lachlan, and perhaps a reading," says
Reverend Forrest. "It needn't be long. But I think you will regret
this if you don't do it. So many of the ladies in the village have asked
if they might provide flowers."

And she hears herself demur and say she'll think about it,
she'll see.

The other man speaks then, as Isabel comes in with the teapot.
"Whatever you decide, Mrs. Lachlan," he says gently, "the railways are very concerned that you know you needn't worry about
your future. There's a compensation payment for the accident,
of course—and also in this instance it's been suggested that you
might take a particular job with us: perhaps you know the library
of the Railway Institute, down at the station? Our librarian is about
to retire, and it's been suggested that you would be ideal for the
position." And he recites the hours, morning and evening, the pay,
the facilities—a heater, a piano—the duties and tasks she'd need
to fulfill.

She watches Isabel stir the leaves in the pot. An evening shift
would change their meal, their bedtime. An evening shift would
change the way their family worked. *So everything changes when one
thing goes*, she thinks, reaching for a teacup to pass to the minister
and hissing as a drop of the hot liquid sizzles against her skin.

The idea of a job: she'd asked once at the pictures if they ever had an opening for someone selling tickets or ice creams, but the manager had laughed and said he'd a brace of daughters and his own wife for such a thing, and couldn't see he'd want anyone else's. As for any of the other places she might have approached—the rubber factory, the nicer ice cream one down south, or an office job with the brickworks, or a shop—it was all shifts and lines and tasks she couldn't quite imagine.

"What do you want that bother for, Ani?" Mac had said. "We're all right as we are—bit of care, now and then, with the shillings, but we come through each month."

The more capable she felt in her own house, her own world, the more she wondered if she'd be any good in the wider space of anyone else's. And so she'd made her home and nurtured her family, polishing the good fortune of her circumstances in her mind as she crafted a pretty quilt, folded a clean sheet, kneaded a good dough, or planted out a garden bed in spring. It was, she told herself, enough, and she relished her life's small pleasures.

But: "It would be nice to have books coming in boxes again," she says at last, reaching for the cup again and steadying its saucer against her hand's unexpected shake. "When I was growing up, out west, our books came in boxes from the city. My father ordered them and they came in consignments. So that would be nice. The piano . . . I don't . . ."

"No, no—it's just part of the institute's facilities," the railways man interrupts her as if he can countenance any objection. "Nothing for you to worry about other than taking the occasional booking for people who'd like to use it."

Ani nods. "All right," she says, with what she hopes is a reassuring smile for Isabel. "But I might not be very good at it—I've never done anything like this before." She passes the biscuits to the two men, to her daughter, letting the rush of the job's details wash over her—who she needs to meet at the institute's library in Sydney;

how opportune it is that the local librarian will be retiring in just a week or two's time.

"What about after school?" says Isabel quietly. "What about my dinner?"

"We'll work something out, Bella, we'll have to. This is how things have to be now." Ani's fingers are clenched so tight around the handle of her cup that she expects it to break in two. She feels Isabel press in against her side and hug hard as the men stand to leave.

"And we'll see you back in Sunday school soon, little one?" says Reverend Forrest, patting Isabel's hair.

"I'm ten now," she says, "ten last week. I'll be able to get my own job soon."

"It's all right, Bella," says Ani, holding her close as the men drive away. "We'll work this out. Maybe you can come with me, or have tea with Mrs. May. There's always a way. Come on now," she soothes with a calmness, a certainty she doesn't feel.

There isn't any other way it can be.

Isabel rubs her eyes, stepping back. "I think I spilled tea on your birthday card," she says at last. "I was making it on the kitchen table this morning and I couldn't get the teapot lid to go in properly."

"Shh," says Ani, pulling her in again. "You're lovely for even remembering my birthday." They stand a moment, swaying back and forth. "I'd forgotten it myself."

From inside the hug, she hears Isabel say, "The trouble is, Dad was in charge of the present—and I don't know where he's hidden it, or even what it is. I wanted . . . I wanted . . . I thought I could use my Christmas money and ask Mrs. May to get you something, but I couldn't get the stopper out of my money box, and . . ."

And Ani starts to laugh—the first time she's laughed in days. "You're lovely, Isabel Lachlan," she says, squeezing her so it almost hurts. "And a card is all I need, even if it is a bit splotchy. But come on, let's see if we can think where your dad might hide a mystery present."

Because it must be here, somewhere in the house; maybe already wrapped, and tucked into or under something that Ani would never think of disturbing. Isabel darts into corners and cupboards—the back of the chiffonier where the special glasses are kept; under the sofa; behind the horsehair couch.

"I know!" she calls, running towards her parents' bedroom, but Ani is already there. The tallboy's doors make a squeaky protest, the drawers, always stiff, a little stiffer for not having been opened for a few days. She pulls out piles of underwear, socks, but there's nothing in the first drawer, or the second; nothing tucked into the shelves; nothing pushed to the back under the rack of hanging shirts.

She tries the closet, the nightstand, the low table beside the bed that still holds the book Mac was reading, its pages pried apart by the larger yellow-bordered shape of a *National Geographic*. A layer of dust has settled around them already: Ani watches as Isabel makes a line with her finger, then another perpendicular to the first, so that the two stripes form an X. But there's nothing in the little table either.

"No X marks the spot," Ani says. "Never mind. Maybe we'll have an epiphany about it tomorrow. Now, we should have something to eat."

But she finds herself standing still and purposeless in the middle of the kitchen, her fingers patting the cover of her husband's last book.

"Will everybody know, Mum?" says Isabel, breaking her reverie. "When I go back to school, will everyone know what's happened? Will I have to talk about it?"

Ani props the book against the teapot, like a marker or a shrine, and sits down with her daughter, taking her hands. "Of course people know—you know that, Bell. That's why they're bringing us all those stews, all that soup." The endless provisioning of their doorstep. "But mostly they'll just want to say they're sorry. Or they might ask you what happened, and you can say you don't really know."

Opposite her, Bella pulls her hands free and picks up her pencil, working hard at the blue sky of her picture, her mother's name spelled out in letters made of clouds. "I was thinking," she says at last, "how all the dads who died in the war will get their names carved into the war memorial. And I was wondering where my dad's name will be carved."

"I think it's up to us to remember your dad's name, love," says Ani, reaching over for her daughter's blunt blue pencil and whittling its end back to sharpness with a knife. "We're his memorial, I suppose."

And Ani's gone again, into that silent, timeless space of inertia, of loss, of dislocation.

"Mum," says Isabel quietly. Ani has no idea how much time has passed. "Mum! You'll hurt yourself—you're chewing your lip."

And Ani feels herself blush, like a naughty child caught out.

"Ah, Bella," she says then, "I shouldn't be watching you make this card—it should be a surprise for the morning." She kisses her daughter once more on the top of her head and goes back into the yard, to lie on the grass, and to wait.

9

"WHAT WILL it be for your birthday then, lass?" The two of them, at work in the garden, on a warm spring afternoon.

"Oh, nothing, Mac. Nothing now." October 1945, two months of peace. What could you ask for on top of that?

"There must be something we can get you, something we can try to find now that the world's supposedly back to normal." Mac laughed at the hollowness of it.

"There is one thing I'd like," said Ani at last, twisting at the tight root of a dandelion, "but I think it will stump even you, Mackenzie Lachlan."

"Try me."

"I'd like to see snow, like my father talks about. I'd like to see white mountains and I'd like to feel their cold." And she wiped the sweat from her forehead, laughing.

Mac leaned on the shovel. "No challenge at all," he said promptly. "I know just the thing—and Bella's going to love it."

～

Look at her, Anikka Lachlan, swirling around on the silky-smooth ice of the Glacarium, her husband surging ahead of her holding one hand, her daughter behind her, holding the other. The air was cold from the ice on the floor and the great ice works in the basement below. And at the front of the giant hall, the walls were bright with a huge mural—an Alpine scene, high craggy mountains, vast cerulean sky.

Around and around, gliding and gliding; wanting to put her arms out to fly. Her husband in front of her, her daughter behind. Around and around through a whole afternoon.

At the end, as they stood on the street with cups of hot chocolate, the air exploded with the sound of bells—"The carillon, at the university, I think, up along Broadway," said Mac.

And Ani laughed. "There should always be bells." Bells for celebration; bells for jubilation. "Happy birthday to me."

Happy birthday.

10

THE MORNING of Mackenzie Lachlan's memorial is clear and bright, capped by an impossibly vast sky. The ocean is calm, its blue as consistent as a wide watercolor wash. A breeze plays with the shapes of the grass, of petals and leaves, and it must be up on the mountain too, because when Ani tries to focus on the trees that mark the escarpment's edge, they're blurred, furry, as if they'd been drawn by a thick lead pencil and then half rubbed out. Yet the air feels still, *stable*, she thinks, like something against which she might test her weight. Her hand moves for milk, for sugar, as it has these past days, to add to her tea, but she draws it back and so takes her tea black, weak and black, the way she used to drink it. The way Mac would know to make it. This morning, for the first time, she woke facing the window, her body turned towards the light, as she always used to, rather than facing the empty space in the bed beside her. This morning, she thought about staying away from the service, as if avoiding its memorial might make Mac more alive.

"You could borrow this, Mum." Isabel is at her side, offering her the brass tube of her birthday kaleidoscope. "You said it was good for seeing things differently."

And Ani smiles, taking it from her and training it on the view over Thirroul. "Perhaps we can share it," she says as the view she's been studying rearranges itself into repeated lozenges of color. She knows she's looking for Mac in the corners of its movement.

And what would Isabel think of staying away from the church?

"What was the last thing Dadda saw before he left Scotland? What was the first thing he saw when he came here?" Isabel asks her questions without pause, and Ani smiles again, but faintly. These are not things she ever thought to ask, and now, of course, she can't.

"Your dad said good-bye to his grannie up in the Highlands and walked away without turning back to wave—he'd promised her that. He took a ship from Glasgow and went through the canal at Suez. Do you remember the stories he used to tell when you were tiny and sitting on the beach together? He'd bank the sand up along one side of you, fold up a little paper boat, and sail it through the sand. That was Suez, he said. Do you remember that?"

Isabel shakes her head, picking at a scab on her knee. "I remember he said he was seasick for a week and that the first night he went up onto the deck he nearly keeled over from the number of stars. And that he sat there and tried to count them all."

This is not a story Ani has heard. "Did he say how many he counted?" She herself has sat with Mackenzie Lachlan, counting the stars, and it feels strange to feel jealous, now, at the thought that he might have counted more on his own, somewhere earlier, somewhere else.

"Two thousand and fourteen," says Isabel. "More than Dad and I counted when it was the war and all the lights had to be off. Remember that, Mum? Remember how late I was allowed to stay up?" Ani shakes her head as Isabel frowns. "But you were there—you must have forgotten. You did have that horrible cold." She takes the kaleidoscope from her mother and points it at her scabby knee, grimacing at the repeat of its image.

"There's an anxious space," says Ani, stilling her daughter's fingers as they worry again at the scab, "between not knowing if you've forgotten something or if you never knew." They will eat their breakfast, put on their best clothes. They will go to this service for a husband, a father. *I do not want to be fifty or eighty or a hundred, wondering if I've forgotten my husband's memorial or if I never knew about it.* "Come on, Bell. Let's have some porridge—'It'll stick to the ribs,' as Dad would say. Let's get ready to face the day."

~

The white wooden church is mostly full and the organ is wheezing when Ani and Isabel arrive. The two Lachlan women, their blond heads caught by sun as they walk along the aisle towards the space where a coffin should be but isn't. It hasn't occurred to Anikka, until now, how awful that emptiness will be. *He has been cremated a week.* She makes herself think it as flatly as she can. *His body is burned, his self gone.* They're injurious statements, like Isabel picking at her scab to keep it weeping.

Walking between the rows of pews, Ani feels the tight freeze of her face's expression, somewhere above a smile, she hopes, but she's tricked herself into thinking she was smiling before and seen her mouth set hard and unwelcoming in a mirror or a window. She looks through the women she passes: Mrs. Padman, Mrs. Bower, Mrs. Floyd—all war widows. Ani remembers how Marjorie Floyd had howled when the news of her husband's death came, howled in the darkness, and then rocked, back and forth, singing him a lullaby. *How strange,* thinks Ani, *that we're here together to mourn my husband.*

She has met each woman, and many others, in the village in the past days, required each time to deliver a telling of Mac's accident, of hearing its news. Three, she discovered, three was the magic number: by the third telling each day she could hear the phrases that worked, the ones that moved the narrative fastest. By the third telling the story felt more like a story, rather than something she was being required to live.

On the end, sitting slightly apart, Iris McKinnon, whose brother, the poet, was the man on the pylon. "It's never what you think," she says, reaching up to touch Ani's arm as if to brush at a speck of dust. "But the living goes on, it always does." And she smiles as Ani ducks her head and blinks.

Once, long ago, she'd described her mother's death to Iris McKinnon—described herself as four years old, uncertain of why her mother had gone away, or where, or for how long. And Iris had leaned forward and patted her arm. *Time heals all wounds*, she'd whispered, and Ani had found herself pulling away so fast her body almost shuddered. *No*, she'd thought, so loud she wondered she hadn't shouted it. *No no no*. Not all of them, not always. There were some things you carried and carried, and now, she is willing this to be one of them.

The organ's notes rearrange themselves from the Twenty-Third Psalm to "Rock of Ages" as Ani follows Isabel into the front pew, thinking about the supposed balm of Iris McKinnon's time. She feels a hand on her shoulder and glances around: the stationmaster, Luddy. She sees shopkeepers, train drivers and engineers, and firemen—even Bella's teacher, tucked away at the back. There's a man sitting next to him, obscured as he reaches down for his hymnbook. But as he straightens up, Ani catches a glimpse of strong shoulders in a dark suit, a ruddy cheek, and speckled-blond hair. *It's Mac*, she thinks quickly, and, *so good that he could get away from work and be here after all*. And her mind lets her hold the illusion for almost a second before she realizes where she is, and why, and that the man she can see is nothing more than a random approximation of familiar shapes and colors. She tries again to smile.

Along the church's north-facing wall its windows are set with panels of colored glass—rose, blue, yellow—alternating along the length of the building. And as the minister speaks, as the readings are read, as the hymns are sung, as heads are bowed and raised again with *Amen*, Ani keeps her eyes on a patch of sunlight coming in through one yellow pane. It inches closer and closer to the place where the coffin should stand, solid and definite. She registers her own name, and Isabel's, in the minister's eulogy. She registers the reading from Corinthians that she loves—*For now we see through a glass, darkly; but then face to face.* She registers the thin-sounding congregation voices that sing, never quite coming into a hymn at the right moment, and with one female voice always rising above the others, trying for a descant. In all her years of sitting with Mac and Bella in this church, she's never identified that aspirant soprano.

The sun inches forward, marking out a perfect rectangle on the carpet. *There he is; there's his resting place.* She swallows hard. *I should have gone to see the flames and the smoke. I should have insisted they take me.* She winces at this and feels Isabel's hand on her knee.

". . . And may the grace of the Lord Jesus Christ, the love of God, and the fellowship . . ."

And then she is a little girl, four years old, watching her father watch her mother's coffin being lowered into the ground. She will never forget the hollow sound of dirt hitting wood when her mother was buried, the look of shock, of distaste and revulsion, that shot across her father's face.

Somewhere close by, she hears Mrs. May talking quietly to Isabel as her daughter moves up the aisle with their neighbor. She hears voices on the porch, and outside, which fade a little as people take their leave or move over to the hall. She hears the rustle of the minister in the vestry. She hears a bus rattle past on the road. Standing carefully, she kneels down and touches the floor's wood where the sun has warmed it.

"Mrs. Lachlan?" The minister is crouching beside her. "Anikka?"

She nods, her fingers moving slowly across the wood as if she were picking out a scale on a piano or counting a clock's chime.

"There are refreshments in the hall, when you . . ."

"Thank you," she says. "I think Mrs. May has already taken Isabel." She looks up carefully. "I will come—I just wanted . . ."

"Take your time, Mrs. Lachlan. No rush, there's no rush at all," he says, patting her lightly on the shoulder as the stationmaster had.

This is how you touch grief, she thinks, watching as a single tear hits the floor and sits domed on its shiny surface. *How long before it soaks in? How long before it disappears?* She has no idea how long she stays there, wondering. She has no idea how often such stillness will come.

"Ani, love? I've brought you this." Mrs. May is holding a cup of tea, a huge scone wedged onto its saucer. "You don't have to do this all on your own."

Ani takes the tea, staring at the size of the floury scone. "Thanks for taking Bella," she says. "I'll come in a minute—I just . . ." She shrugs.

"You take your time, love; I'll keep her busy with the sausage rolls. Always good to have something hot after a funeral—I'll try to keep a couple by for you."

Breaking the edge off the scone, Ani winces at the flurry of crumbs that fall like snowflakes on the pew and the floor beyond. She eats a little—it's still fresh from someone's oven—and then a little more. Mrs. May is right about hot food. Gulping the tea, she tries to sweep up her mess, kneeling down on the floor in front of the pew and brushing at the crumbs with her hanky. Her other hand touches the sunlit space again, and she feels its warmth against her skin, wiggling her fingers in its brilliance.

The magic of light through glass: when Mac got his job on the railways they sat with his guard's lamp lit between them on the table in her father's kitchen, flicking the lens from red to green and back again.

"A shame you can't get other colors," Ani had said. "Blue would be nice—it's how I imagine looking up through the ocean to the sky."

He'd flicked the light back to green so the room glowed with strange, arboreal shadows. "That's how it is, lass, that's how it is," he'd said. "And now I've a beacon for you to find me by."

In the church, remembering this, Ani watches as the sunlight traces the earth's turn to fold over the altar steps, across the communion rail, and on towards the pulpit.

"Where are you, Mackenzie Lachlan?" she whispers. "Where can I find you now?"

11

"WHAT'S THE last thing you see before you sleep at night?"

Ani's voice wavered as a sheet of lightning breached the room's curtains and lit its furniture into stark shapes—the pub's bed, the pub's wardrobe, the pub's washstand, the pub's chair. In the morning, they'd leave the wide Hay Plains and take a train away to the coast together—the first time Ani would see coast or ocean. In the morning, they'd take a train, the new Mr. and Mrs. Lachlan, away from this place where Ani had lived all her life, its grasses as blond as her hair. Now, in the night, their faces close, noses almost touching, her right hand held his left. Here they were, lying with their heads on the same pillow, in the same bed, for the first time.

"The last thing I see?" Mac spoke so quietly that his voice thickened and slurred around its consonants. "It's the ceiling, I guess, or the wall—it's the room where I'm sleeping. Is that what you mean?"

She shook her head, and the gesture made her hair glimmer against the pillow.

"No. I mean, sometimes just before I go to sleep, or when I begin to dream, I see somebody—a figure, a person—caught in a beam of light. Sometimes they're dancing. Sometimes they're just standing there, still, in the brightness. And I watch them for a while, and then the light drops down, and then I'm asleep." At the other end of the bed, her toes brushed against his, and she flinched at the unexpected proximity of another person's flesh in her bed—another person.

"It's all right," he said. "It's going to be all right."

The clock on the mantelpiece chimed once, and Mac frowned; he'd lost track of the time, even the day—was it one o'clock? Two? A Saturday? A Sunday? At least he knew it was almost summer, late November 1935. And there she was, just inches away, his bride, staring into his eyes as he studied hers. There were so many colors in them: grey and gold and a green that was almost metallic. In the center, near the pupil, was a flash of ocher so bright it was almost red.

"Your eyelashes are different colors," she said at last.

"Different how?"

"Different to each other—you've got blond ones and ginger ones and brown ones. Like in your beard. I've never noticed that before."

"Would it have changed your mind about marrying me, my motley eyelashes?" He smiled, squeezing her hand tight, and his legs hugged her feet, her toes. This time, she didn't react.

"Nothing would have done that." Beyond the room, the sky cracked open with thunder and lightning that had been menacing all day, and inside, safe and together, Ani and Mac Lachlan both jumped a little, and laughed. "Some omen, some portent, my dadda would say," said Ani. "Some message from his old northern gods."

"Maybe that's what your people are, dancing and running before you sleep." His accent made the "maybe" *mebbe*; his accent made "before" *afore*. His accent thickened "are" and "running" into rich, fudgy sounds. "Maybe they're messengers from your old country." Tucked this close to her mouth, he could smell her breath as she spoke, and wondered if he might get a little drunk on the perfume of her words.

"That's what my father says—Thialfi or the Valkyrie."

"My gran would say it's the second sight." His eyebrows rose slightly, his lips making the smallest smile. "She'd swear she'd seen any number of happenings before they happened—I'm counting on it that she's seen us married now without waiting for my letter."

She looked so young in this flickering half-light, but they had fifty years of life between them. Because he thought of them as added together now, he realized, rather than two separate tallies of time. It made him feel sure, more secure than he had in years.

Here they were.

"Nice to be inside with you, Mackenzie Lachlan," said Ani as the thunder rumbled.

"Nice to be anywhere with you, Anikka Kalm—no," he corrected himself, "Anikka Lachlan." This new combination of words.

Outside, the thunder collided with the sound of a train; one noise all air and movement, the other all weight and metal. "They're late in with that loco." Mac's eyes focused on the window, as if he might see the reason for the engine's delay from where he lay, warm in his bed. "A good night to be indoors. A good night to be with you, Mrs. Anikka Lachlan."

She leaned forward, kissing his smile. "Thank you."

And later, when she was asleep, he watched the occasional flicker of her eyelids, the rise and fall of her breath. Touching his fingers lightly against her wrist, he felt its pulse. Touching his fingers to her hair, he felt its silk. She was beautiful, without a doubt, and bright too. "She's well able, lad," he imagined his grandmother saying. "And she'll smart you up, my blatherskite." He wasn't wanting for sharpness himself—Mac smiled against the darkness—but he did stretch the truth of things now and then, not an outright lie, but perhaps a rearrangement of a story's dimensions to skate across an ignorance or an elision.

An' look what it gets you—tracing the curl of Ani's hair against the pillow—*a fine, bonny ferlie.*

She'd been ready to love him—he'd seen that—and he her. So what if he talked up the places he'd show her, the prospects he had, the things that he may have dreamed of doing? So what if he claimed her own favorite books for himself? If a man made the right guess at the right time, what harm of it, if it made his girl smile? He could read fast enough to make good the deception, and he'd sort out the settlement of any other promises later on.

The pale fabric of Ani's wedding dress picked up a chink or two of the lightning beyond the drawn drapes, so that one sleeve and a strip around the waist seemed to float above the rest of the dress's material, as if animated by another bride's body. Then the curtains flicked a little in the breeze and rearranged the dress's highlighted illumination, now more, now less, now a whole panel, now a tiny speck.

Her fine clothes, and how fine she'd looked. He'd felt his breath catch when she'd stepped up to him at the altar and let go of her father's hand to take his. No matter a little thing about a fancy novel; a man only gasped at the sight of his true sweetheart.

Beside him, Ani stirred, her free hand moving against his skin. "Sweet dreams," he whispered, feeling certain, feeling foolish. He closed his own eyes at last, while Ani, nestled against the unusual warmth and weight of someone else in her bed, headed deeper into sleep.

And it was Mac she saw this night, Mac in his fine suit, dancing and twirling as he had earlier in the pale lamplight of the pub's dining room downstairs.

Maybe, she thought as the light around him dimmed, *or mebbe it always was.*

12

IN THE vast quiet of the Railway Institute's central library, set at the end of Sydney's Central Station, Anikka walks through the rows of shelving, watching as books are selected and sorted, packed and returned. They pride themselves, these real librarians—that's how Ani thinks of them—on being able to source almost anything for anyone, dispatching volumes all over the state to their various and voracious readers.

"I'm looking forward to all the reading I'll be able to do," Ani says at last, and they smile at her benignly. A common misperception— everyone thinks they'll have that time.

When the meeting is over, Ani stands on the curb outside taking great breaths of the steamy air pushed out by the nearby trains. Her mind is a fug of hours and requirements, this new busyness jumbled against the disappearing rhythms of her days. Before, she marked her hours around Isabel's going to school and coming home, around the changeable pattern of Mac's shifts. Before, she could watch the light move around the house as the day passed, around the garden as she watered here and weeded there. Before, she was the person who had time to think about what was happening to other people—to arrive on their doorstep with a cake or a stew when domestic disaster struck.

When disaster struck elsewhere.

She registers the hands of the station's clock and moves automatically towards her platform, her train, her mind distracted by remembering her father's voice, his anxiety about her money: "I took a boarder in when your mother first died—you might not remember. Another carpenter lived with us awhile. The money was good. And the company. You could think about that—move Isabel in with you and rent out the room." Telephoning from the post office with condolences and suggestions.

Just once, Ani has convinced her father to visit them on the coast, to come away from the plains, to come and see Isabel. When Isabel was just over a year old, he came and slept in the baby's room, while the baby slept in her little crib at the end of Ani and Mac's bed.

"I don't like to be away, Anikka," her father had confessed at last. "I don't like to be far away from where your mother was—I still think of her sleeping there, under the feather quilt my mother sent us when we were married. I miss my bed, Ani; I've never told that to a living soul. But I miss my bed—I feel too far away from my wife." He blew his nose loudly, startling Isabel as she kicked on a rug in front of his feet. "Such closeness to a person, keeping watch as they sleep."

Ani bit her tongue against saying, *More than twenty years, Dadda; she's been dead more than twenty years.* And instead made him his favorite breakfast of porridge with butter and jam—ignoring her Scottish husband's disapproval.

That night, when Mac was asleep, when Isabel was asleep, when her father's snores were shaking the hallway, Ani had crept into his room, turning on the lamp she'd set there when the baby was born. He was tall, still, but stooped a little now, and all the gold and red had finally bleached out of his hair, his beard, leaving him with silvers and the palest white-greys. But his skin was tanned and smooth, and his hands were still busy, even as he slept, flicking and fidgeting on the bedclothes as if he were trying to solve a problem of joinery somewhere.

She'd never thought of it before, about keeping watch over someone, although she'd watched Mac while he slept, and she could not go to bed herself without sitting a moment with Isabel, just looking, just checking, just making sure her sleep was calm and sound. Mac laughed at this ritual—"Do you think she'll have climbed out the window and escaped?"—but Ani knew that he did it too, awake early for a shift, or on the rare nights when she was away from home, or asleep first. She'd laid her hand gently across her father's busy fingers, and they curled around her palm in response, holding her there.

More than twenty years, she'd thought, and his friends' daft ideas of finding him some spinster or widow he could marry. *They mustn't know, they mustn't know the way he carries her still.*

Easing her fingers from his grip, she had pulled down the blind and pulled up the blanket. This inversion of roles, the parent and the child; she kissed his forehead. "*Hyvää yöta ja kauniita unia*"— good night and sweet dreams—as he had wished her every night of her childhood that she could remember. She loved the lilt of those words, the way they swayed.

She opens her eyes, disoriented to find herself in some deep darkness. She doesn't remember boarding the train, let alone the trip away from Sydney, through its suburbs, through the thick bush of the national park, and into her talismanic tunnel. It's the tunnel's dark that presses against her now, as if she was unexpectedly blind or somehow sleeping. She soaks in the noise of the train's progress: she loves the rattles, the thuds, the almost visceral percussion the carriages make, pulled unrelentingly along with the steam engine's exertion.

For thirty years now her father has carried her mother—*forsaking all others*, thinks Ani, almost smiling at the old-fashioned and nuptial phrase. She never questioned that he did, or wondered at his being alone. It hadn't occurred to her that he might have had a choice about it. For herself, she thinks, there will be no boarder, no extra body in the quiet space of her home, no new and unknown being in her bathroom, her kitchen, or triggering the intimate creak of her floorboards, her front stairs. There can be no more change.

Which is—she almost smiles again—*the one thing there must be.* This job, this library, this new, widowed life. Idiotic to believe she can control any of it.

Opening her mouth, she takes in the tunnel's thick, sooty air—she can taste the cleaner steam on its edges—and pushes her nose as far through the open window as she dares to make the noise louder, the taste stronger, the risk (how far away *is* the tunnel's wall?) more precarious.

The carriage rocks and tilts and Ani braces her hands against the hard leather seat, steadying herself above its unpredictability. Once, a long time ago, Mac had told her a story he'd had from his grannie about sending her own daughter—Mac's aunt—down to Glasgow for work. There were strange hazards to beware of, Grannie Lachlan had said. Don't talk to young men. Lift your skirt on only one side when you prepare to cross a road; to lift it on both would reveal too much of your ankles. And when entering a tunnel in a train, put a pin in your mouth to stop any bold young man from kissing you. *And we laughed and we laughed and we laughed.*

"Might I be so bold?" Mac had said then, quiet against the train's roar, although Ani was sure the whole train could have heard him. He was a broad man, and sturdy, and the way he pushed against her sometimes, it was as if she could feel the full weight and momentum of his railwayman's job behind him.

Her mouth opens against the memory of it, and as she swallows a sob, the train bursts out of the darkness and onto the coast.

The ocean is bright and sharp and the sky above echoes the water's deep navy in its own thick color. There is light in the leaves of the trees, blasting them into different greens, shiny and almost metallic, that might belong properly to jewels. There's so much brightness it's as if every light in the world has been thrown on: every flare, every candle, every beacon.

Above the sound of the train, Ani catches the screech of cockatoos with their improperly loud voices. There are cars on the road below too, people walking on the beach, and wreaths of smoke winding up from chimneys, tracing illegible messages across the sky. Color and movement and noise and bustle everywhere and it's life, it's life. *All these stories going on*, thinks Ani, *while I sit in the dark and open my mouth for a kiss I can't feel anymore.* She looks up to the sky, down to the shore, out through the air—looking for kite men; looking for seabirds—and across the face of the escarpment. The beauty of it all, the changing combinations of its shapes and its shades and its shadows: it's as if she's been delivered into the barrel of Isabel's kaleidoscope.

Come away, her father has written again and again, and she lets the sobs come now, thinking of this. *Never never never never.* To lose this moment, this moment in every journey from north back to south. To walk away from this place she had found with her husband. Well, now it will be her shifts that fold around the working of the house, where it used to be Mac's. Now it will be her job that marks the comings and goings in the days. Now it will be her job to sleep alone in her bed and explain to her father that she cannot leave.

Up ahead, the engine sounds its call and the train draws into Stanwell Park. Ani leans back, the brilliance of her realization draining away to an ordinary day as the carriage shudders and slows. She wipes her eyes. She blows her nose. There are other tunnels, she knows, between her and home, but none of them give you this moment, this arrival, this bursting out like magic.

The train pushes south, its line counterpoised between the ocean and the cliffs. Along the horizon, a trick of sunlight turns the water to the color of metal, glistening like treasure or a fine, thin blade.

～

Alighting at Thirroul, Ani stands a moment with her eyes closed against the departing carriages—it's bad luck to count how many there are. As the guard's van leaves the platform, she opens her eyes and catches sight of the guard's arm and the distinct shape—not much more than a dangling trinket at this distance—of his lamp.

Directly opposite, across the tracks, sits the library, a pale, boarded box of a building rising straight up from the platform with one window open and—as Ani watches—the other pushed up to frame the shape of Miss Fadden, the librarian she is about to replace.

"Hello, dear," Miss Fadden calls, waving across the tracks. "I thought I'd let in some air for you." And Ani waves in reply, crossing the tracks to enter her new world, this library.

It's a nice place, not too large, and with big windows that look beyond the railway lines towards the sea. Inside, its floors are oiled up sometimes for a dance, and there's a faint smell of cedar from the shelves, the librarian's desk.

Coming around to its front door, Ani pauses at the porch, raised just half a step up off the ground. Such a strange thing: on the building's eastern side, where it abuts the platform, it sits hard on the gravel, as if the library had been set down on top of it like a child's block. But this porch wants to make a distinction between itself and the ground; the porch wants to hold itself up a little. Ani takes the awkward step, rocking her weight back and forth to gauge its height.

As she rocks, she notices for the first time that the four columns supporting the porch's awning are decorated with pieces of dark black stone, sharply angular. They jut out from the smooth surface with jagged points, and when she presses the soft flesh of her palm into them, she's sure she feels tiny pricks of blood on her skin. Is it basalt? Some sort of schist? Or coal? Can coal look this shiny, this sharp? She's never paid attention to its shape as she's shoveled it into her stove. Coal would make sense: all the mines running back through the wall of the mountain; all the men deep underground, hauling it out. *Call it coal, then*, she thinks, and she steps inside, calling the librarian's name.

Miss Fadden is crouched on the floor, trying to fit a pile of books into a large box like the pieces of a complex jigsaw.

"I've never got any better at this," she says, smiling as she stands to shake Ani's hand. "Perhaps you'll have a gift for it." And she holds out two Zane Grey adventures and a copy of *Kangaroo*.

"Must that one go back?" asks Ani, taking the Lawrence. "I'd like to find it here when I start."

The older lady nods. "There's always someone wanting to read it," she says. "Looking for things they recognize, I expect—and finding them. You can find anything in a story if you look hard enough." She sets it square in the middle of the wide table, straightens her glasses and a pretty little fan just off to one side. "I'll leave it here then, on your desk," she says, and it takes Ani a moment to register the designation.

It comes from the south; a huge surge of noise and movement and the train bound for Sydney is suddenly in the station, its sound amplified by the room. Carriage doors open and close; feet scuffle across the gravel. And then a sharp toot, an acceleration, and it's gone.

Ani looks up to find the older woman's gaze fixed on her, pensive. "I did wonder," Miss Fadden says quietly, "if it was indelicate of them, somehow, to ask you to work alongside such a noise as that all day. When, you know, it was a train that . . ." And she waves her hand, so that it brushes along Ani's sleeve once, twice.

"I hadn't thought of it," says Ani. "I'd rather not . . ."

"Very sensible, dear. Now, perhaps you'd like to have a look at the shelving while I sort out this box." She's through the door and into the smaller room, rustling through paper, before she's finished speaking.

Ani turns carefully, staring across a row of paperback romances—*Bella's happy endings*, she thinks—and other reassuring fictions, while the room sparkles with silence.

13

FROM THE kitchen window of his sister's house, on the corner of Ocean Street, Roy McKinnon stands with his hands in the warm, soapy washing-up water, looking at the ocean itself. There's some trick of perspective in this place, as if the house, the road, the grassy verge beyond were set below the level of the water, as if the sea curved up, the horizon above the line of sight and the water, at any moment, about to cascade down.

A seagull cuts across the window, and Roy jumps, shocked at his own shock—*A bird, buster, it was just a bird.* He checks the clock on Iris's mantelpiece against the time on his wristwatch on the sill—as if to say, *How long is it going to take, to get used to being back in the world?* Behind him, on the kitchen table, is the slender rectangle of an anthology of poems, including his own from the war, with the publisher's polite note about when they might see something new. *What's next, Roy McKinnon?* the man had written. *You know we're all waiting to hear.*

As am I, mate, he thinks. *As am I.*

Pulling the book from its envelope this morning, he'd been unsure where to place it in Iris's neat house—not so much for fear of disturbing any of her possessions but because it was a house almost entirely free of books. There was a family Bible in the hall cupboard, he knew, and three well-thumbed romances tucked under the leg of the settee—he'd found them when he bent down to retrieve a shilling on the night he'd arrived, laughing as his sister whisked them away again like some illicit material.

He smacks at his forehead with his hand, surprised by the wet suds against his skin: the library at the station—Iris had said something about the librarian retiring, and even that hadn't reminded him of its existence, its potential cornucopia. *Sink down into the words of others*, he thinks, plunging his hands back into the warm wetness and feeling around for loose flatware. That poor young widow was starting next week, Iris said. Roy tilted his head, trying again to remember something more of the Lachlans than long-ago football, a quiet spectator. He'd met the man once or twice, he thought—a drink, maybe, or a rack of snooker. But there isn't much to his repository of prewar memories. Sometimes he distrusts that there ever had been times, or places, before the war. Pretty, his sister had said of the widow—"You'll remember her when you see her"— and Scottish, of the husband. "You'd have seen them at the dances," she'd said, "before they had their little girl. It was Ani Lachlan who brought me your poem when it came out in that magazine."

Still, even then, he'd stood wondering what she'd made of it, whether she'd read it. And still, even then, he'd found no way to ask—caught instead by the memory of overhearing Anikka Lachlan's grief.

"Roy? Are you here?" His sister struggles through the door, her basket heavy—he should have gone to help her with the shopping.

A useful thing, you could've done a useful thing, mate. And he lunges so quickly to take the basket from her that he knocks it, sending a paper bag of apples, a bottle of milk, a precious packet of tea spilling out across the floor.

"Oh, Roy." A sharp intake of breath, as if she's trying not to reprimand a child. "Don't worry, don't worry." She takes the dishcloth from him, watching the milk soak into the still-rationed leaves. "Set the kettle on if you want something to do—I think there's enough tea in the caddy for us to have a pot. I'll go back and see what I can sort out."

It's her house that makes him nervous, he realizes, not just its want of books, but it's too neat and too ordered. *There's no living done here,* he thinks, *just Iris and her opinions.* She should have married; she should have had her own children to reprimand, not just take that tone with him.

"I saw Mrs. Lacey today when I was coming along the beach," he says, following his own train of thought. "She said they've got the replacement doctor lined up at last—and you'll never guess, Iris, you'll never guess who she said is coming."

His sister's hand, wiping the cloth across the floor, stops, leaving a wide, white slick on the lino.

"Well, of course it's Frank Draper; I was sure you'd know," says Roy, trying to position the tea caddy exactly as he had found it. "Did you hear from Frank, these past years? I always thought, you and he—"

"Could you get me that towel, Roy, or must I do everything myself? That's a whole pint of milk, you know, a whole pint of milk gone to waste. And no, I didn't hear from Frank Draper. He said it was a lottery, if he'd come back from the war or not, and he told me not to bet on its odds." Her voice is pinched with a fury she's sustained for years.

Roy passes her the towel, wincing at her words as he tries to collect the scattered apples and wipe them clean and dry. Of course he should have known this of her—it's so brutal, clearly, so close to the neatness of her surface. And he remembers suddenly that he loves this about his sister, that she will say things, expose them, with no thought of the cost to herself. There's something clean about her, and something ferocious. He admires that; he even envies it.

"Be good to see Frank," he says slowly, rubbing a piece of the fruit against the front of his shirt and distracted from Iris by the shine it takes on, its freshness, its existence.

"It will be easier to give it a good mop." And Iris is through the back door and away from the conversation. He can see her standing in the tiny square of garden that opens out behind the house, hardly big enough for the outhouse and the chicken run. He can see her standing there, holding the mop as if it were the mast of a ship in a storm. He can see her shoulders, rising and falling, rising and falling, and her dark hair a shadow against the day's light.

Who knows what really happened, he thinks, pouring the boiling water into the teapot, setting it precisely on the mat she keeps precisely in the middle of her kitchen table. *But maybe there's a chance for living yet.*

"I'll leave your tea here, then, dear," he calls, setting it next to the pristine anthology. "And I might take a walk along the beach." Heading through the front door, clamping on his hat, he turns to see her come in at the back with the mop, the bucket, and her sticky, wet face.

"When will you be back?" she calls, although he knows her real question is what could he possibly be doing out there, walking around, or gazing at the water, all these days and nights. He knows she distrusts his freedom, his idleness. And if anyone had told her they'd seen him perched up on one of the pylons around by the old jetty . . . He shakes his head.

Few poems in the middle of a war, mate, and you call yourself a poet.

At least his friend Frank Draper has made something of himself—has a job, an occupation, a profession. Dr. Draper, coming back to the coast to tend to the sick. Roy laughs: *Neither of us with anywhere else to be in the end but here.*

The plans they'd made when they were younger men. "And you'll be a poet, Roy, my friend," Frank would say, ordering up another drink and slapping his friend on the back. The doctor and the poet; the grandeur of young men's dreams, while Frank learned his anatomy and Roy taught spelling and math in forgotten country schools.

Then there was the war, and they'd both gone—Frank to England, Roy all over the place, Europe, and then the Pacific. *Where's Frank been to only just get home?* Roy wonders, recasting his own aimless itinerary.

He pulls up in the shadow of the pool's boxy pump house. Farther down the coast, farther south, he can see heavy grey clouds and rolling banks of squall. There's a storm coming. He turns and waves back towards Iris's house—she'll be watching, through the window, worrying about rain and wind, and him. But it's a while away yet, he's sure of it. And he jams his hat down farther over his eyes and sets off into the teeth of the gale, ignoring the lines of lightning beginning to shatter along the horizon.

14

"THIS IS how it was. I was a wee boy, away with my gran in the north, waiting for the lights."

Mac as a boy, at the top of Scotland with his grandmother; the stories he told were thick with words like "gloaming" and "baffies" and "puddocks." Around the turn of autumn, the turn of spring, the sky might light up with the aurora, sheets of grand brilliance, he called it, all purples and greens and bright shiny whites—sometimes reds and oranges too.

"Better than any of that phosphorescent beach stuff you hanker after," he'd say. "Imagine it, Ani, out across the whole sky."

Once, he told her, he thought he'd seen it in Australia too, taking an engine through a heavy summer night and seeing the sky bristle and shimmer.

But, "A bushfire coming over the plains," the driver had said. "We're all right; we'll push on through," leaving Mac at the locomotive's open doorway, staring at the color, wishing it belonged to something less destructive.

"I dream of a trip to the old country one day," he'd say to Ani. "One more trip, and the skies all brilliant." *His trip*, he always spoke of it as *his trip*, while she worked to carve out her own space in his fantasy by talking about herself meeting Grannie Lachlan or traveling on again to her father's country in that higher European north. It was a daydream, of course: as if the world would ever shrink itself for a railwayman and his wife.

Out to sea now, towards the horizon, the sky lights up with bands of white and yellow: there's a storm out there, and coming on. Ani settles herself against the wall of the porch, watching. Another flare—she strains to hear its thunder. Her father used to tell her stories about the gods and their thunder and lightning. It was their hammer, thrown hard, that caused the brightness; it was their horses, riding fast, that caused the noise.

Ani starts: there is a horse coming along the street, drawing a little trap. She squints, her hand up to block out the rest of the world. The trap's driver raises her own hand in return.

"Mrs. Lacey," Ani calls. "I thought you were my father's thunder god, riding out towards that lightning."

"There's more storm coming up the coast, Mrs. Lachlan. You can see it from our veranda." The Laceys' dairy farm, where Isabel collects their milk, looks south from the back of the hill from which Ani and her house look north. "But I look to be beating it home." She pauses. "I was sorry—"

Ani raises her hand again. "Thank you," she says. She gets her acknowledgments in so quickly now that no one gets past three or four words of condolence. "I can smell the edge of that rain," she says then, changing the subject.

Mrs. Lacey nods, pulling her coat around her. "I was down to meet the new doctor," she says, steadying and readying her horse, "but he wasn't on the train. Frank Draper—do you remember him? They say he's just back from overseas, been on war business all this time. He used to come to the dances down here, before the war. I expect we'll find him much changed after all of this. He was a beautiful dancer—made me feel like Ginger Rogers. Of course that was years ago now."

Ani smiles; she can't imagine anyone making Mrs. Lacey feel like Ginger Rogers. The doctor must have been a magician. "I probably met him once or twice—I think I remember him dancing with Iris McKinnon." She rubs her hands against the suddenly cooler air. "Maybe he'll come tomorrow."

Mrs. Lacey waves again, giving her horse a giddyup, and Ani listens as the percussion of its steps disappears along the street. A new doctor, whose war has gone on three years longer than everyone else's. That will give the village something new to talk about. Yes, she thinks she remembers him, dancing with Iris McKinnon sometimes, and sometimes laughing with her brother. He lived up in the city and came down for weekends and holidays, just as he had when he was a boy—they all did, the three of them. Then there was the war, and Iris came to stay. And perhaps, thinks Ani, she's been waiting all this time; one for Bella's happy endings. But it feels too hard to wish such things, even for other people.

Out at sea, the slabs of sheet lightning are overlaid with sharp forks of other brightness. The wind is picking up, the rain almost here. She's read somewhere that lightning smells like salty air—would the aurora have that smell too?

A swerve, a little skid, and Luddy's car comes up the hill and into the street, his arm through the open window to wave at Ani as he passes, and a man, tall, dark-haired, in the passenger seat. The doctor, Ani assumes, somehow missed in the train's arrival, and being driven round to the Laceys' for the night. The rain begins to fall as the two men pass her fence, its heavy wetness immediately washing away any hint of the car's journey.

Out on the horizon, miles of light break out and hover, luminous, for just a little longer than Ani expects. Her breath catches with their flare—there's something triumphant, magnificent, in it, like a loud chorus or a blast of angels. *For he shall give his angels charge over thee; they shall bear thee up in their hands*: she remembers the psalm from nowhere, and in the instant of thinking of it, the light flares again and she's sure she sees the whole surface of the land and the water rising up a little with its blaze.

"My angel," Mac had called her—twice, maybe three times, in all their years together. She'd liked the nickname, had wished he'd use it more, but it felt presumptuous to ask if he would. It was too much, and in the end, even she hadn't been able to bear him high enough to be safe.

15

"OUTSIDE, LUDDY, outside." The two teams surged along the grass, Luddy with the ball tight against his chest, and Mac just behind him, calling for it, and calling again.

"Here, Luddy, here, over here," watching the stationmaster swing the other way and pass—directly to his opponent. "Help ma boab!" called Mac, pulling to a halt and bending to catch his breath. It was extremities that threw him back into his dialect—in bed with Ani, or when this baby was finally born, he suspected, or when his *dreich team wouldnae play*. He wasn't sure how long he stood like that, stooped and panting, but when he looked up, he felt he was looking at a painting, or a photograph, as if everything from the trees and the people down to single blades of grass had been snapped into stillness. The world was quiet, and he stumbled, his breath thick, almost scared he'd been transplanted into the backdrop, the staged busyness, of someone else's story.

The whistle blew for halftime, piercing whatever moment held Mac fast, and he shook himself back into the world and jogged to the side of the field, reaching for an orange. "What you doin' out there, Luddy? M'a on yer deaf side, mon?" His accent thickened again through exasperation and the fruit, and as he shook his head in disbelief, great drops of juice flew out from his face.

"There's half a game to go yet, Mac," muttered one of the younger blokes. "We're only a point behind."

Mac shook his head again and threw himself down on the grass. "C'mon, lads, I need a win today—last match before the bairn comes, I'd wager." And made a great show of stretching and pulling.

"Wondered where Mrs. Lachlan was," said Luddy through his own mouthful of orange. "Maybe we just play better when we've got her cheering us on."

"Well, Mac plays fiercer when she's not here to see, that's for sure," said the grocer. "You're like a great engine, running us all down on the grass—and that's us on your own team, mate. The way you take off, you'll plow someone into the turf."

"Away w'ye," said Mac with a laugh, standing up and ruffling Luddy's hair. "Daft buggers, the lot of you. There's no danger of me hurting anyone—you know me, lads, couldn't hurt a fly." And they laughed at his heft, his bulk, his wide shoulders and his fast legs.

"Do your worst, Mac," called someone from the opposition. "We've got our own doctor on the sidelines . . ." He gestured towards Frank Draper. "Do your worst; he'll fix us up."

Shading his eyes, Mac looked over to the western edge of the field, saw two men standing, talking, their hats tipped onto the backs of their heads. Draper, the doctor, and Iris McKinnon's brother. He tried to think of the last time he'd seen them—they both worked away, he knew; came down for weekends here and there—but couldn't place it. He frowned: no, it was an odd meeting, somewhere odd, or something odd about it. *Whisht, I dinnae ken, I dinnae ken.* He frowned again at his memory's lapse into old words, and took a step towards the two men as if an extra yard or so of proximity might free a recollection.

Behind them, on the railway line, an engine chugged southwards, hauling a line of freight trucks. *That's a saddle tank*, thought Mac. *What's that doing out of the shunting yard and up here on the lines?* He watched its belch of smoke trace a line above the platforms, watched the clean, round lines of its tank and light disappear around the corner, dragging its load behind it. The doctor and his companion slipped into another crevice in his mind, and he reached for another orange, wondering how Ani was, sitting at home instead of here, waiting through the last days before the birth of their child. *A girl for sure*, thought Mac. *And I'll call her Isabel, for my mum.* Ani, he knew, favored Elise as a name, but it was the only immortality Mac could think of to pass his mother's name on to his daughter; the mother who'd been dead precisely as long as he'd been alive. He just had to make Ani think "Isabel" was her idea.

And I'll know you this time, Isabel. I'll spend the rest of my life knowing you.

"All right, my men. Who's for it? Who's for it?" Mac was halfway across the field, keeping pace with the referee, as the rest of his team pulled up their socks and gulped at their water jars. "C'mon, hurry up, hurry up—it's a braw day for a win."

The whistle blew, the man with the ball paused for the smallest sliver of a second, suspending the world and its time again.

And then the game went on.

16

OPENING THE library door on her first morning, Ani watches the room reveal itself. There's no sign of Miss Fadden, her presence recalled by only the slightest imprint of her glasses and her fan in the desk's dust. Ani opens the windows, first one, then the other, craning her head to see the first train so as not to be surprised by its noise. If she learns when to expect their great loud rush, she reasons, they won't catch her off guard, won't surprise her into thinking about Mac, about shunting, about the solidity of a train against the soft give of a body.

She stands a long time, holding off this last thought, mesmerized by its awfulness. *This is how it is*, she thinks. *Two shifts, morning and evening, and Mrs. May heating up Bella's supper.* Another breath. *All right, all right, this will be all right.* The clock on the wall ticks loudly, and for as long as Ani stares at it, neither of its hands appears to move. Which would be worse, she wonders, a day in which no one came—or a day in which people came and talked with her, at her, about finding her there, about how she is, about the circumstances of her employment?

She had never appreciated before the lovely anonymity of an unremarkable life.

The minute hand scrapes slowly around from five past to ten past. She would take any conversation.

Pushing herself out of her reverie, she begins a circuit of the shelves. *Of course, if no one comes, I really can spend my time reading—what could be better?* And she reaches for *Kangaroo*, left, as Miss Fadden had promised, in its rightful place. But the words blur and merge, her eyes unable to decipher the text. Replacing the book, she tries another and another. It's so quiet, so sepulchral, that she fears for a moment the world has stopped—or perhaps just the world of this one room.

Frozen, here, with time stood still. And if I can't read, if I can't read—the wave of panic that has been building in her since Mac's death finally crests and breaks, and she sits gasping and crying until a northbound train clamors into the platform outside, its noise jolting her back into herself.

A scant quarter hour has passed. She wipes her nose, her cheeks, her eyes, stretching her face into as many contortions as she can manage as if to confuse its memory of her weakness.

She thumbs at the ledgers then, the card files, the neat stacks of paper ranged in the neat wooden trays—a strange topography for her to learn; where things are recorded, how things are traced. She glances at the names of the library's borrowers, names from church, from Isabel's school, from conversations in the street. The lady who owns the dress shop has been borrowing Penguin classics. Mrs. Padman, Mrs. Bower, Mrs. Floyd—their husbands all crossed out of the register; probably Mac has been crossed out like that now too. The two owners of the rival shoe shops had both requested a manual of railway signs—how peculiar is that? Her fingers flick towards *L* for Lachlan: Ani, Isabel—and Mac. And there it is, the list of every book he's ever borrowed, the line now through his name, the terrible sense of a thing reckoned complete and unalterable.

The northbound train pushes out of the station as Ani turns and opens the window farther, catching the last of its sound, its steam. She does love that smell, slightly heavy, slightly mechanical. She loves the way it tastes. And as she tastes it now, she runs her hand along the piano, tucked to the side of the window, and slowly opens its lid. She's slightly scared of pianos, as if someone might expect her to know how to play if she's standing near one. And she did take a couple of lessons from one of the shoe-shop owners when she first came to the coast—he played piano for the Saturday-night dances—but gave up in embarrassment. The only thing she knows how to play is the treble part of "Für Elise"—her father had taught her by rote, numbering the keys so she could remember their sequence, when she and Mac visited before Isabel was born. Ani can still feel the way Isabel kicked and squirmed as she destroyed Beethoven's lovely tune over and over again.

"We could call it Elise, if it's a girl," she remembers Mac saying, standing behind her. "Maybe the baby's trying to tell us that it already recognizes its name."

"Elise or Ludwig." Ani laughed. Mac was always so sure the baby was going to be a girl—*and she was*, thinks Ani now. *There she was.*

She pauses halfway through a bar, goes back to the beginning. Why didn't they call Isabel Elise? It was a lovely name—although Isabel is too, of course, and for Mac's mother, which seems to matter more. She's glad she insisted on that. She hums the melody, a note or two out from the version she's picking out with the index finger of her right hand. *"Für Elise"—imagine being able to hum a tune you knew someone had written for you, and such a beautiful one, so beautiful.* She tries the opening again, and again. Perhaps she could teach herself the piano here—or at least learn this one melody so that it sounds as graceful, as easy, as it should.

Elise Lachlan: that would have been a lovely name. But then perhaps it would have made Isabel a different person. *And what would I change of her? What tiny piece would I want to be different?* Her thumb and little finger pick out an octave, pulsing from higher to lower and back again, louder and louder, until she hears a sound at the door and turns to see Mrs. Lacey, her arms full of paperbacks.

"Mrs. Lacey."

"Mrs. Lachlan, I thought you must have started—I saw Miss Fadden in her garden as I came down the hill."

"You're my first borrower," Ani says, making a great show of taking the books and finding the card.

"You'll get used to it," the other woman assures her as Ani falters then, casting around for what to do next. "Miss Fadden always had a deck of cards in the drawer—she used to play Patience when there was no one around."

Ani slides out the drawer, and there's a deck of cards, the colors garish, with caricatures of Uncle Sam as the kings, and the Statue of Liberty as the queens, Hitler and Mussolini faced off as the jokers. She laughs. "I would never have expected this—I should return them to her; they look like some sort of souvenir."

"We did mark that victory however we could." Mrs. Lacey moves around the shelves, pausing here and there. "I read this when I was a child—always wanted to read it again. Always wanted a daughter that I could call Anne." She pats *Anne of Green Gables'* cover, placing it carefully on Ani's desk. "You won't tell anyone if I borrow it?"

Ani smiles, shakes her head. "I loved these books when I was little. Bella's reading them now—she reads me sentences and I can almost remember what dress I was wearing when I first read it myself, or whereabouts I was sitting in our garden. Such strange particulars, and yet other memories are gone in a minute." She smiles again. "Which is a blessing, I suppose."

But Mrs. Lacey has moved away, scanning across titles. *This is better*, thinks Ani. *Quite nice—quite a nice way to pass the time.* She brushes nonexistent dust from the cover of Mrs. Lacey's book, smoothes her ledger for its entry, readies the library's card.

"And these two," says her borrower. "Iris McKinnon told me this *Timeless Land* was very good, so I'll give it a go."

"I enjoyed it"—Ani nods—"and there was supposed to be a sequel coming—I'll let you know if it comes in—if it's any good." She breathes, feeling her way back towards inconsequential conversations. "Did I see Iris's brother on the beach a while ago?" Proud of being able to shape such pleasantries.

"Yes, he's home—with poor Iris wondering how long for and what he intends to do. Iris says he's no idea about teaching anymore, just talks about wanting to write, and doesn't. I imagine you'll see him in here before long; she never was much of a reader and if you were a poet, well, you must need to read all the time, mustn't you?"

Ani transcribes the titles carefully, not looking up. "I don't know anything of poets, Mrs. Lacey. I'll see if I can get any hints if he comes in here for books." And they smile at each other—*easy; pleasant.* "I was thinking about Iris when you mentioned Dr. Draper coming. I'm afraid I don't remember your dancing like Ginger Rogers, but I remember Frank and Iris—she wore such beautiful dresses then."

Mrs. Lacey settles the books in the crook of her arm and taps the side of her nose. "That's a story still in progress, Mrs. Lachlan. But I know she's lonely, even with her brother home." And she turns towards the door, pausing on its step. "It was lovely to be your first borrower, dear. I hope you like it here—it seemed such a fine idea when Luddy told me. I could imagine you being happy somehow." The words are unexpectedly expansive—Ani bows her head underneath them, and when she looks up again, Mrs. Lacey is making her way across the gravel.

But Mrs. Lacey is right; she does love a library. She remembers once, during the war, getting out of the rain in Sydney—she can't place why she was there or what she was doing, but a great spring storm had come on and she'd run up the stairs of the nearest building to find herself at the new public reading rooms, pushing the heavy doors open with her shoulder.

It was dim inside, dim and quiet, like a church, and then she saw it: a great map made in mosaic, a whole ocean laid out across the floor, with grand ships and blue waves and angels blowing the wind from the southwest, the northeast.

"It's beautiful," she'd said softly as the door eased shut behind her. "Beautiful." In the middle was an old outline of Australia from centuries before when the west coast was mostly rumor and the east coast a single, unvarying straight line—the cartographers' graceful guess at filling a blank. There was no hint of her beach, her coast, her part of the world. It was funny to think that where she lived had been invisible, or missing.

She patted a whale, traced out the accurate shape of Tasmania, and then stood up, moving slowly forward through the next set of doors and into a huge room with the soft light of a pale blue glass roof, and bright stained-glass panels illuminating its walls.

The hush was magnificent, sullied only by the occasional scrape of a chair, the shuffle of paper, and once or twice the sound of a catalog drawer tugged open against its will. Standing very still and quiet, Ani felt like a child in an adult's room from which she knew she should be barred.

She scanned the banks of shelves, the pretty stairs that ran up to higher shelves again, the wide desks nested on the floor. What was this paradise, this sanctuary? And the light through the delicate roof—it was shimmering, and it was gorgeous. Around the walls, the stained-glass windows glowed with images of newspaper presses, of old, old books, of scenes from Chaucer—the pilgrims leaving Southwark, the pilgrims arriving in Canterbury. She tilted her head: was that a koala on the bottom? Were there koalas in Chaucer? Then again, what did she know about Chaucer? Epigrams, really, that was all. *Love is blind. The life so short, the crafts so long to learn.* And, *People can die of mere imagination*, a line that had terrified her when she was at school.

"Can I help you with anything?" There was a tall man at her elbow, a librarian, she supposed. "Was there something in particular you were wanting?"

Ani shook her head. "No, thank you, it was raining, I came in. But it's lovely, lovely to see this."

And the man smiled: "There's something about a room for thoughts and words." It was a statement, simple and direct, but it rang for Ani with the sharpness of revealed truth. "I've always wondered if paradise might not be a little like a library," the man said then. "But that's probably a sacrilegious thing to suggest."

Ani blushed, as if it was, and at the grandness and the intimacy of the words. Her eyes flicked along the rows of men, some women, who sat with their books, their pencils, and their notes.

"It was raining, I came in," she said again. But what would it be like to come somewhere like this for a day's work, instead of the trains or the mines or any of the other noisy, messy places where most of the people she knew went to work? She glanced at the librarian and saw his hands smooth where Mac's were rough and grained with dirt. His shoulders, too, were stooped, and thinner than the straight broadness she was used to. But to come here to work; to sit in that silence, and that light.

She'd told Mac about it that night, as if she'd discovered a new world or uncovered a treasure, and she'd blushed when he laughed at her, at the power she'd invested in the idea of just sitting, sitting and reading. "Well, I do, I do think it sounds like heaven. And I do think about the things other people do, the other people I might be." Which had silenced him, and made him say something sharp about regretting he could make her no more than a railwayman's wife, and made her wish she had never said any of it, never talked about this new and beautiful place. They were rare, these dissonances and petty tiffs. Ani would have walked a thousand miles rather than have had one.

"And how would I have found you, hidden away in a great library?" he'd wanted to know. "There's nowt of adventures and explorers on shelves like those." The stories he loved; the stories, she suspected, he dreamed about living when he dreamed of being someone, or somewhere, else.

There's another footfall on the gravel and Ani looks up, startled out of the loop of that thought—startled, somehow, to find herself in the realization of this library that's suddenly, unexpectedly, her domain. A shadow changes the light in the doorway, and then a man comes in, dark-suited, dark-haired, and rubbing his hands together as if he's come in from the coldest winter.

"You're the widow, then," he says, taking off his hat and drumming his fingers across its crown. "I heard they'd given you this job out of pity."

Ani watches his fingers play over the fabric, beating a tattoo that matches the rise and fall of her stomach. There she is, mired back in the one story by which she might now be defined; she hates him, whoever this is.

"I'm Draper," he says. "The doctor. Come to minister to your sick and your dying, and bring all your new people into the world."

He coughs, and Ani tries to fit his shape to some memory of dancing—but all she can imagine is Mrs. Lacey in a fine frock she saw Ginger Rogers wear once in a film, all swan's down and chiffon, and that image is too ridiculous to belong to anything real. She waits for whatever he will say next, rubbing her own hands together as if to ward off his chill.

"And they've given you all this." He gestures so flamboyantly that there's no doubting how little he thinks of the place. "Which is generous, when not so many women have been able to stay in work since the war." He sets his hat down on the desk—her desk, she thinks, proprietorial for the first time. "Still, there's an argument, I suppose, that it will be better to keep your mind busy than to let it stretch and twist at leisure."

"Dr. Draper," she says at last, "you're not at all how I remembered. But I heard you were coming. And of course I have a daughter to support, and a house to keep." She's blushing, wishing to sound cool and sure. This isn't anyone she can remember; this isn't anyone who would dance or laugh.

"As so many do, losing their men to war—so many women, all over the world, and now the world is supposed to be back to normal, and the men are back to take their jobs, and what happens to those widows who haven't rushed back to the altar with some new man? What happens to their daughters, to their houses?"

Ani feels her teeth clench. "There's Legacy," she says slowly: it feels like an interrogation, an exam. "There are provisions for helping war widows. And as for me, everyone has been very kind. I'm neither ungrateful for this compensation nor"—her voice narrows to a tight spit like his—"unaware of its privilege." She pauses at the squeal of a train's wheels on the tracks outside. "But it's an odd gift, perhaps, to work by the sound of the thing that killed your husband. Not even your war widows have had to endure that." They're unsayable words; she is almost sneering as she watches the doctor's face crease with distaste, but she feels strangely powerful. *What now?* she thinks, defiant. *What will you say to me now?* She's never felt so sharp before.

But the distaste, it seems, is for himself. "My apologies, Mrs. Lachlan." The brash gaze is gone, his eyes focused on his own fingers as they worry at a knot tied in the corner of his handkerchief. "I lost many things in those years abroad, and among them were my social graces. Psychoneurosis, our American friends call it, if you want to be learned about it. People always like to have a label—for a newcomer, an outsider, or a widow. Still"—he straightens up, drawing a random shape on the brim of his hat with one finger—"the nuances of widowhood must be different, of course, when they aren't marked out by the weight of a war—I wonder whether people will regard you as more, or less, available."

Ani stares, wondering how it would feel to slap his face. She's never wished to do anything like that to anyone before. "My husband is barely dead." There's ice in her voice, and as she looks down to make the calculation by the calendar, she sees the date of her wedding anniversary, a few weeks ahead, and tastes something sharp and metallic in her mouth, unsure if its bile is for the nearness of a date that now feels purposeless or the fact that she didn't know, immediate and certain, precisely how many weeks, days, and hours had passed since Mac stopped being in the world.

The train pulls out, and as the room falls silent again, the doctor turns, his gaze panning the rows of shelves. "I expect there's nothing here that I require, but I will come and look another day."

"The hours are pasted by the door," says Ani, wishing she could think of something more cutting or retaliatory. "I'm sorry I don't remember you much from before the war, Dr. Draper. Mrs. Lacey tells me you were a fine dancer—and I think I remember you dancing with Iris McKinnon and laughing with her brother. It would have been lovely to have met you more properly then."

And it is satisfying, she thinks, to watch the color drain from his face, to watch his fingers reach again for his wrinkled handkerchief. "That was a long time ago, Mrs. Lachlan, a long time ago now." In the room's quietness, they regard each other, level. "I don't think I'm much good for dancing or laughter these days."

"Do come, if you think the library might have anything you

need. The hours, as I said, are pasted up." And she watches as he walks away towards the platform, disconcerted to hear him whistle, and wishing she could rinse his conversation out of her mouth.

Glancing up at the clock, she sees that its hands have finally reached the end of her first shift. Pulling the windows down and the door closed—the lock checked twice, three times—she realizes she's never felt more tired in her life. And she hasn't read a single page.

17

SHE RECOGNIZES him at once, the man who balanced on the high, weathered pole, his gaze fixed beyond the white line of breakers, the wavy line of horizon. Roy McKinnon, Iris's brother, the man who wrote the poem during the war. He is tall, she sees, taller than his sister, and his hair is greyer than the color she took it for outside, from a distance, on the beach. Inside, closer up, he looks a little more stooped and weathered. She is scanning the lines on his forehead, around his eyes, and when she realizes he is studying her in turn, she blushes.

"I'm so sorry—was there something . . ."

"Do you keep a poetry section, Mrs. Lachlan?" As soon as he begins to speak, he looks away from her, studying his shirt cuffs, his shoes.

She shakes her head, startled by his directness and fearing another conversation like the doctor's the day before.

"No, no, I don't think we get a lot of poetry through the shelves. Is there something I can request for you?"

He draws in such a deep breath she expects the papers on her desk to shift a little towards him.

"No, perhaps, I don't know. I'm sorry. I just thought there might be something I could take with me now." He's pulled a pen from his pocket and is fiddling with its cap, snapping it on and off, on and off, as he gazes at the shelves. "I'd take *Kangaroo* if you had it."

"For poetry?" she asks, stepping around the barrier of the table, pulling D. H. Lawrence from his place.

"No, just for something that comes from here. Can I use my sister's card?"

She nods. "I admired your poem very much, Mr. McKinnon," she says, opening the ledger to Iris McKinnon's record. "And your sister was thrilled when she saw it in the magazine." She knows this is a stretch, perhaps even a lie. Iris McKinnon had never even acknowledged the verse as far as Ani knew—it's one clear memory she has, handing the cutout sheet to her through her front doorway, watching her take it without so much as a glance, put it on the table beside her, and say that if there was nothing else, she had things to get back to, and close the door. Ani wonders, watching him, if her brother knows any of this.

He says, "You're very kind," and smiles at her, a warm and proper smile.

She wants to say she's never met a poet before, wants to say she saw him perched on the old jetty's pylon, and to ask how he jumped down without drenching himself, or whether he sat through a full turn of the tide.

But instead she says: "It's no trouble to check the book out to your sister's card," and she writes the details into her ledger. She says: "Will you stay with Miss McKinnon long?"

He's balancing the book on one hand as if to guess its weight. "Long enough to read this and work out how it sprang from here."

"You don't like it here, Mr. McKinnon?" And she braces herself for a shrug. "My husband gave me this to read when we were traveling to the coast. I loved the idea that such a story could come from such a pretty seaside town. It felt incongruous or—I don't know—dangerous somehow." It's the first time she's mentioned Mac this casually since—since; she nearly falters—and she likes the ease of it, the sense that it gives him some currency. *Immortality*: she risks thinking the word.

"You didn't grow up here?"

"No, no, miles inland, on the plains, dry as a biscuit. I didn't see the ocean until I was married, until I'd read *Kangaroo*. Were you and Iris children here? I mean"—she blushes, despite herself—"I remember you visiting a little, when we came, in '36, but I don't remember if your family . . ."

He puts the book down on the corner of her desk, the very corner, repositioning it until its edges match the edges of the wood precisely. The silence beyond her words grows and grows, and she's on the edge of repeating the question when he says: "We came for holidays when we were kids, for weekends when we were older. Later, then, our parents died, and Iris came to stay." And then immediately, "And I'll take another novel, to keep me going," so that she knows the other exchange is over. She watches as he moves along the shelves, tilting a spine towards him here and there, pulling out one or two volumes to skim through their pages, his nose pressed close, before he reshelves them—carefully, gently. Then, "I haven't read this for years," and he slides *Jane Eyre* across the desk.

"One of my favorites," she says. "But I expect a lot of people say that. That scene where Rochester talks of sending Jane to Ireland—the cord he thinks connects them, from his heart to hers—" She stops, blushing. Mac had told her early in their friendship it was his favorite book: it was a large part of how she remembers falling in love. And here she is, on the edge of talking about this with a man she hardly knows, just for the sake of bringing Mac into the room.

"I only like reading it now I know how it ends," Roy McKinnon says as if she hasn't cut herself off, and she watches, appreciative, as he flicks to the last page, as if to check that its sentences still tell the right story. "The first time—all that suffering, all that separation; it's a terrible thing to confess but I think I skipped ahead just to make sure it turned out all right."

"My daughter does that sometimes," says Ani, recovering herself. "I like that it matters so much to her that a book's characters end up happy and well."

And he smiles again, tucking a book in each of his coat's pockets and turning for the door. Where he stops, scuffs one foot a little on the mat, and turns again. "It was nice to meet you, Mrs. Lachlan," he says carefully, his fingertips up towards the brim of his hat. "I was sorry to hear—"

"It was nice to meet you, too," she says quickly, across the condolence, and he blushes in turn. *He's shy,* thinks Ani. *I wouldn't have expected that.* Wouldn't it take a certain courage to write a poem? Didn't people talk about his bravery during the war? "And I'll see what I can do about the poetry. There are some new books due to come down next week."

He waves his thanks and goes, and she listens as his feet crunch across the gravel, disappearing under such a sudden rush of a train passing that she jumps.

She pulls a blank sheet of paper towards her, uncaps her pen. How would you start to write a poem? How would you put together a series of words for its first line—how would you know which words to choose? When you read a poem, every word seemed so perfect that it had to have been predestined—well, a good poem. Mac could do doggerel for Isabel, or funny limericks for birthday cards. But a real poem, a proper poem: Ani stares at the blank sheet. *How would you know what to do?*

She smoothes the page, writes the day's date at the top, writes the library's designation, and drafts the request for some poetry, if possible, in the next dispatch of books. "For Mr. Roy McKinnon," she writes, "a published poet, who lives locally in these parts."

18

IN THE bar of the Ryans Hotel, Roy McKinnon and Frank Draper sit down for their first beer together after the war, the glasses cold against their fingers, the room dim and quiet around them. It's a Tuesday afternoon, a nothing time, when men should be working. But here they are, drinking.

"To making it home," says Roy, raising his glass. But Frank, rather than replying, simply drains his drink, and signals for another.

"Impossible, isn't it?" he says, etching a pattern into the glass's frost.

"I never let myself imagine it might happen," says Roy quietly. "Never let myself think about being back."

"What was the worst of it?" They are sitting close, each with his nose near his glass; each with his head slightly bowed. There is something supplicatory about it, as if they were receiving some sort of communion.

"The worst of it?" Roy asks. "The constant expectation of death—killing or being killed."

"Did you kill anyone?"

Roy's fingers tighten around his glass; then he picks it up and drinks it dry. "I can't tell you that; you can't ask me."

"All right." Frank signals across the bar for another drink for them both. "Then the best of it. Was there a best of it?"

And Roy laughs. "I met a bloke who gave his address, on his papers, his enlistment papers, as Thirroul Beach—not just Thirroul, not the village, not anywhere in the streets, but the beach itself, the very sand. 'That's where I belong,' he said, 'and that's where I'll go back to.' Dunno if he made it. Don't even know if I'd recognize him if I saw him."

"Not bad," says Frank. "I like that. My best was a garden of roses blooming a mile or so beyond one of the camps—so normal, so beautiful. They looked right, you know, and they smelled right. They smelled like they belonged in the real world, not those pits of death and misery. Everything else, even after the war ended, everything else was panic and rush—sending people home who could be sent home, the way they clamored and panicked for the trucks, as if someone was going to snatch away their one chance of getting out of there. And just over the hill, this patch of roses was going through the normal course of a normal year. They were blooming as usual, and they smelled so good, I could have eaten them."

They sit awhile, sipping now and then. Roy McKinnon's fingers tap out a rhythm on the bar. Frank Draper rubs his hand through his hair every so often, and lets out a sigh that sounds like *anyway, anyway.*

"So what do we do now we're here?" Roy asks at last. "What happens now?"

"All falling into place, isn't it?" The doctor's voice is hollow. "You must be working on your first book of verse, my poet, and here I am ready to usher in life and death for this village's patients. Just as we always planned."

Roy shakes his head. "I don't know what to write about, now

that I'm here. I don't even know how to write." His fingers circle the top of the glass, the friction between its wetness and his skin making the sailors' curse ring out. He stills himself. "I stand in this beautiful place, on glorious days, and the only images that come are from over there, back then. Not that some of those weren't beautiful or glorious. One night, there was a tiny island and no moon; you know those nights you thank God that you're covered in pitch? We were buzzing ashore in some little boat, looking for the enemy in some new messy swamp, and the whole ocean was lit up with phosphorescence—the way it churned and turned behind the boat, it was like a carpet had been thrown over the sea. I sit and look at the ocean here, and I think of that, on a good day. Other days, I think of other oceans, of what it sounds like when the voices of drowning men finally stop." He takes a long drink. "I should write to someone about that bloke from Thirroul Beach—find out if he made it, find out who to tell about seeing him, if he didn't. That matters, doesn't it, Frank? Those messages must matter?"

He shifts his head, trying to find his friend's gaze, but Frank's eyes stay down, so low they might as well be closed. "I don't know, mate," he says at last. "I don't know. They're not going to bring anyone back to life, are they? Nothing can do that. And that's all anyone wants in the end, isn't it? To change that; to bring someone back. A message—well, I never did set much store by words, you know."

He means it as a joke, and tries to laugh, but no sound comes out of his mouth, and they sit awhile longer, silent, their shoulders almost touching.

"Lawrence the poet, and Yeats's doctor," says Roy quietly. "Do you reckon we still have a chance of filling their shoes?" Their younger selves had set much store by any available precedents, leaning against village memories of renown, a writer from Notts and a doctor from Dublin: if two such men could find their way to this speck in an atlas and *do* something here—well, the young Roy, the young Frank had told each other their own opportunities in these fields might be limitless.

"Don't care whose shoes we fill, Royston, my friend," Frank says now. "It would just be a blessed relief not to be walking around in my own all the time." The doctor pushes back from the bar, shifts his hat on his head. "At least I can sleep," he says at last. "At least I don't tremble or stutter. I mean, my memory's gone, but I'd rather forget than remember—the war at least, and I can't remember when there was anything before that. Saw a bloke interviewed by doctors just last year—that's two years after this is all supposed to be over, and they still can't discharge him from the hospital. You know what he kept saying, over and over? 'I was a solid man before this; I was a solid man.'" He shakes his head, wiping at his eyes. "And Iris? How's Iris?"

"You should see for yourself—" It's harder than Roy means it to sound, so he swallows the end of the sentence with his drink, fixes his own hat, and stands. "I mean, I think she's waiting—I think she's . . ." He shrugs. "You work it out, you two. It's been too many years."

"And you? What do you need to work out, now you're here?"

The two men stand on the curbside, looking along the main street towards the railway line, towards the ocean.

"I need to work out what kind of chump finds poetry in the middle of mud and blood, and can't string a sentence together about this mountain, this sunshine, this sky, and this place. Nothing to do beyond that."

The doctor grips his friend's shoulder, holding him in an embrace for just a moment. "Find yourself something new to think about. It'll work itself out after that."

"Fine advice from you." Roy McKinnon laughs. But it's good to laugh—and Frank, after all, is a doctor; his statements arrive with the authority of prescription. Roy grabs his friend's hand and shakes it, holds it, as a bus rattles southwards and an old horse and cart clatter north. "You were right to come back here—it'll be all right, I reckon."

"Nothing will ever be all right, mate," says Draper, stepping away. "But if I'm going to come to terms with that, I may as well do it somewhere I've someone to drink with."

They walk along the main street together. Frank's face is hard and dark—catching sight of it in a window, Roy doesn't want to know what's happening inside his friend's imagination, or who is there with him. For himself, as he nears the railway station and glances along towards its buildings, he finds that he's thinking about a tall woman with light hair, standing silent among a land-scape of books, and the ocean wild and vast beyond.

He waits for a sentence to form.

19

"THIS IS how it was the first time I saw you."

When Mackenzie Lachlan butted up against the side of Australia, he was twenty-five years old with nowhere in particular to go and no one in particular to be. Walking up from his ship's anchorage on the too-bright, too-blue harbor, he turned at the sound of a Glaswegian accent—more angular than his northerly Scots, but still friendly for being familiar—and found himself talking to a rosy man called Ewan who'd been ashore a month and found a job on the railways. "It's way away, laddie," he'd said to Mac Lachlan, "out in the space where your family must be from," and he punched at his shoulder and laughed as Mac frowned. "A river called Lachlan, man; I'm taking engines out there, to the plains." And Mac Lachlan, who liked a good story, thought he'd like to see the river that ran along in his name.

At the yards the next day, with Ewan still punching and pummeling his shoulders, he was told there were no jobs for the minute, but—a nod, a wink—he might as well travel out with his mate. "Off we go, lad," Ewan boomed as he took a train—and Mac—out through the city's suburbs on their first run. "But y'picked a lousy place to come looking for work, or a lousy time." They left the coast the next day, the engine hauling them south and west through green space, blond space, dust-dry space, and white space that seemed to hold pure emptiness. "But you'll see your family's river," Ewan boomed again and again, and Mac laughed too, the vast landscape and its potential blossoming inside him. He'd dreamed of places this open, this flat, this inviting. This warm.

The ranges and the hills, the slightest inclines and hummocks, behind them, he could feel himself stretching out—wider, wider and wider—trying to see not just this intoxicating stretch of open land but the very curve of the earth he could make out at its edge. He saw birds high in the air; he saw animals bounding along beside the line. He saw mirages and shadows that loomed where there was nothing to throw them, and strange figures that seemed to rise out of the tiny gap where the dirt met the sky, that ran with the train awhile, and then folded themselves back into that liminal rut. He saw different shapes picked out in stars, and different colors marking the phases of dawn, day, and dusk. And when he arrived, he rode out to see this river that was somehow his, its water khaki, its edges soft with the khaki leaves of gum trees. He even passed a tiny place that bore his grandmother's Christian name, Maude, to match the river that marked her surname, Lachlan. And he took all this to mean that this was the place, in all of Australia, that he was supposed to have found.

Back in town, he put out the word for any work and was told to meet up with one of the town's builders early the next morning for a job of roofing that was needed in a hurry.

He slept at the pub, his dreams spiked by tall, thin figures who darted, silhouettes, along the horizon. And when he woke in the morning it was still dark, a frost on the ground, and the sound of snoring all along the hall. He washed his face, shaved, wetted down the worst of his hair, ate porridge in the pub's kitchen, drank a huge mug of tea, and was out in the clear, cold air as the first birds began to call.

He liked the town, the way it pressed together instead of spreading wide in all the room it had, and he liked the sound his boots made on its roads. He followed the instructions the publican had given him, humming here and there, singing now and then—a couple of bars of *Speed, bonnie boat,* a premature snatch of *Morning has broken*—and still filled with the possibility of all the space around him. He was an ocean boy himself—the cuan, he loved it—mucking along beaches for whelks and crabs, swimming as far as the cold would let him, and heading out on the trawlers if he was able. But the span of the sky out here was a close match for the sea—as wide and as blue.

"My bonnie lies over the ocean," he sang softly as he rounded the last corner. He'd reached the edge of the town without realizing it and before him lay the shape of a house, low and spreading, and its roof, triangular and partial, open to the morning. The road dipped down a little towards it, the first brightness of sunrise beyond in reds, pinks, golds: he was walking directly east. "My bonnie lies over the sea."

"Good morning, Mr. Lachlan," a voice called from up in the air, and as he arched his neck to see where it had come from, he made out two figures perched on the roof's narrow frame. "The kind gentleman in the public house said you'd be along early in the morning." It was an odd accent, soft, with the first syllable of each word leaned on a little, like a strangely rhythmic march. It was unlike any he'd heard before, and as his eyes adjusted to the changing light, he made out the man, tall, fair, with a tanned face and thick blond beard and mustache.

"Mr. Kalm," he called, "I hope I've not kept you," and as he raised his hand to wave, it shaded his eyes for a moment so that he saw her just as the ball of the sun came over the crest. Anikka Kalm, standing next to her father, watching the earth roll forward into a new day. Tall, like her father, and fair, like her father, her feet were set apart to balance on the beam—he thought, *She'd stand well on any ship*; he thought, *That's what lissome is, then*—and the bright rose-gold of the moment seemed to burnish her hair, her face, her skin, her shape with light.

"The first time I saw you," he would whisper to her afterwards when he told her the story, "it was just getting light. I took you for part of the sunrise."

But at that moment, in that morning, he simply stood and gazed up at her while she stood above him and gazed out towards the sun.

Oskar Kalm swung down onto the ground, talked about frames and nails and slate and hours, and Mac agreed to anything, paying no attention to the conversation. He heard himself say, "I'm more an ocean man," heard Oskar say that one would have to be an ocean man to find oneself so far from home and in this part of the world. But then the memory of those words, too, disappeared under the sound of Anikka's voice.

"I've never seen the ocean," she said, her voice halfway between the roundness of her father's Nordic accent and the stretch of every Australian voice Mac had yet encountered. "It must be so wide, so blue, so . . ." She fumbled for a word, her fingers worrying at the air as if she might find it there. "So wet." And she blushed.

"My daughter," said Oscar Kalm, "was rudely landlocked by my ending up here." He swung a belt, a hammer, towards his new assistant, calling up to the girl that they needed to be getting on with the job they were there for. And Mac watched as she swung herself down—bending easily to grip the framework near her ankle, dropping down until her toes found the shape of a window below that, and then springing back to arrive standing, next to him, as tall as him, on the grass.

"Mackenzie Lachlan," he said, holding out his hand.

"Anikka Kalm," she said, shaking it firmly.

"I could take you to see the ocean one day," he said, and blushed.

"I could come with you to see that," she said, laughing—although he wasn't sure if the laugh was for the suggestion of the ocean or the red flush on his cheeks. "It's nice to meet you, Mr. Lachlan. I'll bring some lunches out later in the day." And as she strode away, it seemed the sun kept pace with her movement across the ground.

Her blond hair so bright it looked lit from within.

20

ROY McKINNON returns *Jane Eyre* on the day it's due. Ani looks up from a box of books and he's standing in the doorway, scraping his shoes on the mat, taking a little too long to do as simple a thing as come into a room.

"I've brought this," he says simply. "I've been staring at it so long but I couldn't . . ."

"Mr. McKinnon," she says, "I'm so sorry if it wasn't what you wanted." As if she should have been able to guide him, to advise him on a happier book; as if she's failed in her job somehow.

But he shakes his head, seems to shake his hat right from it, and, bareheaded, finally steps inside.

"No, no, it was good; it was good, Mrs. Lachlan, and I've finished with it now. I wanted to hang on to it, that was all. I wanted to keep it close, but—" He smiles, holding it out towards her. "I wondered if I could ask you to get me some particular poets, if that's possible—the British, from the Great War. I thought I might try them."

"Wilfred Owen? Rupert Brooke?" She's pulling names from the contents pages of the one anthology her own shelves hold at home, wanting to sound knowledgeable.

"No, no"—he cuts across her quickly—"not the ones who died; the ones who survived. Sassoon. Graves. The ones who kept living, kept writing."

There's an edge in his voice that she knows from somewhere, but it takes her a moment to place it. It's panic, the voice of mothers when their children can't be found for a moment; the voice of women against the news that their sons, their husbands, are not coming home; the voice of Anikka herself one day when Isabel inched too close to the edge of the station's platform—of Anikka herself, she suspects, in the hours, the days, beyond the accident.

"I made some tea, Mr. McKinnon, just a moment ago—could I get you a cup?" She's on his side of the desk now, pulling out a chair, clearing a space. "Was there something you were looking for in particular? Some poem? Some description?" The way he lowers himself onto the chair is as if he distrusts it, and she wonders whether poets think differently about simple things like chairs and hats. Filling a cup, she wonders if it would be rude to ask.

As she turns towards him again, the tea carefully balanced, the afternoon's light hits that point before sunset where it softens and swells sometimes into a few minutes of rounder, warmer illumination. Through the window, the greens of the trees thicken slightly, the shadows lengthen, and the sky takes on a fuller shade of blue. The mountain, diminished at midday, surges again to its full height; the clouds flare a brighter white.

Inside, the last of the sun picks up the wood of the library's shelves, its floor, its desk, grazing the side of the poet's head and turning his dull grey-brown hair into something flecked by ginger and gold. For the shortest moment, Ani wants to reach out and touch it—to see if it's warm, to see if it's soft—and it's only the cup and saucer that stop her from making this movement.

"There," she says, blushing a little, "it's a magic time of the day when the sun goes over the mountain, don't you think? The way it makes everything glow."

He drinks his tea too fast—she knows how hot it is—gulping with each mouthful, until he reaches the layer of sugar at the bottom. "Is it always like this?" he asks then, china rattling against china as he replaces the cup too forcefully in the scoop of its saucer.

"The light?" she says. "No—I think it needs particular clouds, or a wind. There's something more to it than just the end of the day, but I've never managed to work out what it is."

But he's shaking his head again; she's misunderstood the question. "No, no; I mean, how you say things—the light, the time—is it always like this? It makes you sound like a poet yourself."

The blush goes all the way up to her hair this time. "I don't know the first bit of poetry really," she says, a little desperate. "Although my husband used to read poems aloud to me sometimes—the Scottish ones; they rollicked along. I like to read, Mr. McKinnon. That's all." And she wishes for an instant that she hadn't given him the tea—even though it's already drunk and finished—or the chance of a conversation. It feels heady, or reckless, and she steps back until she feels the solid horizontal of the desk hard behind her.

"It's a lovely light," he says at last, but so quietly that she almost misses the words. "As if it's coming through stained glass—even when you're outside. You know, I've never thought of it like that before." Unfolding an envelope from his pocket, he feels across the surface of her table, his eyes fixed on the middle distance between them. "May I—do you have a pen?" And she slides one towards him, spinning it around so it's ready for him to pick up and write.

"Is this . . . are you . . ." She wants to know if she's watching some act of creation, if something is coming into being in this library that didn't exist the moment before.

"Those terrible stories of the books burned in Germany before the war," he says then. "Do you remember? A city square on fire with great pyres of words—they burned Helen Keller, you know. They burned Jack London. 'Where they burn books, so too will they in the end burn people'—I read that somewhere years ago. And it will be years before we know how many people were truly lost through this war—before it started, when it was happening, and now, even now, when it's supposed to be over." His words come in a rush, tripping over themselves. "How many bodies burned in one city or another country or the whole rest of the world. And now your books, Mrs. Lachlan, are caught by the edge of fire, their spines red and orange, just there, just above you. And it's beautiful." He pushes the pen away, puts the envelope, still blank, back into his pocket, carefully refolded.

"Are you writing now, Mr. McKinnon?" Her forthrightness flares the redness of her face again. "I mean, since you're home—these past years . . . I don't know if it's a question I should ask you or not, but it's always intrigued me how—"

"What intrigues me, Mrs. Lachlan"—there's a coldness in his voice and he's suddenly on his feet, adjusting his hat, and turning for the door—"is what sort of a man can find a poem in the middle of all that, and then come home to a place as pretty as this and find nothing, nothing . . ." He breathes in too long a breath, then tips the edge of his hat. "But I've become monotonous. If you could let me know when those books come in," he says, and is gone.

"I hope you're feeling . . ." she begins to say, into the emptiness. She wonders if he registers the tightness in his own voice.

Taking a deep breath herself, Ani pulls the ledger towards her again, begins to run through the books that will go back to Sydney the following day. *The Grapes of Wrath* has been popular, and Eleanor Dark's *Timeless Land*, while people wait for its sequel, and Zane Grey, as ever. He's dead, but still publishing: what literary medium makes that happen, that writing from beyond the grave? Mac loved him, following his stories across every incarnation of the

Wild West's frontier. And if Zane Grey is still writing books after his own death, maybe Mac Lachlan is still reading them. It feels a dangerously flippant thing to think.

She shakes her head to dislodge the idea, changing the angle from which she looks at her list. If she concentrated on which books were most popular in each batch, would she find the secrets of what this village thought and felt among the stories it borrowed to tell itself? It's a safer thing to think.

She pushes at her temples, unsettled, and sees Roy pulling the envelope from his pocket so that it shakes out to its full size, reaching forward—doesn't matter that it's her pen, her desk—for anything that might make a mark. With her eyes closed, she can make him Mac, the table their kitchen table. She sees her own hand push a pen towards him, sees him pick it up, begin to write.

She can almost see the words as her husband tries to make a poem.

And why not? *Why not?*

She blows a long breath into the empty room. There he is, there he is, Mackenzie Lachlan, her man. He leans forward, finishes his first line with a flourish, looks up into nothingness—she's invisible—and then down again, the pen busy with another line and another. She watches for a minute, knowing she should leave him to do this on his own. No, if she'd had this moment, she'd have sat there, seeing it happen, soaking it in.

His hand slows, stops, and he's blowing onto the words, softly, as if to hurry them dry. What would he say next? Would he read it? Would he fold it up, slip it back into his pocket, promise to read it to her when it had sat for a while? Would he pretend that nothing had happened, that he'd been making a list of the things he needed to remember to do the coming weekend?

He's fading; the kitchen is fading. She's back in the library, staring somewhere between the titles of books she's spent the morning packaging up. Without looking, she pulls a sheet of paper from the stack on her desk, a pencil from the jar. So close, he was so clear. She can do this: she can pull a poem for him out of the air.

> The light is heavy before sunset
> The world encased in thick stained glass

—but that's stealing. That was the poet's line, and she's back in the room with a thud, Mac gone, the poem gone, the light gone, and the evening coming on fast.

The thunder of a train coming down from the north collides with the thunder of one coming up from the south and for an instant, out of nowhere, Anikka is certain they will collide, here, in her station, outside her window, in a great crash of metal and fire and weight.

She hates these thoughts, tries to shrug catastrophe away from her shoulders.

The light is heavy before sunset, she recites. "The light is heavy before sunset." She pulls another sheet towards her, writes out the poet's request for anything by Siegfried Sassoon, Robert Graves. She's read poems by them—she's sure of it, staring at the names until a line comes into her mind: *Everyone's voice was suddenly lifted; And beauty came like the setting sun.*

When Mac was hit, how long had it taken him to die? Did it happen immediately? Did it happen later in the afternoon? Did he go during daylight, in the darkness, or just as the sun set? Was there anyone she could ask? The inquest was coming, she knew, and she'd said again and again that she would not be attending, did not want to sit through the details of injuries and blame. The time, and the light; she'd like to know about those. She could ask the railways man or the minister. She could ask Luddy; he might know. But there is something preserving in the idea that people could know parts of the story that she didn't, as if she didn't need to bear them all at once—she tells herself this and believes it is true.

She folds the request letter, licking so fiercely at the envelope that it slices her tongue.

"Damn it." She's never cursed anything before. "Damn it all." Closing the book before her tears fall onto its pages and make spots on all the lists she's taken such care to transcribe. "Damn and damn and damn."

"Mrs. Lachlan?" Iris McKinnon, the poet's sister, is standing in the doorway. "I'm sorry—my brother forgot to give you this one," sliding *Kangaroo* across the desk. "I hoped it might help him be here, but . . ." She fiddles with the clasp on her bag. "I don't think he got past the first chapters. And he asked me to apologize to you."

"For not reading the book?" Anikka hears a harshness in her own voice and doesn't care if Iris McKinnon hears it too.

"I don't know—he just said to apologize. It's hard, I think, for him . . ." Her voice sounds tired of making her brother's excuses.

Anikka slides the book towards herself so it rests against her belly. "If he's staying with you for some time, Miss McKinnon, he should probably get his own card—so that you can keep borrowing as well." Changing the subject; filling the silence.

The other lady smiles. "Oh, I don't mind—I never need to read as much as he does, and it's nice to think I can do something for him, give him something that might help him . . ." She pauses, awkward. "Of course it's a great blessing that he came home and came home uninjured, and really that's all you can ask for."

Ani taps the spine of the book on the desk, as if its pages needed to be squared, and moves to reshelve it. "There are different kinds of loss, you know," she says quietly.

"Well, yes," says Miss McKinnon, her fingers fidgeting with a handkerchief as if she's thinking about dabbing her eyes or blowing her nose. "As you know yourself, Mrs. Lachlan, after all these years."

Anikka blinks at the thin woman's ferocity—it crosses her mind that she might damn her, and to her face, and this doesn't seem a bad idea, although Iris McKinnon is talking again.

"But as I always say, time heals all wounds—I remember telling you that a long time ago, Mrs. Lachlan, and I try to tell my poor brother every day now as well." Her back is rigidly straight, her face is set, and the weakness implicit in the handkerchief's brief flutter has been stuffed back into her handbag along with the white fabric.

The room darkens as the night properly begins. In the last moments of shadow before she reaches for the lights, Ani hears herself say: "No, Miss McKinnon, no. I do remember you saying that to me, and I've been meaning to say ever since that you were wrong. Time passes, and wounds close over, but the healing is a different thing altogether—and often, I think, you cannot expect that it will ever fully occur."

"Don't say that." The other woman's voice drops to a hiss. "Don't say that they won't all come back, the ones who lived. Don't condemn us all to widowhood, now that you have to make sense of it."

Ani blinks. Is that what she does? Is this who she is? She flicks the switch and the sudden brightness of the bulb above startles them both.

"I'll send a note when Mr. McKinnon's books arrive," she says at last. And the poet's sister turns and leaves without another word.

Ani watches her go, and remembers, in an instant, a day in her own garden, Isabel fiddling with her first flowers, and Iris McKinnon naming each one as her daughter pried their petals apart. These losses, these slips: perhaps it took a larger one to notice all the other people you'd let get away. Perhaps it was only then that you wondered how they happened, if they mattered. *But perhaps I used to be a better friend.*

Ani works the book box closer to the door and kneels down in front of it, checking its contents against its list for the last time, and making sure the books are packed neatly and secure. She wonders if Miss McKinnon has read *Kangaroo* and realizes in an instant that any number of people she knows in this place might even have been here when it was written. They might have seen its writer. Ani would envy them that.

But we were closer, Iris and me, she thinks then. *I was the person who cut her brother's poem from the magazine for her—I was the person who gave it to her so she could read it. Years after Bella was born, I was still the person who would think to do that. I should know what happened with her.*

Perhaps the poem didn't matter to Iris McKinnon; *perhaps,* thinks Ani suddenly, *she wishes he hadn't written it. Perhaps she was embarrassed by it.*

Closing the box and securing it at last, she resolves to be nicer to the poet. And when she walks home, later in the evening, she recites the first two lines of what she's already calling "Mac's poem" over and over in time to her footsteps, like a chant or a spell or a mantra.

21

"LOOK AT this, love." Mac pushed the magazine across the kitchen table towards her, steering it around the mess she was making with some fruit. "Article about the northern lights, see. Did I ever tell you about the time I saw them, a little bairn out in the night with my gran, and all their colors snaking and swirling across the sky?"

"You did, Mac, you did—weren't you going to take me to see their show?" Her reflexive reply, co-opting his fantasy of return.

The house creaked a little, settling its shape in the evening's cool, and Ani waited to hear if this had disturbed their sleeping daughter.

"If we could get round the world, lass, see my gran, and the lights—and then a quick skate across the ocean to your da's country and his people . . ." He smiled. "And all that on a railwayman's wage." The smile widening into a laugh.

She slid the segments of fruit into the saucepan, wiping their bright mess from the brighter red laminate of the table's top.

"Maybe I could get a job," she said after a moment. "Add a few more shillings to our savings."

But he shook his head, his attention back on the pages in the magazine. "What would you want to do, Ani? And what jobs would there be now everyone's back from the war?" He drew in a deep breath. "That smells grand, what you're making—what is it?"

"Just fruit—just some peaches: I thought I'd stew them up so you could have your favorite pie later on." She supposed it didn't matter about the money, and a job might be more trouble than it was worth. Iris McKinnon had been taken off the post round for some returning soldier and was raising hell about being replaced, the grocer said. *Still,* thought Ani, *secretly, she must prefer to have her time back to herself.* Throughout the war, watching Iris heave her heavy satchel along the village's streets, Ani had never thought she looked happy. *She never made it look like a thing you'd want to do.*

"Preserving for the winter." He laughed. "You do take care of me."

She stood alongside him as he sat at the table, pulled him in towards her, ruffled his hair. "Doing my best," she said softly. "Doing my best." The house shifted again, and Ani paused, listening for Isabel.

"She's a big girl now, love," said Mac, noticing her stillness. "Reckon she'd sleep through an earthquake most nights. Remember when she was born and that plane came down on the beach, all engines and kerfuffle, and she didn't even rouse?" He worked his arm around his wife, his other hand smoothing the page he was reading.

"The airplane on the beach? The mail plane in the storm?" Ani frowned. "That was 1936, Mac; that was just after we came, well before Bella was born. Don't you remember Luddy setting out that line of flares to make a kind of runway?"

"It was cars, wasn't it? A row of cars parked along the beach with their headlights on to show him how to come in—and I'm sure Bella was born; sure we brought Mrs. May in to sit with her while we ran down to help." Mac was rubbing at his own hair now, frowning and perplexed.

Ani pushed the pan of fruit to the back of the stove, watching as its bubbles settled into a low simmer. "I'll get my daybook," she said. "That'll fix your lousy memory, Mackenzie Lachlan."

"Your daybook, your daybook," he called after her. "I'm sure it's just a little fallible now and then, Mrs. Mackenzie Lachlan—sure a bit of poetic license creeps in."

Coming back into the kitchen, leafing through the old diary, she raised her eyebrows in mock affront: "I don't know what you mean, sir. I am a mere scribe of events around me . . ." And she ducked as he threw a tea towel at her. "All right, once or twice I might have exaggerated. . . ."

"You had us sliding down the scarp in a tropical monsoon in your telling of our first bushwalk, Anikka Kalm, when it was the lightest shower of rain imaginable."

"Well, it felt heavier, and wetter, and it made for a better story with a bit of thunder and lightning—which I'm sure we *did* have. But I'd never change the year a plane landed on the beach, or whether our daughter was born or not when it did, or whether it was brought home by a line of flares lit by young Luddy or a line of parked cars."

Her fingers leafed through the book's pages, and she paused, reading random lines from its months.

"Here," she said. "One airplane coming down through thick fog and rain, March 1936, with a line of makeshift flares pushed into the sand—we'd only been here a month or so, and it felt like the whole village came out to help. . . ." She paused. "Or were we all just prying?" She held the book out to Mac, tapping its date with her finger.

He hardly read the page, his eyes moving across it so quickly while he said, "All right then, all right," and then looked across at the page opposite, the day before. "See this, though, Ani love." Mac's finger traced the words. " 'And we talked about sailing north, sailing up to see Grannie Lachlan, and how we might find so much money for that.'"

She tilted her head, reading over his shoulder. "I always thought we talked about going later, when we had Isabel, so Grannie Lachlan could meet her. And you see, we could use some extra money—we even said so then."

Mac smiled, tapping at the page. "Yes we did, love: here it is. Written fast in ink." He squeezed her into a hug. "Stories are always changing, aren't they, although I could have sworn I remembered that line of cars—would've told you who'd driven them onto the sand, if you'd asked me. And what do you want with the bother of a job, Ani?" This talk of employment; if she wanted it, he supposed, she should do it, but he didn't want her turning into some hectoring harridan like Iris McKinnon. His Ani, she'd be better than most men at anything she turned her hand to—he couldn't imagine she didn't know this herself.

Ani shook her head, stirring the softening peaches as the sound of a train braking hard cut through the night. "We'll never get north on a railwayman's wage," she said, but she was only teasing, and he knew it—although he felt it underlined by the train's noise.

"She's late tonight," he said. "And in a hurry to make it up too. Shall we get to bed then, Anikka Lachlan? Shall we read a little in the warm?"

And she lay beside him in the dim light of the lamp, listening as he read to her from the famous book about this place:

Then the train came out on the sea—lovely bays with sand and grass and trees, sloping up towards the sudden hills that were like a wall. There were bungalows dotted in most of the bays. Then suddenly more collieries, and quite a large settlement of bungalows. From the train they looked down on many pale-grey zinc roofs, sprinkled about like a great camp, close together, yet none touching, and getting thinner towards the sea. The chimneys were faintly smoking, there was a haze of smoke and a sense of home, home in the wilds.

"The wilds," she murmured. "I never thought of it as the wilds. But home, yes, and the only home Bella has had, compared to our beginnings."

He watched as her eyes closed, as she burrowed her head into his side for the rest of the reading, as she slipped further away from the book in whose subsequent chapters, the ones unwritten beyond the narrative's end, she'd always suspected she was living.

22

THEY MEET in the door of the co-op—Anikka coming out with sugar, tea, flour, and Roy McKinnon going in, his hands in his pockets. Her eyes fail in the sunlight after the dimness of the shop; his strain to see anything in the shadows after the brightness of the day; and for an instant neither can see the other.

They step awkwardly—she to her left, he to his right—so that the doorway remains impassable, and at the moment Ani laughs and Roy's eyes adjust to the gloom so that he can see her, and where he's going, and everything on the busy shelves of the shop, in more minute detail than usual. He's struck by the way she emerges, coming into focus, and by the patterns made by the different bits of produce tucked into their little bays and buckets on the wall behind the shop's counter. There's something to be said, he thinks, about what's available, what's plentiful in this place, in this world, about the great extent of what might be found here. But as he thinks this, he looks at her again and sees that her laugh is distracted, uneasy, in this no-man's-land of space.

She used to love it, the gathering, the provisioning. Now she rushes through the shops she needs to enter, hating the whispers, the stares. Here comes Anikka Lachlan, her basket swinging and her eyes still down—the women pause in their talk as she moves past them, her shopping list tight in her hand. From the counter, they hear her ask for her butter ration and her tea. "She looks tired," says one. "Tired and pale—Mrs. May says her light's on late these days."

"And that job in the library," says another. "Good of the railways to offer it but it must be hard to keep the house going as well."

"They used to play cards with us, her and Mac, sometimes. I miss that. She was always so bright."

They pause as she counts the coins from her purse, pushes them over the counter. And they smile and murmur a greeting as she goes by again. Anikka Lachlan, still in the shadows, not yet found the light. She's cooked meals for most of the widows in this town—now most times she comes home there's another dish, mostly anonymous, set waiting on her porch.

She's no appetite for any of it.

"Mrs. Lachlan." Roy takes another half step towards her and shakes her hand. "I wanted to thank you again—the Sassoon, 'Everyone Sang': just what I needed. That light, that hopefulness, that continuity."

A lady with a broad basket tries to squeeze past them clicking her tongue, perhaps over their obstacle, perhaps over the exuberance of the poet's words.

"'The singing will never be done,'" says Roy McKinnon, still clutching Anikka's hand. "'The singing will never be done.'"

And she smiles at last. "I'm glad you enjoyed it," she says. "We should . . ." Gesturing backwards towards the shop, forward towards the road, as another lady tries to squeeze past. They step as one into the full sunlight, Ani rearranging her parcels, Roy rearranging his hat.

"I was struggling," he says, dropping into such a long pause that she thinks perhaps that's all he wants to say, until, "with trying to write, I think I told you, even all this time after the war, and even somewhere as beautiful as this." His hand, sweeping up towards the escarpment, the sky, loops back to include her in its gesture. "The Sassoon—I don't know, but it helped, and I'm sure I'm closer now to the beginning of something. A new poem." He bows a little with a stately gratitude that belongs in another time, another place.

"I'm glad the library could help," says Anikka, and her smile stretches wider than she can remember. "Poetry is—it's a sort of extremity, isn't it?" she says after a breath. "So whether the extremity comes from an extremely horrific place or an extremely beautiful one"—she retraces his arc across mountain, sky—"maybe both are possible."

A shiny black car purrs along the road, pushing Ani back into the memory of the night she heard about Mac, pushing Roy Mc-Kinnon into his own memory of official visits, important men.

"Are you following the trials, Mrs. Lachlan?" she hears Roy say at last, his voice quiet. "The Japanese ones, the German ones, the trailing detritus of this unending war?"

She had expected war to operate like a tap: on—as it happened; off—immediately it stopped, like life, or like breath, she realizes now. Now she seesaws between feeling that she can never know enough about its aftermath and entrails, and wishing not only to know no more about it but to somehow forget so much of what it has already left lodged and jammed across the wide space of her memory and imagination.

And so the world still arrives folded into a newspaper in her front yard and is carried up her front stairs, and she sits every night after work, after Isabel is asleep, after the housework is done, obediently reading some part of it as if she might be examined. There's a new president in the United States, and Mr. Eliot has won the Nobel Prize in Literature—she knows this, if anyone asks. An American pilot is dropping chocolates and other sweets into West Berlin for its children, and seven Japanese men have been sentenced to death for their roles in the war. Yes, she's following the reports. She reads as much as she can in the evening; she cuts a strip from here, a story from there, to stick into her daybook. And then she sets the rest in the combustion stove, putting the world out of Isabel's way.

All this she says to Roy McKinnon—but the words are too much and come too fast, as if she hadn't spoken like this for a long time and is afraid she might have forgotten how. "It's to do with wanting to know what happens next," she says, "with feeling like something could be rounded off, or made better, although I don't know how it can be. There was a man who danced through Martin Place when the war stopped—I saw him on a newsreel; he danced and danced for joy. But what were we celebrating? The awfulness of its finishing? All these articles about war that still leach out into the newspapers now, three years later: there wasn't a full stop, was there? The story just keeps unfolding."

"Perhaps it's something to do with seeing it all as a kind of continuity," says the poet. "There is no beautiful now, no terrible then, just these trails of things going on and on. Which perhaps means there are some things you can write about, and some you have to leave alone." He watches the slow progress of the local bus as it draws in, collects its passengers, and pulls out, heading south. "There's some comfort in seeing things go on; birds keep singing, buses keep running. But if you want those things to continue, per-haps you have to accept that the other kinds of things, unhappier, even horrific ones, will continue too. And that's harder."

His hand moves to wave as the bus passes and Anikka, turning, sees the face of Frank Draper, sees his hand wave in return. She looks away, shifting the weight of a small bag of sugar against her arm, wanting to make no acknowledgment of his gesture.

"He was there, you know," says Roy, over the chug of the bus's motor. "He went into one of those German camps with the British. Did you know that?"

"Dr. Draper?" She shakes her head. "No. Mrs. Lacey said he'd stayed in service well beyond the war's end. She didn't mention anything else."

"He was one of the first men in—went into one of the worst of them, I think, if you could designate any better or worse. We hung round together, years ago: Frank, me, my sister, dances and the beach. Frank and me would have a beer and spin our dreams: he'd do his medicine; I'd start to write. And we'd end up here, somehow, when we were old and practiced." The bus hauls itself up the hill to cross the railway bridge, and disappears around the bend, taking its laboring engine with it. "Hardly recognized him when I first saw him. But then I wonder if he had the same trouble recognizing me."

"I remember seeing you, before the war, but I didn't recognize the doctor. And he's become quite . . . abrupt," says Ani, taking care with the word. "But no, I didn't know where he'd been." Dr. Draper would know what a body starved, a body shot, a body hanged looked like. And probably a body mashed and squashed by something huge and powerful. She winces, and the poet sees the edge of it in her shoulders, her widened eyes.

"I've been puzzling at memory myself, Mrs. Lachlan," he says, trying for something that will bring her out of whatever dark place she has slipped into, "and how it is that I can remember your husband here before the war, but not you, never you. You'll forgive me," he says gently, "but you're someone who would have been memorable."

She brushes away the compliment as if it were a fly. "I didn't know you knew my husband," she says.

And it's Roy's turn to brush at the air, to clarify the words that hang there. "I wouldn't say I knew him, but I met him, certainly. And of course there was that wonderful story about him and his blackberries—the railwayman jumping down to pick a bucketful of fruit, and his mates unhitching the engine he's in charge of and leaving it, while they drive on with the rest of the train. He takes off after them, full pelt, and runs into the back of their train just around the corner, where they're laughing and playing cards on the side of the track, just wanting to give your man a fright."

"My man?" She has no idea what the poet is talking about.

"That famous story about your husband," he says. "You know, when he jumped down for some fruit, and the rest of his train made off without him. He had us in fits telling us about it."

It's shocking to think that this poet knows some story about Mac that Ani herself has never heard. "Of course we've picked blackberries," she says slowly, "the three of us, up in the bush; we went every summer. But I don't know what you mean about . . ."

"It was well before the war," says Roy, "maybe even before your little girl was born." He turns away from her a little, as if he's trying to see far enough along Thirroul's main street to look into those days, those times. "Mr. Lachlan, as I remember, was working a bank engine to shunt trains up the hill and from one main line to another. He'd got a good long train up there, and then rather than going on with it, he hopped down to fill his bucket with berries instead. The blokes at the front of the train saw what he was doing, uncoupled his engine, and took themselves on—just having a joke, you know. But when Mac looked up and saw his engine all on its own, he panicked, jumped in, and went after them hell for leather. Came round the corner expecting to be on the run after them and didn't have time to stop himself before he rammed into the back of their vans—derailed them, derailed his own engine's wheels. Got six weeks off the engines and back on the platform for that, he said, before someone interceded and said he could go back to his job. But I wonder if the berries were worth it, if you don't remember how he came by them."

Ani frowns, her basket heavy on her arm. "I just don't see how it could have been Mac, if it's a story that I don't know." It's hard enough accommodating death as the thing that interrupts a story you care about, let alone the shudder of realizing that there must have been more stories of life beyond the ones you'd actually heard.

The poet smiles. "There must always be things we don't know, mustn't there," he says, as if her thoughts are written across her face. "Impossible to know every moment of a person's life, every instant of their day. And would you want to, in the end, if it was stories about that bloody war—I beg your pardon, Mrs. Lachlan— rather than stories about berries that you had to take on? They're the hard ones to put behind you," he says. "Perhaps you never do. My sister tells me Frank Draper's not even sure about being a doctor now, although that's what's brought him here. Well, at least they're talking. 'First, do no harm,'" he quotes from the famous medical oath, and his own wince mirrors Ani's. "Who knew how far a group of doctors could move from that idea in the name of some dreadful politics?" He shrugs his shoulders, the tops of his arms, as if to dislodge that abhorrent ideology and all that it spawned. "But what a thing to be saying to you, Mrs. Lachlan, on a day like this, when I really just wanted to thank you for the poetry."

"Come down to the library whenever you like," says Ani, trying to put the blackberries from her mind as she shakes his hand again. "I can send a request for anything you'd like." A train's brakes grate on the lines nearby, and she raises her voice, ignoring the interruption. "You know when we're open, don't you?"

She's never referred to herself as the library before—*you know when we're open*—and she likes the sound of it. Walking away, she finds herself reciting the Sassoon poem as she turns and heads up the hill:

Everyone suddenly burst out singing;
And I was filled with such delight
As prisoned birds must find in freedom,
Winging wildly across the white
Orchards and dark-green fields; on—on—and out of sight.

"And I was filled with such delight," she repeats, her steps slowing a little as she begins to climb. But her smile twists and stiffens. *No delight for Anikka Lachlan*, she thinks. Not now, not ever, not ever again.

In the brief instant of her eyes closing to blink, she sees an image like a black-and-white photograph of a body, dead, distended, horrible. And the worst of it is not knowing if she's imagining Mac, or remembering the poet's powerful wartime poem, or looking at some shard of the horror that the rude doctor had found, one of the first Allied liberators to walk into one of the worst places on earth.

But Mac did bring berries home from work sometimes, she thinks suddenly, turning the corner into her own street and marking her own house halfway along. *Buckets of berries picked beside the tracks.* She can even remember the first one, and how anxious she'd been when he told her about jumping down, running into the brambles, and rushing back to catch the engine he was working on before it went too far. *If anything should happen*, she'd said, and he'd said, *But what could happen except berries for our teatime?*

How long ago would that have been? And was it something as stupid as fruit behind the last accident? Stopping again, she hates him for a moment, for whatever stupidity ever sent him off after blackberries when he should have been working, and whatever inconsequential stories he'd told to other people and never told her.

As she climbs the stairs to her front door, she sees a paper bag on the step and opens it gingerly, afraid of more tiny purple berries that might appear out of nowhere, delivered somehow from the past. But it's round blue plums, three of them, and a note from Mrs. May. *Because of your anniversary, and because they were always his favorite,* she reads. *These ones looked so fine.*

Plums? His favorite? All she knew about was peaches, his peaches. *Mac's* peaches. And their anniversary? Their *wedding* anniversary? How could she have forgotten the date?

It's some kind of assault. Struggling with the key in the lock, she's through the door and dropping everything—including the plums—hard on the floor, where she sits and cries for everything forgotten, unknown, and undone.

Which is where Isabel finds her when she comes home, the pulpy plum flesh sharp and sticky, and Ani sitting with her fingers pressed into her eyes and her throat dry from crying.

23

"DOES IT bother you, Mrs. Lachlan, to ride in these murderous things?"

Spinning around at his words, Anikka doesn't know—never knows—what to expect from Dr. Draper. In the handful of times he's called at the library he's been charming and obnoxious in equal measure, complimenting her on a bowl of flowers one day, and berating her as an idiot another when the book she'd requested for him proved to be the wrong one. He came once with Iris Mc-Kinnon, too, and leaned against the shelves, scowling, as the two women transacted the business of the books. It was the first time in such a long time Ani had seen Iris smile—a bright contrast to the doctor's face—and she wanted to wish them well for it. But then Iris had made another grand claim for time's balm, and left Ani hating them both.

Now, she shakes her head and tries to laugh, determined not to cloud another meeting. "I wouldn't have much of a life left, nor much of a world, if I let that happen, would I, Doctor?" She will not tell him how impossibly huge trains seem sometimes, or how she freezes, sometimes, in the middle of a journey, wondering if this engine, carrying her along so reliably, is the one that took Mac away from her. The one that killed him.

"You're of Miss McKinnon's school, then," the doctor continues, moving closer to Ani on the platform. "The old 'time heals all wounds.'"

Against the glimmer of a smile on his face, she steels herself and proceeds. "No, no—I hate that phrase, hate it. All the forgetting in it, all the ignoring, the papering over, the covering up, the pretending." Which is more than she means to say.

He glances at his watch and then down the track.

"Perhaps we're traveling up to Sydney together," he says, indicating the oncoming engine. "If you don't mind the company." The train slows, stops, and he steps forward, holding open the compartment door.

"Of course," says Ani, "of course," wondering if it might have been possible to say anything else. She'll have to concentrate on him now, on whatever he wants to say. Out of nowhere, she wishes Roy McKinnon were traveling instead. *What would it be like, to travel with a poet?* But there's something treacherous in that thought, and she bats it away with her list of tasks for the city. Of course, she wishes no one were here. She wishes herself alone.

Settling into the forward-facing seat, registering the photographs opposite—the Blue Mountains, the Harbour Bridge, the famous roundhouse at Junee—Ani smiles at Frank Draper as if their meeting is the happiest coincidence of her day, and hopes he might nod off soon, as some men do in trains.

"Roy McKinnon speaks very highly of you," he says then, smiling back. "And your library," he adds, and she hears in his tone some implication that this second point, at least, is quaint. But he looks polite enough, with his dark suit, his hat, and she gives him just a little more latitude as he goes on: "I am sorry I've upset you on some visits to your library. McKinnon says I must have left most of my manners on the other side of the world when I came home—and I think sometimes he's right."

"He told me, Mr. McKinnon, about the work you did—about where you were, at the end of the war, I mean." Navigating things she suspects are probably best left unsaid but wanting some sense of how far he might be pushed in return, she blinks at the glint of the roundhouse's glass as it passes her window. There are rainbows in its corners, small sparkles of treasure.

"He told you about hell, did he?" The doctor's voice is coated again in ice, and Ani pulls herself into her seat, the boundaries clear, and is thankful to be able to look out of the window and see the next station, and who might be on the platform, who else might be making this trip. "I'm sorry," says the doctor as the train begins to move. "I find myself unable to say anything useful about it, so I wonder sometimes how it is that other people can tell its story for me."

The landscape through the window begins to blur with the train's speed, the texture of the cutting changing from the roughness of individual rocks and layers to a rush of one uniform color. "You get used to people telling the version of your story that they want to hear," Ani says, quiet. "Well, you get more used to it than you might have thought you would."

"How long has it been now, Mrs. Lachlan? How long has it been for you?"

But it's still only months, the math of her story, and his—she knows—is years. "It's like Miss McKinnon's recuperative sense of time," she says, trying to change tack. "It's not right, it doesn't heal, you don't forget, but you find some kind of accommodation. Don't you? Don't you?" She's making it worse, she can see, as he frowns and is silent. The train shapes itself around a curve, and she sees its engine away up ahead, dragging them on. She's never noticed this before—must never have looked out of her window at precisely the right moment to see it happening.

"I like that," he says suddenly, pointing towards the back of the train where the last carriages can now be seen curling around the track's wide arc. "That sense that we're all being safely carried along. It's all we want, most of us, isn't it?" The coldness has gone from his voice again, and Ani recoils from this latest change. These slams that skew from placatory to hostile: it's going to be a long journey.

"Sometimes it's nice to feel carried along," she concedes. "But mostly it's nice to know we can jump off, don't you think, if we want to, if we're going too fast, or too far?"

He snorts a little and stares at the ocean, until Ani wonders if she might get her book out of her bag without being rude. "Do you want to know, Mrs. Lachlan," he says abruptly, "do you want to know what it was like when we went into that place? Do you want to know how far it was from here, from where you were, from your safe little village with its ordinary lives and deaths, its distant understanding of the scale, the mess of war?" And there's no ice, no coldness in his voice this time, just a great sense of tiredness.

"I think we know how far it was, how unlike here, anything here, anything that has ever been here, Doctor," says Ani carefully. "And now we hear more and more about it, and we understand less and less of how it could possibly have happened." She wonders how much he might tell her, and how much she might not want to hear. "I sat with women whose husbands had died, whose sons had died, whose brothers and fiancés had disappeared—none of them there; none of them where you were. But they seemed such individual deaths; there were still particular people attached to them. The way my husband is my particular story, the death people particularly associate with me." She smiles, quite a small, tight smile. "But where you were, what you saw, that was beyond—beyond anything, I think. Anything, perhaps, except those bombs at the very end."

There's something about the accountancy of death, about how to look at more than one scale at the same time: hers now, for Mac;

Mrs. May's, say, during the war, when her husband died making a railway in a jungle; the thousands in the bright blasts that ended the war; the thousands upon thousands in the long stretch of horror that predated it and has outlasted it. She doesn't know how to say this without making the war sound like a problem of mathematics.

"They sent me to the sick bay when we got there," says the doctor quietly. "I couldn't tell you how many people were there—it would be almost better to say there were none. There were remnants, shadows; there were bodies whose state, alive or dead, could hardly be distinguished. You have no idea, Mrs. Lachlan. I don't mean that to be anything other than a simple statement of fact: your world, your grief, what you understand of death. You have no idea. And there we were, the liberating army, to tell them it was over. To tell them they had survived, they had endured." He coughs. "Five hundred and fifty-five of those survivors died after we arrived. Five hundred and fifty-five people endured everything up until that point, and we could not heal them, could not make them whole, could not lead them back into the world that they must have been promising themselves the whole time. I heard it was three thousand a day, in one place. Three thousand deaths, every day. I don't—" He puts his hand up quickly as she moves to say something. "I don't speak of this; I don't usually speak of this. And I'm very sorry for your loss, Mrs. Lachlan. I understand that everyone is, that it's a certain tragedy, and that it has a certain weight for them—and of course, of course, for you. But I carry those five hundred and fifty-five people; I carry their weight. The doctor who found them and failed them."

He fits the tips of his fingers together while his lips purse and twist. "And I sit in this place, seeing people with their colds and their burns and their boils, and I find it impossible to think of doing anything for them, when I failed the people who needed me so much more desperately."

He coughs again, a thick, heavy cough from somewhere deep

in his chest, and she rummages for a small paper bag of cough drops—the smallest gesture, but she's glad to be doing something—and holds them towards him.

"Would you like—"

He shakes his head, clears his throat, straightens himself so that his shoulders are pulled back and square and his hands rest flat on his knees.

"We had this plan, me and Roy McKinnon," he says, "when we were kids down here for holidays. Me, off to be a doctor, and he had this mad idea to be a poet. I knew there'd been a medico on the coast who'd come from Ireland—knew Yeats, someone told me, and was a fine doctor, a good doctor, the kind of doctor who kept all the good people from this good little place alive through that terrible influenza in 1918. That's for me, I said. I'll be that man—and our boy Roy will be a poet.

"So we'd go off and make our way in the world, and we'd come back, older, respectable, with wives and children and yards of stories behind us. We'd come back here, and we'd talk about the world, where we'd been, what we'd done, and how it was to end up in a nice little place like this. We had it figured for a pretty good life too."

"Did you like his poem, Dr. Draper?" asks Ani, and frowns as the doctor shakes his head.

"I'm sorry—I don't mean I didn't like it," he says at once. "I mean, I didn't read it. I heard that it had been published, of course, and I did drag myself out of whichever mess I was in and write to him, saying that I was waiting to see it, to see what he'd done. He sent me a poem by Yeats instead: 'On Being Asked for a War Poem'—do you know it? I don't remember all the lines, but it starts, 'I think it better that in times like these, a poet's mouth be silent.' It took months for my letter to find him, his to find me. I never replied—never expected, I think, to see him again after that. I mean, I never expected to see anywhere like this again."

The yellow-grey stone of the escarpment flashes by on one side of the train; the different blues of ocean and sky flash by on the other. *Perhaps there are different kinds of death, or dying,* thinks Ani suddenly. Outside, there's not a cloud to be seen, and the sun's light picks out the different stripes and blocks of the world's colors at their most perfect pitch. Perhaps there are different kinds of resurrection too.

Tilting her head towards the window, she catches another glimpse of the engine surging forward, pulling them on.

"I was up in the city—years ago, before the war, before my daughter was born. And when I came onto the platform at St. James, the driver, a mate of Mac's—of my husband's—asked if I wanted to ride in the engine. I don't know how many times I'd gone through those tunnels, peering out at the black walls, sometimes seeing the face of a workman staring out of an alcove, waiting for us to pass. But to ride up the front, to be looking into the tunnels head-on, rather than from the side, to see the way the train's lights pushed out against the darkness, illuminating the places I'd always seen as shadow—and then to see the day growing bigger and bigger once we'd passed through Museum Station and were on our way back out into the open. It was like I was on a train in another world. It looked so different, so exciting, from up there. I'd love to ride up the front around here one day—cutting through the trees, the tunnels, over the bridges."

From his side of the compartment, the doctor almost laughs, caught instead in another bout of such hacking and coughing that he has to lean forward and brace himself against it. "Perhaps Roy McKinnon is right about you," he says at last, taking one of her cough drops this time. "Has he started writing poems, do you know?"

Anikka shakes her head. "Really, Dr. Draper, I've only spoken to him a few times. There's an etiquette . . ." Her hands flail and she blushes. "I don't know. But I know he's reading a lot of poetry, because it's all coming down in the trunks from Sydney—I've got another request list from him to drop in to them today." She doesn't tell him that she wonders about the mechanics of writing poetry, about the way a poet's hand might hold its pen. But she does say, finally, that she hopes he will write something soon; she does say that she hopes she'll be able to read it.

"Good old Roy," says Dr. Draper, leaning back and settling himself in the corner made by the seat and the window. "I guess it's something that we both made it back here. Whatever we might fail to do with ourselves after that."

As the train crosses the high viaduct near Stanwell Park, sunshine cuts stripes through the trees outside and Ani presses her fingers against her eyes so that sparks flare behind her lids. The train slows, stops, and she listens for doors opening and closing before the whistle sounds, and the engine begins to pull away. They'll be in the tunnel soon, cutting away from the coast, away from the ocean, and on the long run up to the city. In the seat opposite, the doctor closes his eyes, and is asleep.

She watches Frank in the light before the train plunges into the mountain—he looks tired, she notices, but probably doctors are often up all night, with one thing or another. Keeping watch over someone—who said that, about the grace of watching someone sleep? Reaching out, she surprises herself by moving his hand a little before it drops from the armrest of his chair, and she's astonished by the weight of it, the solid, dead weight. She's astonished, too, by how much his hand feels like Mac's—*Although of course*, she thinks, *he's just a person, another person*. And she feels Mac diminish a little, this fraction of his being so easily replicated.

It's shocking. Ani pulls her hand away, tensing and flexing her fingers in a silent exclamation. But it's no more shocking than the next thought that comes: *What would Roy McKinnon look like as he slept?* she thinks, and more safely: *Or when he laughed or leaned back at the end of a good meal?*

They're still neither of them well fed nor well rested, these men, and in a flash of neighborliness, she thinks the village should be doing something about that. Taking care, keeping watch—that, she tells herself, is what her interest, her concern is all about.

24

ANI HAS been walking a good quarter of an hour before she realizes she has looked at nothing but her own feet, one stepping in front of the other in the stoutest shoes she could find—the muddy boots she uses for gardening, their familiar dark-soil mud now brightened by the orange clay of the track that winds up from Austinmer to the top of the escarpment, hundreds of feet above.

There's a group of them, a dozen or so from the church: the new minister—Reverend Robinson, young, enthusiastic, and known to own his own compass—has organized the outing, or "the hike," as he refers to it, and Ani has pretended to be merely acceding to Isabel's pleas in agreeing that they will go. It's a Saturday. It's gloriously warm. And it feels good to stride out, her legs stretching and climbing, and to know that she will lie down tonight properly exhausted.

"I wasn't sure you'd come, Mrs. Lachlan," the minister says, catching up to her as she climbs beyond tree ferns, sandstone boulders, a little marsh of reeds and bulrushes such as Isabel might hope holds fairies. "I mean, I wasn't sure," he corrects himself, "if the library kept you busy on the weekends."

Ani steps carefully over a fallen bough. "No, not all the weekends—they leave me something." She makes a show of indicating the view so she can catch her breath. "There's just more and more of it, the higher you go." She points out towards the sea, makes her breathing deep and slow.

"Have you ever traveled over the ocean, Mrs. Lachlan?" Reverend Robinson asks, following her gaze.

"No, no." She shakes her head. "My father came from Europe, and my husband of course. But I've always had the ground beneath me—apart from a little boat, here and there, a day's sail." She hears Isabel behind her, laughing with someone from school. It's lovely to hear that laugh. "Should we . . ." And she clambers over a scatter of rocks, pressing on.

The path tacks and weaves, straight up with ladders here, running along the cliff's face there, out in the sun on some stretches and tucked into dankly fecund pockets of rain forest in others where the air is thick with the rich smell of the leaves, the vines, the growth all around. Below is Austinmer, the neat rectangles of its rock pools pushing out, constrained, into the ocean. Just south, Thirroul, with its busy space of rail yards, and the straight streets of houses running east to the coast, west to the base of this scarp. Farther south, beyond Wollongong, sit the steelworks, belching and sprawling—she had been so scared of their heat, their power, the ferocity of their furnaces and ovens when she first came to the coast. And then, during the war, her dreams had rearranged them to mirror its heat and ferocity. She was always grateful it was the trains, not the steelworks, that paid her husband—*even now*, she thinks, *I guess, even now.*

A plume of white steam pushes up from one of the stacks. One of the last stories Mac told her was about a group of Baltic steelworkers with a grievance against their German foreman—she didn't know if the grievance belonged to this part of the world or had traveled with them from somewhere else—who'd taken the opportunity of some construction work to push him down into a smooth tablet of wet cement. "They'll find him one day," Mac had said, and she'd hated his casual unconcern. "There's always a war going on somewhere, I suppose."

She takes in the smell of the turpentines, the straight grandeur of one or two remaining cedar trees, and turns her back on the steel. *The war is always going on.*

"And good morning to you, Mrs. Lachlan." It's Dr. Draper, with Roy McKinnon at his side. "Beneficial to be out on *the hike*." His voice mocks the label, a parody of doctorly advice. "Plenty of fresh air; plenty of exercise; you know what they say." His skin is still sallow, his frame malnourished, and the darkness under his eyes is darker than even the worst crescents Ani has seen smudging her own face.

"Dr. Draper." She smiles, set on friendliness after their train ride together a week or so before. "And Mr. McKinnon. You couldn't ask for a better day for a climb, could you, although I suppose Reverend Robinson has more power than the rest of us to guarantee the weather."

The poet smiles, adjusting his hat. "It's the sort of day you dream of, yes," he says. "But my sister's not one for heights—or hikes." He laughs. "I used to do this each year we came when I was a boy, racing up here, trying to make my time faster and faster. When you burst out at the top, and you turn, and you see the whole coastline unfolded below you—that's something, don't you think, Mrs. Lachlan? That's a thing worth racing for."

Ani nods. "It's years since I was at the top—I remember feeling I could see all the way to South America. It seemed possible; there was so much world out there." She starts to walk, and the two men fall in step behind her. "Are there mountains along the coastline in Chile? I always meant to look that up, to find out what I was looking at, all that way away."

"Well, you've the perfect opportunity now, all those books at your disposal." Roy McKinnon leans forward to pull a low branch out of Ani's way, and Frank Draper steps through after her, changing the order of their line.

"And all that time," the doctor says quickly. "I often wonder who uses that library—it's almost always empty whenever I look in. I wonder how long the railways will keep it up, if there aren't enough readers for its books."

This talent he has, thinks Ani, *this talent for finding some brusque thing to say, some criticism.* "We've a good number of readers for a branch our size," she says, a little surprised by her defensiveness. "They're talking of changing the hours and circulating the books more quickly between branches—and we're taking more requests now, which our readers like. Mr. McKinnon"—she smiles back to him—"has often availed himself of this, of course."

"She can get you anything, Frank," the poet calls. "Anything you like."

But the doctor doesn't smile. "I wonder if your daughter isn't too young to try a climb like this—you must be more fearful, more protective of her now." They round a corner and there is Isabel herself, half hidden behind a rock with two giggling friends, waiting to jump out at whichever parent passes first.

Ani laughs. "You can ask her, Dr. Draper, but she looks all right to me." She tickles her daughter as she goes by and, glancing back, sees the poet tickle the top of her head as well. Isabel giggles again and ducks.

"See you at the top, Mum," she calls.

Up ahead, the first knot of walkers disturbs a tree full of white cockatoos, and they rise up, protesting, their vast wings reaching across the sky.

"Did you see, when we were climbing, a whole tree of them, those cockatoos? We were up above it, looking down. It was like looking down into a Christmas tree, with row after row of candles." Roy McKinnon has swapped places with the doctor again, and walks close to Ani. "I was looking for the angel to put on the top—an angel was all it was missing."

"And the fact that it's not yet December twenty-fifth," Frank Draper adds, louder again. "That does work a little against your metaphor, Royston, my friend—you always were premature with your celebrations."

"My father always cooks a Christmas meal for the pitchest night in winter," says Ani, "as dark and as cold as he can get, to remember the old country. Apple bread and herring and Christmas mustard—*joulusinappi*—although I could never work out what made it different from the mustard he ate at any other time of the year. Or where he found herring in the backblocks of Australia."

There's a bustle on the path behind them and a couple of women overtake, greeting the doctor as they glance at Ani and the poet, and asking Roy about his sister as they glance coquettishly at Frank.

"Say it again, the mustard word," Roy McKinnon says as they pass, and he stays her steps with a hand on her shoulder.

"*Joulusinappi?*"

"It changes, your whole voice changes when you say that—a different sound, a different pitch." And he steps back, letting go. "As if a whole other person was speaking. I wonder who you would have been, Mrs. Lachlan, if you'd grown up speaking that language instead of this one."

"I'd have been someone even more enamored of this sunshine than I already am." It's good to feel the stretch and reach in her muscles, and there's a sort of warmth from the climbing too—or the talking. And although she thinks she can see the lip of the escarpment, the end of their climb, not too far in front of them, she wishes she could go on striding and climbing, ascending forever. "I don't know as much of the language as I should," she says, slowing down. "I meant to learn it before I came away from the plains, from living with my father—now he writes the odd word, here and there, in a letter. Like *käy pian* . . ." She smiles at the poet's blank face. "It's 'visit soon.' But I never seem to get away."

The path straightens and steadies and reaches the top. Ani pauses, staring at the pine tree that she usually sees from so far down below.

"Here we are then"—the doctor arrives, Isabel and her friends hard behind—"and the minister has made good on the promised lunch." He strides over to the picnic rugs, already spread and waiting. "Satisfaction, at last. The repayment of repast. There you are, Roy, that's almost a rhyme for you."

"Your rhythm's all wrong." Roy laughs, sitting himself down beside his friend.

And it is good, Ani knows, to sit and eat and laugh—to look out across the view of the coast and not have every thought bound up with the last time she was here. It is good to see Isabel, smiling and playing. It is good to talk with the minister, with the poet— even with the doctor, although she wonders what entertainment he allows himself out of scaling an escarpment, as out of anything.

But she smiles herself, and she chatters. When the poet mentions his plan to see a movie with the doctor the following week, and asks if she'd like to join them, she smiles again and finds herself nodding—"Yes, I'd like to see that film; yes"—although she hasn't, until that moment, ever heard of it. And when another tree lights up with cockatoos and the matter of Christmas is raised again, and Roy McKinnon wonders aloud about celebrating it, Ani talks about inviting him and his sister to join in their meal. And thinks it a fine idea.

Reverend Robinson says grace, and they eat, quiet and busy with their sandwiches, their pies, their fruit. To the south, the steelworks sends up another column of thick white smoke, and then another. Farther south again, Ani sees a band of grey clouds—a storm coming up; it seems so preposterous in the middle of such a rich, warm reservoir of sunshine that the picnickers ignore it, relishing their food.

But up it comes, so fast that they're only just packing the last of the plates when the first drops of rain fall, heavy and huge.

"If some of the ladies would like to drive back in the car that brought the picnic?" the minister calls, and there's a rush towards the parking lot. Mrs. Floyd giggles and touches her newly set hair; Mrs. Padman holds a tiny handkerchief over her head. The minister pauses, gesturing towards Ani, but she shakes her head.

"I'll walk back down—me and Isabel. We'll get a bit wet, but we'll be under the trees most of the way." She takes her daughter's hand and they make for the track's mouth, both of them laughing.

"Come on then, come on!" The doctor, of course, and the poet. And they set off, the track's sticky clay already a little more slippery, a little more malleable than it had been when they made their ascent.

Isabel darts ahead, Ani steadying herself here and there on rocks and branches as she tries to keep up. She sees her daughter sit down and slide a little way, and as she catches up to her, she sits down as well, feels the wet ground pressing up through her scruffy trousers.

"This is great, Mum," Isabel shouts. "Isn't this great?" Thunder breaks out overhead and another nest of cockatoos rises up, protesting. "Your Christmas candles are back, Mr. McKinnon," Isabel says, stopping to let her mother pass. "I've always wondered what they do when it rains—isn't it bad for birds to get their feathers wet? Doesn't it make it hard for them to fly?"

"But what about seabirds, Bella?" Ani says. "What about cormorants and albatrosses and oystercatchers?" She takes the first rope ladder as fast as she dares, the uprights chafing at her skin as her palms rush over them. She can't hear the poet's answer, if he gives one, and for a moment she relishes the feeling of being completely alone and here, in the bush, in a storm, tucked in against the side of her mountain.

She pushes water out of her eyes and jumps down another stand of steps, and another—she hasn't felt this light, this nimble for the longest time. There's a crash in the undergrowth to the side of the track, and she sees the back of a little swamp wallaby, with its delicate ears and tail, bounding away.

"Bell?" she calls. "A wallaby. Did you see it? Did you see?" Her sweater, tied at her waist, is heavy with water, and her shirt clings and sticks to her like another skin. *A sight we'll look, when we get to the bottom*, she thinks, hearing her daughter whoop and laugh. She springs down another drop, and another, takes the next ladder almost at a run, and slides away on the seat of her pants again, wanting to whoop as well. What would her father make of the poet, she thinks out of nowhere. *What would my dad make of a man like that?* A man like that, running wet, in the rain, running home, needing to be warmed, needing to be dried. Needing.

She stops, hot and breathless, despite the drenching.

"Bella? Isabel? Are you all right up there? Are you coming?"

What is she thinking, out in the rain, her daughter soaked to the skin and running down a mountainside with two men she hardly knows? What is she thinking, being here at all? It's another minute before she remembers the wet walk she took with Mac, and the way they pushed themselves together afterwards. But it comes, this memory, and just as quickly goes: she's making a new story here, not reliving an old one.

The bath's water, clean and hot, is going to feel magnificent.

A call—a *coo-ee*—echoes around her; the doctor's voice, then the poet's, and then Isabel's. And they come around the corner, one close by the other, and catch up with her, pressing on together to the track's end, to the point where they began.

"Now that," says the doctor, shaking his hair like a drying dog, "that is what I call *a hike*."

And for the first time, Ani sees him really smile.

25

STRETCHED OUT in the bath, on the night of Isabel's tenth birthday, Mac ducked his ears under the water again and again. "Just listening to the house," he said as Ani watched his head dip and rise, dip and rise. "There's such noise under the water; you can hear the pipes and the pressure and all manner of other sounds like some great machine pulsing away. When I get my deep-sea dive—no, now, Ani love"—as she shook her head against this mad desire—"when I get my deep-sea dive, I reckon I'll be able to hear the machinery behind the whole world. You're an embarrassment to us coast dwellers, you are, keeping your head above the water all the time." And he ducked away again, his eyes wide in mock ignorance of the words she was saying into the room's air.

"Come up, Mackenzie Lachlan: you come up and listen to me. I don't mind your underwater thing—you can read about it and dream about it all you like. You can dive down from the highest board at the pool and you can duck your head under the biggest breakers that the surf pushes up. But under the sea, properly under the sea, so far down and so dark, so dark—I just don't know why you'd want to do something like that."

"You're still a landlubber after all these years, aren't you, pet?" he said, ducking fast under the bath's surface again as she threw a washcloth, a nail brush at him. And he stayed under this time, blowing a few bubbles, and then holding his breath until she leaned forward, her frown anxious, and scolded him again.

"I was going to offer to read to you while you're in there," she said then, "even from your silly new underwater book. But now . . ." She shook her head. "Your shenanigans." But she was smiling.

Mac pulled a towel from the side of the bath, rubbed the water from his hair, his ears. "You'd like the book, Ani. The creatures they see, and how beautiful it is down there. Even when I was little, I'd swim out into that cold grey Scottish water, peering down to try to see what was underneath—my gran had all these stories of the ashrays and the selkies and the blue men of the Minch, and I was after a glimpse of them as much as any sort of fish or shells or proper sea life." He shivered, although the bath water, straight from the copper whose little fire Ani tended, was steaming hot. "I cannae tell you how cold it was, how cold, out there in that water. And I'd swim and swim with my fingers numb, then my hands, then my arms all the way up to the elbows—I probably wasn't in more than a few minutes each time." He closed his eyes and saw himself as a small boy, shivering across the shale on the other side of the world. "My gran always had the fire high and the soup on the stove when I gave up and came in. And she'd warm me up and fill me up—and tell me the next round of stories about the water lovers to get me ready to go again." He laughed, reaching for the soap. "But read me a bit, lass; there's a lovely bit about the color and the light—you'd like that part, I promise."

"This part?" she said, flicking through the pages. "'At six hundred feet, the color appeared to be a dark luminous blue'?"

"That's it, Ani. That's it." He slid his shoulders beneath the warm water again and closed his eyes.

At 600 feet the color appeared to be a dark, luminous blue, and this contradiction of terms shows the difficulty of description. As in former dives, it seemed bright, but was so lacking in actual power that it was useless for reading and writing.

There are certain nodes of emotion in a descent such as this, the first of which is the initial flash. This came at 670 feet, and it seemed to close a door upon the upper world. Green, the world-wide color of plants, had long since disappeared from our new cosmos, just as the last plants of the sea themselves had been left behind far overhead.

At 700 feet the light beam from our bulb was still rather dim; the sun had not given up and was doing his best to assert his power . . .

She paused. "Do you want the next bit, about worms and things?"

"Just the color, Ani, just the color." His voice was low, his eyes closed, and his mouth smiling.

" 'At a thousand feet,' then, here," she continued.

At 1,000 feet . . . I tried to name the water; blackish-blue, dark grey-blue. It is strange that as the blue goes, it is not replaced by violet—the end of the visible spectrum. That has apparently already been absorbed. The last hint of blue tapers into a nameless grey, and this finally into black, but from the present level down, the eye falters, and the mind refuses any articulate color distinction. The sun is defeated and color has gone forever, until a human at last penetrates and flashes a yellow electric ray into what has been jet black for two billion years.

In the quiet room, the space behind his eyelids replicated the shape of the bathroom light, the pale rectangle made by the bath itself.

"I think," said Ani, as Mac opened his eyes to look at her, "I think that I was afraid of the dark, when I was little. I remember, after my mother died, my father used to sit with me until I went to sleep, and sometimes I had a lantern in the room at night—I must have called out." She smiled, closing the book. "But I suppose your blue sounds lovely—your luminous blue. And I suppose I could trust you to a bathysphere for one ride down to see it, if you really had to go." This was Ani, he knew, doing her best to be generous.

"My birthday treat one year," said Mac. "I wonder if they'll ever have them available for rides? I could go down off the coast here, see all the coal ships lost off that old jetty, and the deep, dark drop where the continent falls away. That'd be something, to see what's down over that edge." But she was frowning again. "Too much? Too far?"

"No, no, if you like . . ." But he could tell she was humoring him. "I was just thinking of all the other ships trapped under the water now," she went on, "all the lives stopped down there. And would there be mines? Would there still be mines? How long would those mines go on floating in the ocean—and how would you know where they might end up?"

Mac eased himself out of the bath, dried off, found his pajamas, and kissed her, very slowly and gently. "Things needn't always come back to that war, Ani love. It's over now; it's over. You mustn't always be remembering it." And he kissed the top of her head, taking the book from her lap. "I'll make you some tea," he said quietly, and she nodded, brushing at her eyes.

Stoking the stove, he shook his head. She could just say something about wanting a dress made of luminous blue—which would be beautiful; a dress for dancing, if ever there was one. Why must the war still feel so heavy for her, and so close? Three years now, he wanted to say—he almost wanted to shout it. *And we came through, we came through, love. Here we are. Together.* He hated the way she carried it with her, the way it surfaced so easily in her mind. It made him anxious; it made him fearful.

Tossing a handful of kindling into the firebox, he registered the spit of flame and the hiss of steam as a drop of water from the kettle's spout hit the plate.

"But could you not have a nice landlocked daydream as well?" she said, nestling in behind him with her arms hugging his flannelette waist. "A nice landlocked daydream that wouldn't make me worry about the dark and the depth?"

He was quiet awhile, measuring tea out of its caddy, setting the cups carefully on their saucers, thinking of different things he might say—how they might sound, what they might mean. The tea was drawing, the milk poured, before he spoke.

"If I do have a dream," he said, "it's that I might make a poem—just one, just one. I was thinking about it when we saw Roy McKinnon. Imagine that; making a set of words so perfect that had never been put together that way before. I've never told anyone that, not even my gran. But it's something I'd like to do; I'd like to make a poem." It was magical, the way such a thing could make her smile—the way she'd smiled when he said he loved reading *Jane Eyre*, all those years ago. Such a little thing, he thought, it made no odds. And he knew it would mean the world to his wife.

The kitchen was still, ruffled only by the occasional crackle from the combustion stove, the occasional drip of water from the tap. Watching her across the smooth red table, Mac raised his cup and paused—the smallest toast—to drink. *That is marriage*, he thought, remaking yourself in someone else's image. And who knew where the truth of it began or would end?

"Thank you, Mackenzie Lachlan," Ani said. "Thank you for telling me that."

He watched the darkness of her eyes sparkle and change as she slipped into a daydream. Well, he would write her a poem, if he could—*or mebbe she is my poem*, he thought, *her and Bella.* Still beautiful. Still his. He didn't always believe that could be so in the bloody mess of the rest of the world. Which wasn't a thing to say aloud.

"You're lovely, Ani Lachlan," he said, reaching out to stroke her hair. "You're lovely, my angel, my golden-sun lass."

She reached across the table, took his hand, and kissed it.

"There you are," she said. "Right there. I'd say that was the makings of a poem."

26

"MUM?"

"Mmmm?"

"Do you wonder sometimes, do you wonder where Dad is?"

The two of them, stretched like starfish in the backyard, their first Christmas morning without Mac, under the early blaze of a summer sun.

Anikka props herself on one elbow, looks at her daughter, looks at the length of her as she lies there—longer every day, if that's possible—at her stillness, at her calmness.

"I mean, I hear you some nights," Isabel goes on, "I hear you crying when you go to bed. And I wish . . . I wish you didn't. I wish you felt like he was somewhere good and quiet and peaceful."

Sitting up now, her back straight, Ani says: "Is that what you think? Is that where you think your father is?" Picking at bits of grass with her fingers, folding their stalks, and flicking them towards the run where the hens peck and mutter.

Isabel sits up in turn, stretching higher and longer again. "I don't mean a Sunday school kind of place," she says, "just somewhere quiet. You know, somewhere that he'd want to be." She pauses, looking past her mother into some infinity. "You know that book he had, about diving and getting right down to the bottom of the sea? I think he's there. It'd be so quiet there, and all the fish and shells and things he could see, like he always said he wanted to."

Like he always said he wanted to.

Anikka remembers the book, remembers the day it came, wrapped carefully in brown paper, all the way from America. "My undersea explorer," Mac had said, smoothing its cover, flicking through its pages. "Remember the magazine story? The man in the bubble going half a mile down? This is him; this is his book." And Ani had smiled and nodded, scared, for the first time, that she might find her husband with weights tied to his feet, practicing holding his breath at the bottom of the big, tiled municipal pool. Scared, in an instant, for Mac and the sea.

And this is where Isabel imagines him. Ani leans over, brushing dried grass from the back of her daughter's frock. "What does he do down there?" she asks at last, wondering at the steadiness of her voice. "How does he spend his time?"

"He draws the fish and the squid and the other strange creatures that go past. He writes down the things he sees to send in to the *National Geographic*. And he works out ways of keeping his light going—because you know, the men who dived, they were talking about how dark it was, and how long their light might last. I think Dad would have worked out a way by now to have the light on so that he could make days, and then turn it off when he wanted to sleep at night."

"I don't like to think of him being in quite so much darkness," says Ani. "And maybe not somewhere so far away, so on his own."

But Isabel shakes her head. "Oh no, I think there'd be lots of people down there—they'd have ways of talking to each other, one bubble to the other, maybe like those strings that connected the bubble to the surface. Maybe they talk through those, or maybe they talk to the stingrays and the squid and the stargazers."

"Stargazers?"

"There's a fish called a stargazer—its eyes are on the top of its head. Better for counting at night, I guess."

Ani laughs. "Maybe I should read that book after all—I never . . . I never got round to it." If that's where her daughter thinks Mac has gone, maybe it's not for Ani to tell her she thinks it sounds dark and lonely. "When I think about where your father is, I think about a room at the very top of a house, with a wide view through a big window, and the most comfortable bed in the world. And he's curled up in the bed. He's comfy, and sleeping. Just sleeping.

"He might wake up sometimes; you know, when you wake up somewhere that's not your home, and it takes you a minute to recognize where you are. But he's never awake long enough to wonder about any of that, although he can look out of the window and see the stars, the moon, think about the tides. Then he snuggles down and goes back to sleep. Waiting for the morning." She's making it up, and she's sure Bella knows. Mostly, if she's honest, she doesn't yet quite trust that Mac is dead; mostly she avoids thinking of any of this at all.

Isabel leans back on the grass, recovers her starfish pose. "It's lonelier, yours than mine; mine's got electric light and conversation."

"Mine's got dreams," says Ani defensively. "And there will be a morning—one day." *When I get to wherever he is*, she thinks. *Even if I'm an old woman, breaking down the door.* She stretches up herself, her fingers mimicking the starfish shape she and Isabel have cast on the grass. "We should start thinking about this Christmas lunch for Mrs. May and everyone—setting the table, checking the pork." And she stands, holding a hand out to Isabel, who springs up like a jack-in-the-box.

"What about all the men in the war, Mum?"

"All which men in the war?" Knowing perfectly well.

"All the men—all the people—who died? Do you think there's enough space for them all to have somewhere to go, or maybe even more than one place, like Dad, who's got a bubble under the sea, now, and a bedroom with a view?"

The woman whose son died when his plane tumbled into the sea, who imagined him floating on its wing, floating on the surface of the water, surfing a wave here or there, as if he were a young chap on vacation again. The woman whose husband died when the building he was in was bombed out of existence, who was sure he'd been blown all the way home by the blast, and was somewhere out in the garden, checking on the last plants he'd put in before he left, and leaving her messages about watering here, pruning there.

"More than enough space, lovely," she says, keeping hold of Isabel's hand as they walk from the bright yard to the cool, shaded house. "It's probably like your kaleidoscope: you look at one piece of space, and every tiny twist or turn multiplies that into somewhere new—somewhere different. More than enough room for everyone to fit in somewhere, to be doing the different things we all think they ought to be doing."

She pulls her daughter into another hug, noticing her tallness again. The evening shifts she works in the library, the nights Mrs. May gives Isabel her tea, the nights Isabel's asleep when Ani gets home. Sometimes Ani feels she's lost her daughter as well as her husband. But then she pays her bills or buys the growing girl a new dress or sends a little money to her father.

She has to trust that this is the right thing.

Now, she hugs harder. "I miss you, Bell; I miss how things were." And then, quickly, against anything else that might be said, "But will you make the custard later, the way Mrs. May's been teaching you?"

And as she irons out the tablecloth, rubs up the silver, chops the potatoes, rinses the tomatoes, she sees Isabel back in the yard, her kaleidoscope to her eye and the lens up at the sky, turning it by the smallest of increments, remaking the big blue space.

Ani flicks the white linen across the table and the world disappears for a moment behind its movement. When she focuses again, she sees Mac's book, the diving book, perched on the edge of the sideboard, as if it might have been there since she read it to him in the bath on the night of Isabel's birthday. Perhaps Isabel's been reading it; perhaps that's what made her think about where Mac was. Ani pats its cover, but cautiously, as if some fanged fish might shoot out from between its pages, nipping and biting. Then she picks it up and it falls open, and she begins to read:

I sat crouched with mouth and nose wrapped in a handkerchief, and my forehead pressed close to the cold glass—that transparent bit of old earth which so sturdily held back nine tons of water from my face. There came to me at that instant a tremendous wave of emotion, a real appreciation of what was momentarily almost superhuman, cosmic, of the whole situation; our barge slowly rolling high overhead in the blazing sunlight, like the merest chip in the midst of ocean, the long cobweb of cable leading down through the spectrum to our lonely sphere, where, sealed tight, two conscious human beings sat and peered into the abyssal darkness as we dangled in mid-water, isolated as a lost planet in outermost space.

Ani slams the book shut. Cold and deep and dark and lonely, with that string, that fragile cobweb of string, the only connection. *It is as if I had a string somewhere under my left ribs*—it's *Jane Eyre*, and it's Mac's voice, Mac's voice saying the words for her memory—*tightly and inextricably knotted to a similar string situated in the corresponding quarter of your little frame. And if that boisterous Channel, and two hundred miles or so of land come broad between us, I am afraid that cord of communion will be snapped.*

That cord of communion, that fragile cobweb, whatever it is that still connects her to Mackenzie Lachlan. *I am afraid that cord of communion will be snapped.* She bows her head, patting at the side of her body, feeling the exaggerated landscape of her rib cage. She has to remember to eat.

So long since she made a meal for anyone other than herself and Isabel—she's forgotten how nervous it can make her, and the dead space before the first guest arrives when she's sure the food will taste dreadful and no one will have anything to say, when she wishes, more than anything, that no one is coming, and is terrified, the next moment, that no one will. *And then what would I do with all this food?*

A saucepan of apples sizzles as some of its juice spits onto the hot surface of the stove. It's Christmas Day. There's a table to be set. People will come and eat and laugh and be together, speckling her white tablecloth with food and festivity. Mrs. May, of course, and Isabel, and Roy McKinnon and his sister. And Dr. Draper— scooped into the invitation at the end of the bushwalk. *Sit him next to Mrs. May*, she thinks as she sets out the cutlery. *She knows enough stories of undiagnosed illness to keep him busy for a week.* She places the glasses—wishes Mac could carve the pork, and then swallows hard against this automatic thought.

She'll put Isabel on the other side of the doctor; give him a dose of childhood and its optimism.

In the middle of the table, a small pile of gifts sits clustered around a bunch of Christmas bush with its starbursts of dusty pink flowers. A special gift for Mrs. May, for all her help, and a little something for everyone else to open. A box of shortbread each for the men—the first time Ani's attempted Mac's proper Scots recipe—and a jar of homemade jelly for Iris. She's noticed them more and more, Iris and Frank, walking together, and Iris with that smile. *Some rapprochement*, she thinks; some recovery or some beginning—she's heard the edges of its story whispered in the post office and the shoe shop, and politely turned away. Of course she wishes them the world.

Isabel has wrapped the gifts, prettying them with ribbon and little sprays of the flowers. *So the table looks busy with treasure*, thinks Ani, *and everyone has something to take home*. In the dim room, she stands a moment, scanning the sideboard, the linen press—she pulls out a chair and is standing on it, leaping so quickly she might have flown.

"What are you doing up there, Mum?" The back door slams as Isabel steps forward, steadying the chair on which her mother is balanced. "What are you looking for?"

Ani blushes up to the roots of her hair, her tanned face hot and prickled. "I just thought—I didn't know if we'd looked—"

"Your birthday present," says Isabel glumly.

Ani sighs. "I'm sorry, Bell; I shouldn't. And not on a day when I've had such nice surprises already." Her fingers brush the star-shaped coral brooch her daughter had given her that morning. "It's greedy of me—I don't know what I was thinking." And as she steps down, one of the chair's legs bows, its wood splintering. "And now look what I've done. . . ." She drags the chair onto the back veranda, worrying about who might mend it. Of course the table will look scrappy now, a kitchen chair pulled in to make up the numbers—although she'd spent half an hour setting and unsetting an extra place for Mac, and left it, in the end, set, but with no chair. Her table had been just big enough to seat the living.

Leave it alone, Ani Lachlan, she tells herself, packing up the extra place. *Leave what's lost alone.*

But the guests come and sit and eat and the pork is perfect and the pudding sweet and the conversation easy. Iris McKinnon tries to toast to absent friends, and Mrs. May distracts her with an anecdote about someone's son who arrived home unannounced after the war to be just in time for Christmas lunch. "And you know, his mother had set a place for him every single meal he was away."

Thank you, thinks Ani, smiling at her neighbor. She doesn't want to cry.

They pass the afternoon with games—charades and codes and Chinese whispers. A film; four words; and the doctor is miming *Gone With the Wind*, blowing up a storm until his cheeks are red and his veins popping. A book; one word; and Ani's jumping around the room like a kangaroo. Towards evening, they cluster into the kitchen to sort out the washing-up, Frank Draper with his hands deep in hot water, and everyone else busy with tea towels and stacking and putting away.

Turning from the ice chest, Ani feels a surge of gratitude for this busyness, this festivity, for the very noise of its process. She stands a moment, watching her Christmas guests, red dress, blue dress, two suits, and Bella's bright golden hair; she sees flickers of their colors and shapes in the kitchen's windows, in the facets of the dresser's reeded glass doors. She stands a moment, still and pale, a light calico apron tied over her pretty white dress. She feels herself smile, and catches the edge of Roy McKinnon's smile in return as Mrs. May steadies her heavy brown camera and clicks.

"A memento of our Christmas, then," Mrs. May says.

One last game of charades, one last cup of tea, and slices of pudding wrapped up to take home—Ani and Isabel stand on the front steps, waving their guests along Surfers Parade.

"Still no sign of my surfers." Ani laughs, one arm around her daughter's shoulders, her other arm looped through the crook of her neighbor's elbow.

"It was nice to have everyone," says Isabel, "and Dr. Draper was funny, wasn't he? He told me and Miss McKinnon the funniest jokes—I thought you said he wasn't very nice?"

"Well, he can be a bit odd," says Ani, squeezing her close. "But perhaps it was his Christmas cheer."

Later, as the night vibrates with the sound of the summer's cicadas, Ani lies back on her bed. *A good day, mostly*, she thinks, *and a happy one*. Which seems surprising; she's glad that it's over. Someone along the street is playing a recording of Christmas carols, fruity voices singing about stars and angels and joy. The needle stutters and jumps into the next song. Ani closes her eyes, and it's Isabel she sees, perched on top of a Christmas tree, her arms out, like an angel.

A comfortable bed, a quiet room, a sky full of night stars, and, one day, a morning. *That's better*, she thinks as the light falls away. *That's better.*

27

BY THE time she passes Austinmer, heading north under the hot sun of a New Year's Sunday, the tide is running out, the dints and crevices reemerging in the rock pools below the Headlands guest-house. It's silver this morning, and although the tide is ebbing, a thin sheet of the ocean lies across the rock shelf so that a fisherman walking out from the land with his line looks as if he's walking on the surface of the water itself. The sky is silver too, overcast but glowing bright with the hidden sun. Behind Ani, beyond the edge of the escarpment and to the north and south, wild bushfires are burning—the smoke is part of the air's silver thickness, and she can taste it every time she takes a breath. But down here, on the level of the sand, the silver-grey ocean curls down around the lip of the horizon. The world falling away.

The fisherman reaches the edge of the platform, bends down to busy himself with something, and then casts his line out so that it leaves the smallest trace of a signature across the air. Mac was never a fisherman, never liked the flapping and thrashing that was the end of the fish's life; never liked the way the knife sliced so easily through the flesh for gutting—although he did it, when he had to, when they needed it for eating. Ani had always meant to offer to take on the task, imagining herself as someone more able to do it. But as she stands and watches the fisherman now, as she watches his line tighten and arc as he flicks it clear of the water with the slithering exclamation of a catch writhing on its end, she knows she'd have been just as bad as her husband. Or worse: she'd have thrown the fish back and settled for toast.

Beyond the rocks, a great wave builds and builds and finally breaks as Ani holds and releases her breath. It's the sense she has whenever she sits with her daybook, trying to retrieve another recollection of Mac. The store of memories had filled and grown for a while, just like this swell. And then, instead of breaking, it froze, suspended, not a drop more water to push into it, not a single extra moment or memory to be reclaimed. She cannot remember the last words he said to her. She cannot remember how much breakfast he ate that last day. She is trying to make her peace with these gaps, these elisions—pushing away her journal and pulling towards herself any story by anyone else instead, as long as it has a man and a woman falling in love; as long as it has a happy ending. She disappears into the safety of these pages and reads herself towards sleep, where it's never Mac she sees now as the light goes down and she begins to dream.

Beyond the fisherman, farther north, smaller waves crash against the edge of the continent, flaring into anemones and chrysanthemums. And farther north again, there are surfers, three of them, slight shapes against the movement of the ocean, and then suddenly upright and balanced, riding improbably in towards the shore. If Mac wanted his bathysphere, wanted deep and down, he could have it. She'd take this any day, walking on water—or flying; maybe it was like flying.

She watches the pulse of the waves, trying to feel their rhythm and then predict it. Her breath catches a little when she senses that this one, *this one*, is going to rise up high and smooth, and sees two of the riders rise up with it, as if in confirmation. They're suspended then against the silver sky, cresting and gliding on the silver water, and as she follows the line carved by their heavy boards, it intersects with the straight black dart of an oystercatcher, diving down, hunting and hopeful.

They'd taste of salt, the surfers, when they stepped out of the ocean. *In the nicks and folds of a surfer's body*, she thinks, *there'd always be the stickiness of salt, the way I could taste soot and smoke on Mac when he came home from work—here.* She raises her hand to her lips, her tongue touching the crease where her fingers join her palm. *Soot and smoke here.* Of course she hasn't forgotten him: he's here—his smell, his taste, his being.

It's the sun, hard and bright as it pierces the smoky clouds, that breaks her concentration, blinding her for a moment so that she calls out, shocked, when she blinks and sees the fisherman walking towards her and quite close now, emerged from the blazing radiance.

"I said if you wanted a fish . . ." he repeats, gesturing towards the bucket brimming with fins and scales and the cloudy dead end of so many dead eyes. "You're Mac Lachlan's wife, aren't you? Seen you walking along the sand sometimes. Think my wife brought round a pot of food when we heard the news—but then I guess every woman around here was doing that. It's what you do, isn't it, food and so forth. Did you want one of these?"

Ani shakes her head, frightened of the fish, of the idea of carrying one home, and wondering if the man has seen her standing there, gazing out across the water, and licking at her own skin like an idiot.

"You're very kind," she says, and pretends to laugh, "but I'm not sure how I'd get it home."

The man shrugs. "I could fetch you some paper from up home, if you wanted." He gestures towards one of the low weatherboard houses set across the road and Ani, turning, is sure she can make out the shape of the casserole-cooking wife by a window, watching this conversation and trying to conjure its words. Once, when she and Mac weren't long married, she'd sat in a railway carriage, its windows jammed shut by too much paint, and watched the mime of Mac talking to a woman with gorgeous red hair; Ani had never seen her before, not in town or anywhere nearby. When Mac came into the carriage, he pointed back towards the platform. "Woman who came out on the same ship as me—cannae believe she'd turn up out here, of all places." And Ani had smiled, and laughed too, and said something small about coincidence, intrigued by how frightening, how unsettling, it had been to watch her new husband have a conversation she couldn't hear with a woman she didn't know.

Now she makes a small wave up towards the house. "If you could thank your wife for the casserole—I was very bad with writing all the notes I should have written. But you take the fish; you take the fish. I'm not sure how long I'm going to stay here before I walk back." The water has retreated well beyond her feet now but she can feel the bottom of her dress pressed wet against her calves.

"Must be troublesome, not having a man about to do for you," the fisherman says as Ani watches him trace the line from her ankles, up around her wet hemline and the length of her legs, across her belly, her breasts, and up to her neck, where he stops, coughs, and turns to look out across the water.

"You've not much choice but to get on with it," she says, her hand at the V of her dress. "Ask any war widow." It's a harder thing than she means to say, but she gets a twitch of satisfaction from the man's blush.

"I'll get these home then," he says, pointing again to his house, the idea of his wife. But as he turns to go, he pauses, the bucket swinging from his hand. "There were a group of us used to take a drink in the wine saloon sometimes—your Mac was there once or twice; some of the boys home from the war had a hankering for the sherries they'd had overseas. And Mac said those thick drinks almost touched the edge of the whisky he remembered. He'd be on his way home, calling in—I'm not sure you knew." His eyes are fixed on his own feet now, his downturned head dampening his voice as much as the sound of the nearby water. "He sang us a Scots song once, his booming great voice and all the words about light and heather and the wide ocean. Brought a lot of us to tears. But I could never remember the tune when I set out to hum it, and I never had the moment to ask him if he'd sing it again." And he touches his forehead, the barest implication of a salute.

"There are days I can hardly remember the sound of his voice, the way his breath broke up sentences, the way his accent changed some words." Ani is staring into the nothingness, barely conscious of what she's saying. "If he was famous, someone would have made a recording of his voice—singing, or saying something. A little bit of a movie, or a gramophone record you could play over and over. I can remember the way that man danced along Martin Place when the war was finally done with, but I can't remember the way my husband said his own address, where he paused, where he spelled things out." She shakes her head and peers into the bucket of fish. "I will take one of those, then," she says, "if you don't mind about the paper, and if you wouldn't mind gutting it too. You're right; there are things you miss having a man to do." And she clenches her teeth as his eyes sweep her body again before he goes.

Alone on the sand, she watches the oystercatcher coasting in the shallows, its head ducking under the water every so often. The surfers have gone, ridden in, she guesses, and now standing warm in the sun with their big planks of wood drying next to them. But she feels such a hum in the air that she wonders if she hasn't committed herself somehow to trying surfing, walking out across the water and gliding along with the rim of a wave, elegant and aloft and free.

And all this from a conversation about Mac and a dead fish.

She takes the parcel from the fisherman, nodding. "Thank you for this," she says, placing it near her feet, "and for the story. Makes me feel a bit of a beachcomber, hunting more bits of someone I thought I knew everything about." She waves across the road to the house, to the implied wife, as well—an extra thank-you. Behind its tin roof, the mountain puts up its high, solid wall, the facets and faces of its rocks lit by morning's sun, and the smoke thick along the top. "Will it come down, do you think?" she asks, pointing to the traces of the inferno.

The fisherman spreads his hands like a question. "Must be due a burn through there," he says, "and it's been a blessed hot summer for it. But there are a lot of houses between us and it; a lot of people would try to fight it down before it reached the beach. If it does come over the top." He squints. "You never really know how worried you should be, do you? You never really know what's coming next."

And as she watches the fisherman go, an anyone in his rolled-up trousers, his smeary shirt, his felt hat, she squats down in the sand, next to the fish, her back to the sea, and one foot tucked beneath her so that it pushes hard against the hard bone, the soft space, between her legs. *His skin would taste of salt*, she thinks as he crosses the road and scrambles up the bank to his house. *And he has a wife who might taste that.*

She licks at her own hand, and tastes tears.

28

HALFWAY THROUGH a lap of Thirroul's pool, Roy stops, letting himself float like a starfish. The sun is a bright disk—a nasty red—through the haze of the bushfire's smoke, and the air tastes sharp and bitter. This waiting for a fire to come, or not: he'd forgotten the powerlessness of such time, and how unbearably it stretched. Ducking under the water, he opens his eyes and kicks out towards the pool's edge, hooking his forearms up over the concrete and dangling, his back to the water, his eyes on the mountain. Through the previous night, he watched the red glow of the fire beyond its rim, wondering what he should do—or might do—if a runnel of flame suddenly leaped down over its edge. Wondering how glorious it might look if the whole face of the scarp was bright and ablaze.

Behind him, a kid comes hurtling down the slide and into the water, dowsing him with spray. "Oy!" Roy hears his own voice, too loud and too angry. "Oughta watch where you're splashing."

"Oughta watch where you park," the boy calls, spluttering water and kicking away.

Kids on vacation—what kind of a bloke'd scold a boy for leaping? Roy leans forward on the concrete, its sharp edge pressing hard between his elbows and his wrists so that his forearms shake uncontrollably. He watches them spasm, mesmerized. *And what if that kid'd hit me? What if he'd knocked me under and held me there? Or pushed me down so my head slammed the concrete? What if I was down there now, down under the water, the life shaking out of me, some kid pushing me under, and all this, all this life and light almost over?*

"You all right, mister?" The slippery-dip kid pulls himself onto the wall, alongside Roy, pointing to his quivering arms. "You having a fit or something? My grandpa has fits. You want me to get someone?"

Roy shifts his weight, pulling himself out of the water and holding up his recovered arms like trophies. "I'm all right," he says. "See how far out you make it on your next go." Sending him back to the ladder, the leaping, the joy.

There was something beautiful in the boy's smile, Roy thinks as he jogs across the grass to his sister's—it's the first time he's had a nice thought about a kid, he realizes, since the war expelled him from his classrooms. But it's replaced in an instant by the more beautiful idea of being held under the water, his limbs still. He kicks at a stone and wants to shout and cheer as it lands directly between two of Iris's potted plants.

"Is that you, Roy?" she calls as he scuffles at the door.

Who else? he thinks, calling, "Yes—I'll just hang out my towel." She's in the bathroom, the air thick with the competitive smells of eucalyptus oil, vinegar, and methylated spirit.

"You don't want a wash, do you? I'm halfway through doing the bath—didn't expect you until the end of the day." Kneeling on the lino, she's hunched forward over the tub and scrubbing so hard he can see her muscles working through the fabric of her dress.

"It's a hot day for cleaning, Iris," he says. "Can I get you something cool to drink?"

"Well, there's nothing else that wants doing today, so I thought

I'd get on and do this. Didn't expect you home until nightfall," she says again, and he nods in acknowledgment this time, giving her half a smile.

"All the smoke out, it's no weather for walking. And the pool's full of kids on their vacations. Almost brained by one of them, little bugger." He watches her arm drag the scrubbing brush back and forward, over and over. What would she say if he told her about the tranquillity of drowning? What would she say if he told her the boy's smile was beautiful? Then, "Any of that Christmas shortbread left? I could get you a piece, with a drink, if you like."

"There's lemonade there." Iris leans back on her haunches. "A jug of it. But I'll finish this first, you go on." They watch each other a moment, a strange staring contest while Roy tries to pick what his sister will say next. Something about lunch, or a job; safe bets both.

But, "Frank Draper dropped a book in for you." Her hand wipes across her eyes and fusses with the edges of her hair. "*Kangaroo*—I told him you'd had it already from the library and hadn't made much headway. But he said you needed it until he could get you some Yeats."

Roy grimaces. "Bloody Frank." Every second time they saw each other, Frank was loaded up with mementoes of their dreams, their plans, as if an accretion of these might cajole Roy back into his vocation. Every other time, Frank's mood hovered somewhere dark and bleak, his conversation snapped and icy, his observations weighed down with despair.

Roy saw his friend on the same seesaw with Iris: there were days when Frank walked out with her and smiled at the smiles of the town, and days when he snapped at the very mention of her, and Roy knew he'd snap at her in person too. *Just kiss her*, he wanted to say. *Just walk down here now and get this over.* The man of action, the man of motion: that's how it used to be with Frank. If anyone was hesitant, or reticent, Roy knows it's himself.

"Look, how hard can it be to start?" Frank had blustered at the pub one afternoon. "One sentence, right now, top of your head, worst thing you saw: get it out—don't think about it."

And I said, the way a man looked nothing like a man when he'd met a machine gun; the way no woman would meet your eyes when you were carrying one.

"Okay, good—that's a start; that's a start." Frank had drained his beer in a gulp, signaling immediately for another. "Now the best thing—best or most beautiful. Top of your head. Come on."

The way the ocean glowed green some nights; the way the little boats used the light of the Milky Way, used its pathway, to navigate.

"There you are—write that down. I reckon you're on to something here, Roy. I reckon you're cooking."

Even now, Roy knows, the scrap of paper on which he obediently wrote these ideas is folded neatly in the top drawer of his bedside table. He unfolds it every morning and rereads it, waiting to see what will happen next.

Now, in Iris's kitchen, he opens the box of shortbread and breaks the last piece into two, reaching for a glass with his other hand. "I'm taking this around the side," he calls. "Want to keep an eye on the fire." He drops the shortbread into one pocket, Frank's copy of *Kangaroo* into the other, and settles himself against the wall beneath his bedroom window, where he can see the mountain to the west and the wide reach of the beach to the east.

There are more flames now, licking at the scarp's edge; you could never say aloud that it was exhilarating, thinks Roy, *but it is, it is.* He reaches in his pocket for a pen—there might be something in this; the anticipation, the terror, the threat of conflagration—and finds the paperback instead, watching as it falls open at a dog-eared page:

Cripes, there's *nothing* bucks you up sometimes like killing a man—*nothing.* You feel a perfect *angel* after it. . . . When it comes over you, you know, there's nothing else like it. *I never knew, till the war. And I wouldn't believe it then, not for many a while. But it's there.* Cripes, it's there right enough. Having a woman's something, isn't it? But it's a flea-bite, nothing, compared to killing your man when your blood comes up.

What is *this?* Roy rakes at his hair, at the air, at the mushy mess of the shortbread he spat onto the grass when he began to read these words—to feel them, to taste them. *You feel a perfect angel*: what the devil thing is that to say? Where's Frank's fancy-sounding psychoneurosis taking him now?

Roy stares at the page until the words blur into grey lines against the yellowing paper. *You do bloody not feel like an angel, mate, and the last thing you think you can ever do again is trust yourself with anything as gentle as a woman.* Something moves across the road, and Roy sees the boy from the pool padding along, a bucket swinging from his hand like the arc of a pendulum. All the nights Roy's tried to swing himself to sleep with his watch; all the nights he's watched the back and forth of its face. And they awoke the next day *refreshed and able to carry on.* That's what the paper said.

Bunkum.

Turning his head from side to side, Roy lets his gaze pan from the fire to the water and back across the landscape in between. *How long before I find my deep and refreshing sleep?* he wonders, his head jerking still as he sees her step out of the brightness to come along the beachfront: Ani Lachlan, her pale dress wet around the bottom and a lumpy newspaper parcel held awkwardly across her body.

That's why he hadn't read *Kangaroo* when he borrowed it from her—all those lurking traps of violence and brutality when all he wanted was the scenery of it, this place. As for killing a man . . . Roy snorts. Frank Draper could hold those five hundred souls on the knife edge of his conscience for as long as he liked, but it was nothing compared to seeing a man, and lining him up, and pulling a trigger, and watching him fall.

From the top of the mountain, a single line of flame picks its way down through the trees, slower than Roy had expected, as if it is considering its every move. Yet even down here, the smoke is thicker for its incursion, stiffening the air and sharpening it somehow.

You do not use a word like "angel" in a sentence like that. He tears at the offending page of the novel, ripping it out of its binding and screwing it into a ball to throw away. The word "angel"—he looks out through the infernal day, beyond the limitless sea—the word "angel," the very idea of such a being: that belongs to someone like *her*. And Roy raises his arm to hail Ani—"Hullo"—the word swallowed by the width of the road, the sound of the sea, the purposefulness of her stride. The look of her on Christmas afternoon, soft and gentle in her light, white dress, and smiling as if she'd just realized there was life in some place she'd thought otherwise desolate.

And there it is, the beginning of his poem:

Let this be her.
A folding of the light
And she stepped through, candescent messenger

"Candescent messenger." He uncaps his pen and scrawls the phrase across the endpaper of Draper's wretched offering.

"Mrs. Lachlan," he calls again, but her head is down and she doesn't turn.

She looks, he thinks, *like an angel in a lost world.* Is that who she is—his muse? But he closes his eyes and sees her as she was on Christmas Day, and he knows there's something more to it than inspiration.

"Desirable," he whispers, "lost, and lonely, and desirable." It would be something, he thinks, to make her smile, and he lets himself imagine her, her hands out to receive a gift from him—a sheet of paper thick with words that she's inspired. There'd be such light and joy in her face.

If he's going to be a poet, he'll give her this one thing a poet can give; he will write a poem for her. No, better: he will make her a book full of beautiful verses and set these words—his words for her—as their climax, their culmination.

He smoothes the paperback's rough page, folding his first new sentences over and over in his mind until they are certain and secure, embedded in his imagination.

"Let this be her, a folding of the light," he says again, and loudly, his gaze moving between the surreal red trickle of the bushfire and the last glimpse of a woman going home.

29

HE WAKES early, before dawn, but with no intention of going to the service. Anzac Day; the dreadful glory of that war that was going to end all wars. Not even for his sister will he pin on his medals and walk about in the smell of rosemary. No, Roy McKinnon is not for that sort of remembrance. He turns in his covers, feeling them twist tight around his legs, his body, until he almost panics.

What's wrong with you, man; what's wrong with you? Shaking himself free, he stands to stretch by the window.

In the next room, Iris is awake and dressing—she will go to the service. She will say, *Someone should; it's our duty.*

Let her go, then, thinks Roy. *She can do her own remembering.* He watches through the window until the front door clicks, and she is hurrying away along the street. *And let Frank be there,* thinks Roy, *waiting for my sister.*

He pulls on a sweater and trousers and goes into the kitchen to make himself some toast. So rarely hungry, he must have dreamed good dreams to wake up and want to eat.

And perhaps she was in them, he lets himself think, turning the bread as it browns on one side. *Perhaps she was there.* He glances up the hill, towards the street that runs along its crest. From Iris's back door, he can glimpse the front of Ani Lachlan's house. *She will go to the service*, he thinks. *Ani Lachlan would care about those things.* Not letting himself touch the idea that she might go for the chance of seeing him.

The way he's carried her, these three, four months since he found the first lines for that poem; the way he's crafted her and shaped her, forming a suite of stanzas so right, so perfect, it almost takes his breath away. The poem's final draft on a sheet in front of him, he lets his fingers rest gently against the lines of which he's most proud:

> . . . her white dress,
> So light she might float clear,
> Were she not tethered by the limitless
> Surprise of being here.

The limitless surprise: he sighs. It's as if he's been in the deepest and most intimate conversation with her—and it astonishes him, every time he sees her, to remember that she has no knowledge of it. Yet.

On the table in his room, the thing he's been making is finally finished—transcriptions of great and stirring poems by great and stirring writers, and his own new poem, right at the end. He's typed them out on thick, creamy paper, reveling in the fake sound of industry coming from his Remington Rand. *Not my words*, he thinks he should say when his sister remarks on the busy clatter, but there's something reassuring in being thought productive at last.

The poems complete, he found some fine red silk thread in one of Iris's sewing boxes—the remnant of long-abandoned embroidery—and stitched his pages together, binding them hard with two pieces of card covered in red. At school, he remembered, he always loved the presentation of his projects as much as composing the words that filled them, and as he sat cross-legged on the end of this narrow bed in his sister's house, with his meticulous needlework, he was a kid again, all happiness and potential. *So maybe this morning*, he thinks, steeling himself. *I could sneak it in while she's away.* The thought of her face, the thought of her smile—these daydreams have collapsed into the possible embarrassment of shame, or her displeasure, or of having offered something unwanted. He's not reassured enough to face that, he thinks, flat.

"And then what?" he asks himself aloud. "What happens then?" The unknowable thing. But he makes himself leave the house before he can change his mind again, is up the hill, through Ani's gate, and around to the back door before the sun has cleared the horizon.

Ani's house is empty; he knows that immediately. She and Isabel are certainly not here. Very slowly, Roy eases the door open and steps inside. His heart is pounding, his hands damp against the rough, red linen of his gift.

Into the lounge room, over to the mantelpiece; he is ready to shove it in anywhere and leave, when he stops, pauses, and takes in the volumes the shelf already holds. She spoke of this, the books she and Mac shared—she told him the story of unpacking them like a dowry and putting them here. *You're a rude bugger to want to muscle in on that sort of memory*, nodding at the authors, the titles. *All the places she's been through these pages, all the people she's met.* Where else would she have ended up but in a library?

Stepping back, he looks around the rest of the room. There's an engraving of Edinburgh Castle over the fireplace, and another of a three-master on a high sea over the chiffonier. A pair of slippers, some pencils, and a drawing sit abandoned on the floor—he reaches for the paper, admiring the likeness of the house he's standing in to the one in the picture that Isabel has made. *She's a bright one, that one,* he thinks, setting it back on the ground, and for the first time in almost a decade, he misses the bright girls he used to teach in tiny schools. He misses teaching them how to dream.

He moves towards the hallway, noticing the way the light comes in through the stained-glass panels in the door—when Ani is here, it's always propped open for the breeze. On the sideboard, a small white bowl holds four blown-glass Christmas ornaments—two red and two blue—so delicate, the lightest touch might shatter them. Beyond these, two photographs. The first is Mac, in a smart suit and tie—Roy is almost tempted to turn it facedown. *At what point is it appropriate to court a widow?* he thinks, clinical. *And who's the appropriate person to do that courting? Not some sneak who breaks into her house, not some twit terrified of his own shadow, not some fellow who wants to swim out to the horizon and keep going, mate.*

He stares at the picture, remembering Mac's size, his momentum, the way he strode along a street or ran along the football field. *You, one of those men of motion; bet you never thought it would come to this. Bet you never thought I'd be the one alive, and standing here—* as if Mac would have thought of him at all. Which seems a pity, somehow. He'd have liked Mac Lachlan as a friend.

Because he did like the man, he thinks suddenly, and remembers all at once standing shivering in a cold predawn, talking with Mac about the mess of the world. Before the war—was it '37, '38? And what had Mac said? That he wouldn't go, if it came to fighting; that it was *nowt to do with him,* and he'd stay here with Ani. *And wouldn't you, wouldn't you,* thinks Roy as he turns to the second photograph, Ani and Isabel, taken by a street photographer in Sydney.

That's Martin Place, he thinks, smiling at the silly sunglasses, the silly smiles both are wearing. Must have been during the war: Isabel four years old or so.

"Nice way to spend an afternoon while we were out saving the world," he says aloud, as shocked by the slam of his mood and the iciness that freezes around his voice as he is by the words' presence in the still, quiet house. *Makes me sound like Draper.*

Turning again, he sees the doorway to Ani's bedroom, and stops. *What the blazes are you doing here? What if she comes home? Take the book and get out of here—give it to her yourself when you see her, you great fool*—all this, as he mistakes a sound for footfall on the porch stairs and hurls himself back through the house, towards the back door.

And stops, hearing only silence.

All right, Roy, all right. Back at the mantelpiece, he slides the thin red book in between two paperbacks, and then turns and runs, tripping on the mat, leaving it disheveled, half looking for her reflection in the corrugated surface of the kitchen cabinets as he skirts past—their plates and glasses rattling a little as he goes—and on, through the back door and through the gate before he has time to draw breath.

The inverse of burglary, he thinks. *And now, now what?*

He can't hear for the sound of his heartbeat in his skull. He can't stand still for shivering against the autumn's chill. But he's pleased with it, this thing he has made—the best of the world's best poems, as he sees them, and the finest new thing of his own. Then, clear and complete, he remembers that autumn night, twelve years before, when he and Frank Draper huddled over a radio for news of a bombing in Spain. *More than a thousand dead, they said—and how few that number sounds now.* It was shocking, the way his head had pounded then with his own useless vitality. *Women and children, going to market.* And they'd stood and talked of it with Mac. He stops, breathes deeply, tries not to retch.

From across the village, he hears the sound of a train, and then, high above, the purr of a plane's engine—it's all he can do not to dive under a hedge for cover.

It doesn't get any better, he thinks, making himself keep walking. *It doesn't get any easier, the being here, or the being.*

Twelve years since that bombing and the mood Frank had been in when they'd heard the news and walked home through the night. So dark, so bleak, so pessimistic.

So right.

How many women and children since? How many market days? Back at the bottom of the hill, he takes a deep breath at his sister's front door, his pulse quiet, his sweat dry. Across the road, someone is surfing on the wide sheen of the ocean, riding the smooth waves up and in, closer and closer, only to drop down out of sight at the last moment, before the break, and paddle out to do it again.

There's something futile in it, and something quite beautiful.

One day, thinks Roy, *one day I will try that. I'll take a board out past the breakers and see what the sea makes of me.*

A car honks as it passes, and he spins round as if he'd been caught in some terrible act—bloody Frank, with his new wheels, and probably off to deliver some baby. *Ah well, Iris will be disappointed.* On it goes. But there is consolation, even optimism, Roy tells himself, in the fact that he presumes it's birth, and not death, that has his friend on the road so early.

He closes his eyes, the image of the surfer overlaid now with an image of Ani Lachlan, rising and falling on a sunlit sea. *You're gone, mate, completely gone.* He's done all he can, he tells himself—written the poem and delivered it to her bookshelf. He breathes out, as if his breath has been held tight for years and years on end. The surfer stands, rides the glassy wave, drops down, and paddles out again.

Going in, Roy keeps him in his sights as long as he can, almost shocked when the closing door finally shuts off his view of the water, the light, and the surfer's body, miraculously aloft.

30

SHE DOESN'T know how many times she's looked at the mantel-piece, how many times her eyes have scanned its books, taken one out, or another, and read it, and replaced it. But she's never noticed this before, a thin red paperback like one of Isabel's schoolbooks, its silk-stitched spine unblemished.

Her heart lurches as if she'd stepped forward and found no floor to stand on. And as she looks around, quickly, she catches an unexpected movement—but it's only the curtain blowing against the window.

All right, she thinks. *All right*. But she cannot quite reach out to take up the book.

She's tired, that's all—it's Anzac Day. She woke at dawn to watch the sun rise, the men march, the women weep or cheer. Standing so still as the parade passed by, Isabel's hand held so tight, that she wondered if she was turning into something like the rock from which the cenotaph had been carved. *Important to remember; it's important to remember.*

"Good morning to you, Mrs. Lachlan." As the last of the march-ers rounded the corner, Ani had turned to see Iris McKinnon standing quietly alone. "I wasn't sure you'd be here—it must be tempting to sleep in when you don't need to get down for the library. And you were always keen to avoid being part of the war."

"Miss McKinnon." Ani had held out her hand, ignoring the largeness of this small woman's words. "Iris, good morning to you. It's a large turnout, isn't it? The library, yes, it's busy, and then there's Bella . . ." She ruffles her daughter's hair. "I don't know where the weeks go." She looked around for the doctor, expecting to see them here together.

"He's not here," said Iris McKinnon, riffling through her bag for a handkerchief and blowing her nose. But as Ani murmured something about the unpredictability of medical demands, Iris cut across her and said, "Not Frank, I mean my brother. My brother will have been sorry not to come." Then she blew again, and Ani jumped at the sheer force of the noise. "I think it means a lot to him, having someone like you here—I never was much for reading, you know. I never know how to talk to Roy about these things, or trying to write." She sniffed, and Ani wondered if she was crying, but she turned her head away. "Still, he seems better for being here now, and being busier with your books and things. It's all you can ask for, isn't it, that these men find their way back home."

Ani blushed. "I'm pleased to be able to find him the books he's after—it's what we're here for, after all." She gestured beyond the stone statue of the soldier to the railway and its library beyond.

"I'm not sure I mean the library," Iris McKinnon said slowly. "I think it's more than that. He thinks the world of you, you know—I'm not sure I should tell you that, but there's something wrong with a world where such things aren't said."

And it was Ani's turn to fumble for her handkerchief, to bring it up to her face, to look away. "Well, I've had a bit of luck in getting books down from Sydney," she said. "I'm sure that's all it is."

They stood a little longer, neither saying a thing, before Iris

McKinnon took half a step forward, reaching out. "Whatever it is, it helps," she said softly, taking Ani's hand and holding it a moment before she walked away.

Isabel circled, grabbing onto the hand that the poet's sister had just held. "What's 'thinks the world,' Mum?" she asked her mother as Iris McKinnon walked towards the war memorial. "What does that mean? How can someone 'think the world'?"

Somewhere behind her, Ani could hear a group of women talking—something about a wedding, and a bride being married *by* the man she loved, instead of married *to* him. "Years of silence," someone said, "or willful misunderstanding."

And then there was talk of the poor speeches, a desultory dance, and a short honeymoon in a flash hotel in Sydney. "And he doesn't know, the groom, the poor fellow. He just thinks she's a nice quiet girl, and he's lucky in his choice."

"*His* choice?" another crowed. "He had no choice about it, and never will." They laughed, although Ani, unable to identify whoever the story was about, could not quite see the joke. *It's too hard*, she thought blankly, *trying to keep track of all these different situations.*

"I like it, 'thinks the world,'" she heard her daughter say. "It's like some funny riddle. 'What would you think about to think the world?' The answer'd be twenty-four thousand, nine hundred miles, maybe, which is the world's circumference at the equator, or maybe fifty-seven and a half million square miles, for how much land there is."

"No one likes a braggart, Bella," said Ani quietly. "Let's go home. It's just a thing people say." And she'd spent the rest of the morning planting out rosemary bushes, Mrs. May passing seedlings from the basket, until the garden pulsed with that pungent, particular smell.

Now, as the sun clips the top of the scarp and slides through the west-facing windows of Isabel's room, the street is quiet. In the shadow of the living room, Ani steadies herself against the mantelpiece. She had planned on going to the pictures that night, on seeing the latest news from Europe. Sometimes she meets Roy McKinnon there; sometimes she meets Frank Draper with him, who, once or twice if it's a comedy or a musical, has had Iris on his arm. And sometimes they walk home together, talking—the two men sometimes stammering, sometimes inappropriate, sometimes caught, one or the other, in a long, silent hiatus—about the movie, the news, the night.

"We are all too old for this," the doctor had said once, and Ani had seen, for a second, their middle-aged parody of four young folk out for a night on the town.

He thinks the world of you: she isn't sure she wants to know what that means, or what she'd like it to.

And now, the day feels overwhelming. *I'll stay in, take a long bath, forget the news of the world.* So tired, she thinks, that she can't even reach out and work this unfamiliar little book free from its place on a shelf.

This thing she's been looking for, and she's found it on this day of remembrance. But her hesitation has nothing to do with tired- ness, she knows. *You're afraid, Anikka Lachlan. You're afraid of what you've found.*

The house is too still, too silent. For a moment, she thinks there's someone standing behind her, but when she turns to look, it's only the curtain again in the late-afternoon breeze, and Isabel's slippers, forgotten by the sofa with the picture she was drawing the night before. She spins slowly, scanning the room, and sees the pho- tograph of Mac facing her from the sideboard, as if he was peering around into the sitting room, waiting to see her react.

A deep breath, and another. Ani lays her hand along the other books, walks her fingers across their creases and ridges until she reaches this new red thing. She feels its stiff cloth cover, slightly longer, slightly wider, than the papers it holds. She opens it, feeling the texture of paper that's thick like velvet, and rough-cut. Luxurious.

Here it is, here it is at last. This untitled volume: what else but the present Mac meant for her? She pulls it out quickly and sinks onto the floor, cross-legged, patting at its bright shape.

There's no title, no author, no words of any kind—she opens to the endpapers, the frontispiece: all blank. A journal? she wonders. Or was it the beginning of something he never had time to finish?

But as she balances its spine in the lectern of her two hands, the covers fall open and there is text inside, typed, the letters pressed hard into the first page. She tilts it towards the light. Where had Mac ever found a typewriter? How had she never heard its keys?

But still, here he is. Here he is.

Holding her breath, she opens the front of the book again and finds a one-line inscription—*For Anikka Lachlan*, written neat and careful—before she turns to read its first poems: Shakespeare's lover like a summer's day; Byron's walking in beauty like the night. She skates across lines she doesn't know, and lines she does, and on through stanzas and verses to Elizabeth Barrett Browning counting the ways of her love. *And, if God choose, I shall but love thee better after death*. Line after line of love, and of longing, and of other places and times. Title at the beginning, author at the end, all carefully transcribed for her.

She turns the page, almost at the end of the book, and finds the last poem, "Lost World." Such a lull in the room. The curtains hang still and outside there's not a breath of air, not a single bird. She leans back to look through the front door: not a single leaf is moving, nothing.

She's holding her breath.

> Let this be her.
> A folding of the light

And she stepped through, candescent messenger
Announcing to my sight

Another sense,
In this lost world whose color
And form flared round her, ever more intense,
And as she passed grew duller.

I took this place
For some cartoon of hell,
Among whose mud and mayhem I would pace,
The ill-drawn sentinel.

Instead I found
The water and the light,
Light on the water, light in which the crowned
Escarpment trees ignite.

I looked for loss
And found what pledges are:
Pale hair, brown cheeks and stone-grey eyes, across
Her breast a coral star

As silver-pink
As dawn. Life's vortex spins
Around her. Come, she offers. Eat and drink.
Each door and window twins

Her moving presence,
Alive with promises;
She speaks, she laughs, among the iridescence
Of all her likenesses.

And her white dress,
So light she might float clear,
Were she not tethered by the limitless
Surprise of being here.

Still. She may throw
A shadow, but bears more.
I saw her too, too quiet, to and fro,
A figure on the shore,

Or in the snare
Of some wild dance, head back
And flailing, frenzied, almost unaware,
Almost demoniac,

Or heavy with
A sorrow not to quell,
The painting of a deity from myth
Lost on the lip of hell.

Which is not here,
No matter where I gaze.
With her the reckoning might well be near,
The tally of our days.

From where she stands
A single line's drawn out,
Weightless meridian that from her hands
Will loop the globe about.

All this in her,
All things, all places furled

And folded in her, the bright messenger
Who comes for a lost world.

And then she's glancing ahead, to the next page, and the next. But there's nothing more, and no author at the bottom.

Squaring her shoulders, she reads it again from start to finish, only letting out her breath when she's done.

Mac's poem, she thinks. *Mac wrote me a poem.*

A folding of the light, and she stepped through. And *her moving presence, alive with promises.* And *the limitless surprise of being here.*

The limitless surprise.

Small noises fill the room, fluttering as if they've traveled a long way. It's only when she leans forward that she realizes they're coming from her own mouth, like *oh, oh,* and *oh.*

The miracle of it—not just the present found after so much looking, but that it's this, *this,* as if she has somehow been allowed one more conversation with her husband, one whole new exchange. She presses her fingers lightly against the words and is certain, absolutely certain, that she can feel the pressure of his fingers pressing back as they set these letters onto this page—only now, right now.

And what more could you ever want, she thinks, *than the chance of just one more conversation?*

"Sweetheart." The word rattles around the empty room. *There you are. There you are.*

She touches her fingers to the poem, word by word, and then reads it in a kind of rush, taking whole lines in a gulp, before she sits, quietly, her fingers stroking the fine red cover. Opening the cover again, she finds her own name—*the writing,* she thinks, *I thought Mac's* A *was more triangular, where this one loops around.* But it's a careful and considerate script—*and he would have concentrated; he would have wanted to make the penmanship perfect.* Who knew that he could make such a thing? Who knew he had it in him?

she wonders, wincing then at how discourteous, how impolite it is to imply that a poem was beyond him. A poem, any poem, *let alone this beautiful thing.* And where had he found a typewriter?

Before a quarter hour has passed, she has it by heart. She wants to run into the street and shout to everyone about her discovery. She wants to hold it close to herself and share it with no one, not even Isabel. *That's right,* she thinks. *That's better.*

Her fingers pick out the letters that form her name from random words in the poem, the way Isabel used to find the letters of her own name in any words on any page when she was first learning to read. *Would he have read it to me? Was that part of the gift?* And she can hear it in his voice, so clearly, the thickening of "lost," the softness of the *g* in "messenger." No trouble remembering those sounds today; it's as if their echo is rising up from the book.

After this, she thinks, *everything changes. After this,* she thinks, *nothing can change.* This strange feeling, as she reads the lines again, that she's somehow been confirmed with him, connected to him—that all the aching, all the grieving can be put aside to make room for him, him himself, returned somehow, and revitalized.

It matters that he had the chance to do this. It matters that he had the chance to make this thing. He's alive in it—she can almost feel his breathing—and when she presses the page against her chest, she can almost feel the shape of him again.

She stays there, sitting on the floor, and when she hears Isabel coming up the stairs an hour or so later, she pushes herself up, all stiff and awkward. Slips the book back into its place on the shelf as the screen door opens, and has her arms ready for a hug.

"What a day, Bella, what a glorious day. I was just thinking about a quick swim before dinner—I know it's late, but what do you think? Will you come?" And she swings her daughter into a kind of dance in the middle of the room, like she used to when Isabel was small enough to be swung entirely off the ground, laughing when Isabel starts to laugh. "And a baked custard for supper, I thought. A baked custard—the way you like it."

"Like a special treat?"

"Like a very special occasion." Ani squeezes Isabel close, rests her chin on the top of her daughter's head, wonders how much longer she'll fit in that way. *You have these things for as long as you have them*, she thinks, *and then you get something entirely new.*

But as they make their way down the narrow steps cut into the cliff, the sea roils and swells, enormous, from the shore below.

"I don't care," Ani calls above the pounding surge. "I'm going in."

But, "Mum," Isabel calls, high and excited, "your green—look, your shiny green." The water is picked out with swirls and spreads of shimmering light.

Luminous, thinks Ani. *Glorious*. On top of the poem, it's almost too much. She stows her shoes, her dress at the bottom of the stairs and skips towards the water like a girl of Isabel's age.

The water is colder than she expects, but she ducks her head under and laughs at the way the shining color runs down her body, her wet hair as she surfaces.

"Come on, come in, it's beautiful," she calls, dipping down again as Isabel walks tentatively towards her. "We won't stay long; we won't go far." And she watches her daughter's head duck down and come up. *What a crazy thing to do.* The two of them diving, again and again.

They stand then, as still as they can among the movement of the choppy ocean, watching the lustrous carpet ebb and flow along the shore, Isabel tucked in against her mother, held warm and close.

"So there's your phosphorescence, Mum," she says, cupping her hands to carry the exquisite water ashore. "Maybe it was here lots of nights and we just never looked at the right time."

Ani smiles, wrapping herself in her towel, her clothes, and feeding her sticky feet back into her shoes for the climb up the cliff.

From somewhere deep comes the idea of asking Roy McKinnon his professional opinion of her husband's first poem, but something in the thought makes her throat grab. *Because it's mine*, she thinks, possessive: *I want no one else to see it, to be able to breathe its words.* Maybe one day, years from now. Maybe then. *There's always time.*

31

ON THE first anniversary of the war's end, Mac worked an early shift and walked the long way home, looping down to the library via a quick drink in the billiards hall and a haircut next door. *To celebrate*, he told himself. *Lest we forget. Et cetera.* He slid his books across to Miss Fadden, taking care not to knock her half-worked game of Patience. *Not a bad life*, he thought, *to sit in a room full of books and have time for a card game now and then.* He could think of worse ways to pass the time.

"If you'd like something new for Bella," said Miss Fadden, shuffling her cards away in an approximation of busyness, "there's a lovely book came down today about a little French girl called Madeline—made me think of Isabel; I think she might like it." She set it in the middle of the desk with Mac's card on the top, waiting.

"You're good to keep an eye out for her, Miss Fadden," said Mac, running his finger along the shelves. "But what about for me? Any nice books about French girls for me?"

He liked to make Miss Fadden laugh. "Here, for you," she said, when she'd had her giggle. "A new Hornblower—and I do believe he sails up the Seine, so you can keep an eye out for your own

Madeline while you're reading it. And tell Mrs. Lachlan I still can't get her *Brideshead Revisited*—I think everyone must be wanting to read it at the same time."

Mac smiled, pulled two more books from the shelf, and pushed his pile across the table, complete. "And what are you reading, then, Miss Fadden? If you've any time to read at all among the busyness of the library?" He wasn't sure he could remember a time when there was another borrower in the room beside himself.

"There's a lovely new Georgette Heyer romance I'm waiting for, Mr. Lachlan, and I always like to read the children's books, to make sure I know what I'm recommending. Lovely things, when they're well written—but you'd know that, from reading with Isabel. How is she, little pet?"

"It's just an excuse for me to read them, of course." Mac laughed, tucking the books into his satchel. "And she's grand, she's grand. I'll let Ani know about her book and tell her to keep her fingers crossed for next time." He waved as he went, whistling across the yard and calling to Luddy as he passed the stationmaster's office, "Will there be fireworks down here tonight, mate? The anniversary? The victory day?" He gestured over towards the empty football field where effigies had been burned and bonfires lit.

Luddy shook his head, coming out onto the platform. "Doesn't feel like anyone's making that much of it," he said. "To be honest, I think most people want to forget it ever happened."

Mac sighed. "I didn't even fight in the thing and I reckon we should do better than that." He glanced up at the mountain, at the afternoon sun. "What do you reckon, Luddy? How many years of eternal peace will this one get us?"

But Luddy waved him away. "You go home and make your own memorial. It'll be years before they sort out the statues and the sandstone."

Coming across the football field, Mac broke into a slow jog—

years since he'd played a game, but he could still hear the calls of his team and the sliver of a crowd that turned up to watch. *You're an old man now, with your rickety knees and your daughter outrunning you.* He slowed, crouched down, and sprang out across the final yards of the field. There it was, the rush, the surge of acceleration he used to love, flying down the wing, heading for the line.

Mebbe I'm not so old after all.

He climbed the hill and turned into his own street—*Surfers Parade, and Ani wondering when there'd be a parade of surfers coming along with their great, long boards.* It sounded like a dream, or an apparition, but he'd like to have seen it himself. They could run along the road and dive out from its end—maybe they'd clear the rock shelf if they sprinted fast enough, flying with their boards out over the open water, away behind the waves.

Like Isabel, when the war ended and the barbed wire along the beach came down; she stood for hours watching surfers hover on the lips of unbroken swells. "They're standing on the water, Dadda; they're riding it. They're riding it. How do they do that? Is it magic?"

And he'd wanted to tell her it was, wanted her to think that there was magic in the world.

32

ON A winter's morning in June 1949, Ani wakes suddenly in the darkness, wanting to be anywhere but in her bed, in her room, in her house. She used to joke about it with Mac, that latent Scandinavian sense of long, cold days; the uneasiness she felt in even this most temperate place. Now, she pulls on any clothes, any shoes, and one of his sweaters—the only one she's kept—before she turns to see Isabel standing in the doorway.

"The beach?" Ani asks, and her daughter, already dressed, nods.

Two apples in a bag, the end of a loaf of bread, a piece of cheese, and a jar of water: "I hate waking up this way," Ani whispers as she pulls the door behind her. "Let's get down to the sea." And they run along the street, hand in hand, around the corner, and down the stairs to the sand, almost tumbling with haste.

A smooth ocean to the east; a sliver of moon hanging over the dark escarpment to the west. Isabel flies along the shore, her hair shaking free from its plaits as she runs, and Ani stretches her legs out so that her steps match the footprints left by her running daughter. Isabel turns a cartwheel, another, and another, and Ani laughs. *That's better*, she thinks. *Much better.* She wishes she were brave enough to try one herself, but she's never quite understood how to push on her arms so her legs will spin up and around her body. She's forgotten how light she herself used to be, springing all over the unfinished houses her father worked on—up to their highest point, and down again in just a step or two.

"Just try, Mum, just try." Isabel is running towards her, spinning again, and springing into a somersault.

Slowly, deliberately, Ani puts down their bag of breakfast, pushes up the baggy sleeves of Mac's sweater. The summer Mac had taught their daughter how to cartwheel, Ani had absented herself from the training; someone had to be ready with bandages and ice wrapped in tea towels. *The two of them*, she thinks now, *they always made it look so easy*.

"All right," she calls. And then, quietly, "All right." And before she can think about it, she reaches her arms high up to the sky, leans over to plant her right hand on the ground, kicks her legs out hard, and finds herself standing again, standing and laughing, brushing the sand from her hands.

"You didn't look much like a wheel, Mum," Isabel says with a laugh. "But it was a good try." Then, "Try again," she shouts, making another cartwheel. But Ani shakes her head.

"Maybe tomorrow," she calls. "I'll need to work up to it." And she makes a great show of gathering the bag, settling its contents, looking up and down the beach for any unexpected spectators.

She sees him then, ahead on the sand, and probably looking straight along at her, at her mad jumping—she can't tell, with the glare of the sun. She points: "And anyway, there's Mr. McKinnon." She nods towards him and waves. "He doesn't need to see that sort of thing at this time of the morning."

"I don't think he'd mind your cartwheeling, Mum." Isabel is balanced on her hands now, her feet pointing up towards the blue. "We never laughed at him about him perching up the pole, did we? Remember when we saw him? On my birthday? With Dad?"

Ani shakes her head. "We didn't, no. But still, I don't think he needs to see such an amateur display before breakfast." *If he wasn't here,* she thinks, *if the beach were empty, I'd do it over and over.* There's something embarrassing about his having seen; but there's a tiny part of her that's exhilarated by the idea of it too.

As for the cartwheel, the great loop itself—that had almost felt like flying.

"Anyway, where are we walking? Along to the jetty or . . ." She trails off. Beyond the southern headland, beyond the next beach, sits the cemetery where the small box of Mac's ashes has been placed. Maybe today, maybe this morning, maybe after a cartwheel and a bread-and-cheese breakfast, she can manage to go there at last.

Isabel nods, following her mother's gaze. "We should go, shouldn't we? He'll be wondering why we haven't visited."

And Ani flinches at the pragmatism of it, at the implied neglect.

"Have some food, love: let's sit here and have some food, and then we can walk along and find . . ." She can't say *and find him.* She can't say *and find what's left of him.* She can't say *and find his tombstone,* because there isn't one yet—she's not sure she wants there to be.

She spreads their towel on the sand, slices the bread, the cheese, the fruit, and watches as her daughter eats. *One of the greatest happinesses,* she thinks, *feeding a child—no one ever tells you that.* And only as Isabel finishes her second helping does Ani begin herself.

At the cemetery, they jump over the low fence, heading for its coastal edge. "This is Catholics," calls Isabel, matter-of-fact. "And there's Anglicans down here, and Baptists," walking farther east again. "Kids' names at school," she says to answer her mother's unasked question. "Look: Raffertys and Larkins and that old lady who lived behind Mrs. May. Here are the Presbyterians."

Ani glances at the stones on either side of her, at the shorthand of their names, dates, relationships. *In memory of my darling wife. My beloved mother. My son, Tommy, aged nine, killed on his way home from school*—"Oh Lord." She clutches her hands together. The date is more than a decade ago; the stone still as polished and shiny as if it had been set only yesterday. *Our mother, and our father*, she reads: Is that her future, then, dug in here beside her long-dead husband? She feels Isabel pulling at her hand.

"Here, Mum, I think. Here." After all this time, there's a pile of wizened brown petals heaped up in a rotting mound, a small white cross with his name written in black.

Don't think about it. She almost says it aloud: *Don't think about it.*

Crouching on the grass, she presses her fingers into the rich, dark soil. Two rows over, Isabel's bright hair bobs up and down among the stone angels, the granite blocks, the urns and the pillars and the open marble books. *Life*, thinks Ani. Her fingers fiddle with a loose pile of earth. *And what comes after.* She shakes her head. She cannot imagine that there is anything to do with Mac in this place. She cannot imagine any remnant of him being here.

Still, taking a deep breath of the salty air, she brushes some loose dirt from the little cross and murmurs, under her breath, the lines of his poem—"Life's vortex spins around her. Come, she offers. Eat and drink"—while Isabel paces and prowls between the headstones and monuments, giving her father a wide berth. A few rows away, a spark of rosellas lights up a tree like tiny fireworks, their feathers brilliant reds and blues. Mac never tired of their brilliance or their beauty: "There's nae a lass as bright as you in all of Scotland," he'd call to them, scattering seed across the grass in the backyard at Surfers Parade.

"Nice that you're here," Ani whispers to them now. "Nice that you're near him." She closes her eyes against their movement and her mind flares with the colors of their plumage. *How long does a bird live?* she wonders. *Did any of you see my husband in his prime?*

"Bella?" She sees her daughter pause and turn towards her name. "I think I want to get home, love. What do you think? Can we make tracks?" And she's sure she's taken care not to pass again the grave of that small boy killed on his way home from school, so shockingly accidental, until she glances sideways as she walks and reads, this time, its full inscription.

> He left for school as any day
> No thought of death was near
> There was no time to say good-bye
> To those he held so dear

The morning sun dries the tears on her cheeks as her running feet clear the cemetery's boundary and reach the sand again. "Maybe there'll be dolphins on the way home," says Isabel, catching up to her, and Ani kisses the top of her head, catching her breath, wiping her eyes.

"Now that would be something, Bell," she says. The pod of dolphins they watched on the day Isabel turned ten, at the beginning of the last week of Mac's life. How impossible not to have known that's what that week would be; how impossible not to have seen that coming. How impossible, now, that Bella was heading towards eleven.

Cresting Sandon Point and heading north, Ani remembers the great marble map on the library floor in Sydney, the beauty of its waves, its ships, its angels and dragons, the straight line that stood in for this coast she's walking now. *Walking along a coastline that didn't exist.* The size of the oceans, the size of those old ships: what were the odds of anywhere being discovered?

About the same odds as a man called Lachlan crossing a country he'd just arrived in to see a river that had borrowed his name.

"What chance your dolphins?" Ani calls to Isabel. "What are the odds we'll see them?"

Isabel shakes her head. "I don't really understand how to do odds and chances yet—although Dad tried to tell me using this long story about billiard balls."

"Billiard balls?"

Isabel nods. "He said whenever he went to play billiards he worked on the theory that he had a one-in-four chance of winning every game and about the same chance of sinking the balls. There was something about the eight ball and who else was playing and . . ."

But Ani has stopped in the middle of the sand. "Billiards?" she says. "Your father never played billiards in his life."

Isabel looks at her feet, twisting a little so they disappear below the sand.

"He said he never played at the hall on the western side of the railway, but sometimes he'd pop in to the one near the shoe shop, on our side, if he finished early. It was a secret." Her voice drops to a whisper. "I wasn't meant to say. But I saw him coming out one day. That's the only reason I knew."

Ani closes her eyes, sees a wide green table, a triangle of bright balls in the middle. Someone leans in and breaks the balls' triangular pattern with a single swipe of a cue. She hates the crack the wood makes as it strikes the hard, shiny Bakelite. The balls fly away, running in all directions, a muddle of color and motion. She opens her eyes.

A cloud passes across the face of the sun and she shivers instinctively. Out in the water, a single dolphin leaps and dives. The beach is empty; there's not so much as a seagull along its length.

"I wonder what other secrets your daddy had," Ani says then, as lightly as she can manage. That word, "daddy"; they never used it. It sounds spiteful now, and mean. But it still throws her to realize she'll learn nothing more directly from her husband, only second-hand anecdotes about him. And such things can never be hers to claim.

Isabel paces out the beach, kicking an empty bottle that she's found in some seaweed to make a strange, syncopated beat. Behind her, Ani makes hard work of her footsteps, deliberately laboring in the soft sand. *What does it matter—a game of billiards? What does it matter, now and then?*

"I don't mind the game," she calls at last, aloud, to her daughter's running back, "or even the secret of it. I just wish I'd had him longer, to have learned these things from him."

"I never knew husbands were for learning from," says Isabel, slowing down to fall in step with her mother and taking her hand. "Does that mean it's easier if you marry a teacher? At least you get someone who knows what they're doing. Maybe that's an idea, when you marry again. Try for someone who knows about teaching."

Ani shakes her hand free, pushing her daughter away. "Damn it, Isabel, you say some ridiculous—" And she sees the girl shrink into herself, her shoulders hunched, her head dropped down. Ani drops the bag and kicks it, relishing the pain as her toes strike the thick glass jar. She can feel her teeth grinding against each other, and she wants to run and run and run. *The second time I've yelled at her*, she thinks, desperate at the thought. *The second time I've yelled at my gorgeous little girl.* "Bell? Bella?" She holds out her hand, but Isabel shies away.

"It's all right," she says, her voice very small against the beach's great space. "I know you're sad; I know Dad's dead; I know it was a horrible thing to see the tiny space for his ashes; I know it was a stupid thing to say." And she sets her pace just ahead of her mother's, staying out of reach until they're almost through their own gate, when she works herself under her mother's arm and lets herself be held.

At home, in the bathroom, Ani runs the cold water until her hands stiffen. If only she could curl herself into the white curve of the basin and numb her entire being. *I yelled at Bella; I yelled at Isabel.* She stares at her eyes in the mirror, shocked that they look the same—grey, wide—instead of the flashing glare of some terrible monster.

On the afternoon Mac died, before she headed for the station, Ani had stood awhile, surveying herself in this very glass: her suntanned skin; her spots of freckles; her cheekbones—"Your mother's," her father always said, "she was known for them"; and new lines, deepening, around her eyes and the edges of her smile. Isabel had turned ten, and Ani had scanned herself, candid, for any evidence of that particular decade.

Now, nine months later, her skin is paler—less time spent out of doors—and the lines are deeper. The whites around her fine grey irises are specked with red, messier than she remembers, and thick smudges of tiredness reach down towards those famous, inherited cheekbones.

She's never felt time so etched across her skin, and she rubs at it hard, pushing it up and around, trying to see the old face, the other face, the person Ani Lachlan used to be.

33

IT COMES from nowhere, the sense of being watched, and when she looks up she sees him through the library's window—Roy McKinnon, looking in, but looking through her, beyond her, so that she's not surprised when she raises her hand and smiles to no response. How long has he been there? Or is Ani herself no longer there, disappeared somehow? She pats at her cheeks, her collarbones, to check her own existence.

A train pulls into the platform opposite, and Roy draws in a deep breath, pulls back his shoulders, and turns away. Behind him, in the gap between two carriages, Ani sees passengers moving towards the southbound train. *He must have been almost against the wall to have been looking through the window in the first place*, she thinks. *And staring at what?* She pats at her hair, brushes down her skirt, self-conscious, almost smiling.

Roy McKinnon, she thinks. She likes it somehow, the idea of knowing where he is, of talking with him about his books and the world. But then, people do say the silliest things, turning simple friendships into galloping gossip and noisy surmise, *in which I am now cast as librarian and relict.*

The other week, running into him at the pictures with his sister and the doctor, she'd sat beside him in the darkness and watched the way the light from the movie refracted and lit up his hands, his lap, the cracked leather on the arms of his chair. The way a film's images jumped around—a shot from one camera, the reverse angle from another. It would be nice, Ani thought, to be able to shift so smoothly to another person's point of view—to see what her hands looked like, perhaps, if you were a poet, or what this dark room of picture watchers looked like from up there on the screen.

"Are you all right, Mrs. Lachlan?" His voice had been low and quiet, near her ear.

"Yes, yes," said Ani, in the too-loud response of any word spoken in darkness. "I just . . ." She gestured towards the screen. "My mind was wandering—sorry to disturb you." And as she watched, he raised his hand, and she half expected him to take hers, to grip her fingers, comforting. She had to work against a sense of disappointment when he didn't, brushing at something in front of his eyes instead.

At the picture's end, they stood apart from Frank and Iris in the foyer, unraveling the movie's plot and trying to remember other films in which they'd seen its stars. Then, "I wondered what you made of that bit-part engine driver," Roy McKinnon had said. "He seemed a brutal man, and I would never have thought it a brutal profession." It seemed an oversized observation for a small and inconsequential character.

Ani had frowned. "I didn't really think about it as if it was anything real," she said—she'd hardly noticed this character at all, or anything much of the film. They never drew her in the way books did, as if her imagination functioned better when it had to make up its own pictures, its own movements, rather than having them all laid out in front of her. But she liked the pause they gave her, the opportunity to sit still in the dark awhile and not have to think much at all.

"What I envy the railwaymen," said Roy McKinnon, "is all that motion, all that movement—the sense of spending your day traveling from one place to another and back again. I found the classroom bad enough, pacing around its four walls, but at least I had the children in there with me. Now it's me, and a desk, a blank page, and nothing else. Perhaps I should write for the pictures— perhaps I'm attempting the wrong form. What do you think, Mrs. Lachlan? A picture show set here, with all the trains and the coal and a writer at work on the edge of a cliff."

Ani laughed. "I think I know what you have in mind," she said. "But I'd come and see it. I'd love to see this place all big and silver on the screen. I wonder if I'd see myself anywhere." And she'd smiled to see him blush, almost say something, and then hurry forward to help Frank with their ice creams.

"The first time Bella saw one of these," Ani said, taking a choco-late-covered ice-cream heart from him and holding it with care, "it was after the war—Mac had told her about them, all her life, when of course you couldn't buy them. And she couldn't believe such a treasure would really exist. 'Chocolate and ice cream,' she kept saying. You'd've thought he was handing her the stars."

And they'd talked then of things that had seemed wonderful to them when they were children—the delectable softness of pussy willow catkins, said Ani; the perfect sweet thickness of a custard's skin, said Roy—and of the strangeness of realizing that somewhere, sometime, for no reason either of them could remember, these things must have stopped feeling remarkable or special.

"I miss that," he'd said, gazing out from the theater's front steps as if he was trying to pinpoint the source of something wonderful now.

Their ice creams eaten, the other two dispatched, they'd walked the long way home, with Ani telling the story about the night at the end of the war when she and Mac had danced along the sand behind the loops and curls of barbed wire. "I can't remember how long it was before they took it down," she said, "but I remember being shocked that it didn't happen immediately."

"Did you trust that it was over, when they said it was, when you saw the man dancing along Martin Place? Did you really think a thing as vast and awful as all that could just stop?" There was a tightness in Roy's voice, and a sharpness.

"Of course," said Ani quickly. "It was what we'd been waiting for for months." She looked across at him; he'd ducked his head down so his eyes must only have been seeing the forward steps of his own feet and the strips of road on either side. "Look, look there, I think I just saw a shooting star." A half-truth—she hardly knew what she'd seen; it might have been a gull in the light—but it made him look up and smile.

He stopped then, gesturing towards his sister's house. "Here I am," he said superfluously. "I won't offer to walk you home; I know the way people would talk."

And Ani had smiled—"of course, of course"—and said something about hating town gossip. "I'm used to it now, hearing the same story about myself, told over and over. I suppose it's a way of getting used to what's happened, when you realize you're hearing about your own husband's death, or even talking about it yourself, and you hardly even register the conversation." But walking up her own stairs, five minutes or so later, she wished she hadn't finished with a story about herself, about Mac. She wished she'd taken her leave with the story about wonder.

The air shakes as the northbound train arrives, and through the window Ani sees Roy McKinnon straighten his coat sleeves, his hat, and step into one of its compartments. Does he look better now than when he first came? she wonders. Is his face a little tanned, a little rounder? Or is it that she knows what he looks like now, and is no longer surprised by his lightness, how whittled down he looks, how insubstantial?

The train whistles as it prepares to pull away. Ani raises her hand again in acknowledgment, and when Roy McKinnon—through her window, through his—tips his hat, she's not sure if it's a response or a coincidence.

Settling himself on the train, Roy tips his hat to the empty platform, to the edge of the library and his reflection in its window, to the beauty of the mountain rising up behind it. He has something at last, something to show, and he's heading up to the city to meet a man at a magazine and pass on his poems. His first new poems in more than four years—written arduously, daily, in the weeks since Anzac Day. All that, for four or five he's happy with. Four or five, that is, apart from Ani's poem; he's kept that back. That's his; that's hers. But four or five new poems nonetheless.

The thought of it almost makes him laugh.

The compartment's framed pictures offer him the Hawkesbury River, the Blue Mountains, and the view up the coast, from Stanwell Tops, where box kites were launched. *Three options, where would you take her?* He usually avoids thinking so directly about Anikka Lachlan—it's too much, mostly, to look head-on at so bright a muse or messenger—but it's as if, this morning, a new recklessness, a new confidence is seeping from the lines he's written into the center of himself. *This is what Iris would call "feeling better,"* he decides. And perhaps there's something to be said for plain language. Stanwell Tops is too close to Ani's world. And she came from the plains, he knows that. Maybe Katoomba, or the Hawkesbury—the mountains or a river. It would be something to take her somewhere new, to show her that other places exist.

The most direct, the most proprietorial thing he's ever thought about her. He wants to call out with the daring of it. But instead, he pulls his poems out of his pocket and skims their lines again. They're a start, a good start, neither as sharp nor as fluid as the ones he managed during the war—and perhaps neither as lucid nor as elegant as the one he wrote for Ani. But they're feeling their way on towards those things, he's sure of it. All they need is to step clear of the last of the mud and the bodies.

Which is what the editor says, looking over them quickly a couple of hours later while their lunches sit, untouched, in the middle of a rather grand hotel dining room. "You've got to get past the war now, McKinnon. You've got to find other stories to tell." And he slides the pages back across the table, pinning them with Roy's fish knife as if a strong wind might rush through and blow them away.

Roy stares at them there, a white rectangle under a silver bar. It seems disrespectful to take up this paperweight and start eating his fish, but he's not sure what else to do. He shifts the pages to his bread and butter plate, flattened by the man's easy dismissal but enjoying the fact that his unworthy words have almost disappeared.

"I thought it might be too soon to show you," he says, awkward and blushing, "but I just wanted to feel as if I was . . ."

"Absolutely, of course." The editor has almost finished his fish, is most of the way through his vegetables—three or four chews per mouthful and a swallow that makes his whole face shudder. "You wanted to feel you were back on track, back in your world. And you are, sir, you are on your way." He sits, a forkful of potato poised midway to his mouth. "You're just not there yet." He chews. "But there must be something new you want to write about in this place you're living down the coast?" And he tells Roy the story of an envelope he'd received from another returned poet that had spilled the hard, parched landscape of some remote place across his desk that very morning, enough trauma and pain in it to sense what the man had seen and survived, but nothing explicitly, overtly military. "I accepted the poems immediately."

Roy nods slowly. *Enough of this now, that's what they all say. Enough of this.* "It's a beautiful place, where my sister is." He closes his eyes to see it. "This lovely escarpment folding into the Tasman Sea, the water and the light, and the trees. And there are people there, good people." He smiles, his eyes open again but seeing Ani's brightness. "I've started writing about them already."

"Well," says the editor, wiping his plate with the corner of a slice of bread, "I'll wait to see those. And if Lawrence could manage it, I daresay you will." It's a generous comparison, a generous endorsement, but Roy can see it on the man's face: *It's the least a chap can do, throw another chap a chance.*

The editor raises his glass. "There are fine poems to come from you yet, Mr. McKinnon. If the war unearthed their source in you, the peace will make it flourish." He's used this line on more than a dozen young men in this very dining room.

Roy makes his way through his fish, his vegetables, as quickly as he can, aware of the other man's empty plate. The editor is rattling through gossip from the publishing world—authors Roy knows only from spines and title pages, although the editor talks about them as if Roy is surely at all the parties and gatherings he himself attends. He invites him to one or two, and presses him to say he'll accept when Roy demurs: the length of the train trip he'd have to make, the difficulty of getting up from the coast.

In the hotel's lobby, the editor stands on one big black tile while Roy shakes his hand from the middle of a big white one: they look like pieces stranded on a chess board. *Remember this*, thinks Roy, feeling for his pen as soon as he's on his own in the street, and he scrawls the image on the back of the rejected poems and makes his way towards the station.

Everywhere, the city is busy with lunchtime, and he stands a minute in the shade of the post office's colonnade, watching as surges of people come and go. This is where she said it came from, the image of the man dancing at the end of the war. This is where someone had caught happiness for Anikka Lachlan to watch on a newsreel.

And his happiness? He closes his eyes: Anikka Lachlan turning a cartwheel on the beach—a gift of a moment, beyond acknowledgment, beyond words.

He opens his eyes and the city bustles on, a few shouts and sharp calls, the occasional horn, and not so much as a smile on most faces. *That happiness, that big thing ending,* thinks Roy: *you'd think that joy as big as that would have hung around in this place always.* But had he danced and spun when the news of the war's end found him? No. He'd crouched on a beach and cried awhile, for the waste of it, the time and the death and the waste.

Stepping into the crowd, he sees a tall woman with blond hair striding out in front of him, takes three fast steps to catch her in case it's Ani, fumbling awkwardly with his hat, his lapel, when he draws level with her and sees that it isn't. *Of course.*

That's his poem, he knows. Or rather, she is. And it's the only one that's any good, the only one that's real. He'll send it to the editor tomorrow; he'll show him he has found something beyond the war.

It's nearly two months since he secreted it in Ani's house—two months' torturing himself that she hasn't found it, or that she has and can't speak of it to him. He hates himself each time he takes his leave from her without asking about it. *A poem's nothing without its readers,* he thinks, recklessly. *And she can't ignore it if it's in the world.* It's a simpler thing to stamp an envelope than say "I wonder if you've found . . ." or "I made you this thing."

Settling into the train's first carriage as it pulls away from

Central, Roy unfolds his newspaper and distracts himself with its stories—strikes and blackouts, foreign ministers arguing in Europe, new missiles being built. *June 14, 1949, and it's as if the war never stopped.* He turns the page: a denazification court has commuted a sentence for a top German banker—*Denazification: that's a mouthful of a word. Should have hung them all.* And a father has confessed to throwing his two-year-old son onto a concrete path in a temper.

Roy closes his eyes. *This world, this bloody world.* What chance could you have of happiness or joy? He pulls his papers from his pocket, crumples them one by one into misshapen balls, and throws them through the open window as hard as he can to clear the tracks and the wind the train drags in its wake.

But then the train shudders, the wheels screeching against the rails as Roy scans the racing results with their grainy photographs of tiny horses. *Such names,* he thinks: *So Happy. Jovial Lass. Full o Fun. Amused.* He closes his eyes and sees Ani's clumsy cartwheel against the morning sun, startled as the carriage lurches suddenly to a stop. *All we want to be—So Happy. Full o Fun.* There's an eerie silence; the noise of his newspaper hitting the floor is too big, too amplified to seem real.

Have they stopped the train to pick up my rubbish? he wonders half seriously as he looks back along the track for his jettisoned papers.

A shout; a whistle; and then another cry. Roy opens the window as far as it will go, leans out as far as he can to look ahead.

"Someone's been hit," the driver calls from the engine. "At the crossing here; someone's down."

"Is there anything we can do?" He's swinging down onto the tracks before he's finished asking the question, his feet uncertain on the uneven ballast.

As he draws up to the engine, the driver leans down. "You a doctor?"

And Roy feels himself nod. *Why not? I've seen enough bodies.*

"He came from nowhere"—the driver gestures towards the fender. A mangled bicycle, a mess that had been somebody, shoes flung away, and a pair of glasses glinting on the other side of the tracks.

"I see," says Roy. "I see." He leans forward, unsure if he should touch the man, trying to imagine what Frank would do or say.

"Is he going to be all right?" the driver calls, pale in his high-up cabin.

Roy tilts his head, noncommittal, taking off his coat and covering as much of the accident as he can. He's not sure if he can see the man's chest rising and falling, or if this is just terrible, wishful thinking. *Either way*, he thinks, and says, "It would have been very quick." And, "Are you all right up there?" He likes the command he can hear in his voice.

And the driver nods.

Crouching down, Roy picks up the cyclist's glasses and wraps them in his handkerchief. There must be a wallet in one of his pockets, something to give up the man's name, his identity—but Roy draws back from touching him, certain now that he can see a tremor, a shudder, rattling through the body like alarm. Someone with real authority can take it from here; somebody with real authority can feel for a wallet. Still, he reaches for the man's shoes, unsure where to place them.

A couple of currawongs land beside the tracks and watch him; a car's horn blares nearby. He touches his fingers to the smooth, warm metal of the railroad tracks, and thinks of Frank Draper's stories. At the end of the war, at the end of a railway line, a camp full of leftover pieces of people, mostly dead, the rest close to dying, among mountainous great piles of the everyday things they would never have thought twice about before—sturdy shoes, good traveling bags, and useful pairs of spectacles.

Along the line of carriages now, windows and doors open, and passengers crane to look, pulling away as they realize what's happened. *Nothing to do with them*, thinks Roy, *just a delay on their way to or from somewhere else.* He closes his eyes, sees Frank's mess from the other side of the world, so far from here, from the sun, and the air, and the pleasant day passing. He can't imagine that those camps would have felt any more real on this side of the world, even when that war was under way and being fought.

Now there's this train, this engine, this driver, and how could anyone not know that this is happening? Yet even in the next street, people would be living their day without the slightest idea of this hiccup, this accident. *The world is so many individual bits and pieces*, thinks Roy. Millions, he supposes. Millions and millions.

Bits and pieces: his eyes focus on a splat of blood, then another, and another. Who cleans up these things? Would the railways dispatch people with buckets and mops, or someone with a hose and a broom? Years ago, when he was younger, he saw a team of scrubbers on the pylons of the Sydney Harbour Bridge—it must have been just before it opened—washing away the blood of a worker who'd fallen to his death. Roy was sure he could still see the mark on the silvery granite when they'd finished and gone home. He'd never felt safe crossing the bridge, seeing that, as if that stain might have tarnished or weakened it somehow.

If he thought of his own war, he thought of bodies on beaches, facedown along the shoreline where the ocean leached the marks and stains away. He has little sense that there was blood, but he knows this can't be true. Perhaps he's hosed it into some dark part of his memory where, if he's lucky, it will never breach its levee.

He wills himself to stare directly at the cyclist; he wills himself to see a glimmer of life. And can't. How quickly it can stop, then, just like that. *So you have to take your chance, Roy; you have to chance your arm.* Make sure Ani Lachlan knows her poem. Send it to his editor for the rest of the world to read. Anything to shatter this inertia.

Damn it but he is sick of the waiting, and it's exhausting, he sees suddenly, to be unaware of something it would be so simple to find out. Maybe she hated the poem. Maybe she was embarrassed by it. Or maybe she simply hasn't seen that there is something new sitting among her other books. *Wake up, mac*, he thinks, startling himself with the inapt appellation. *Do something, once and for all.*

And so he moves the dead man's shoes, placing them next to each other and aligning their toes: it seems an appropriate gesture to make. *What was he doing here today?* Roy wonders. Where was he going—and what was he thinking that he didn't see the train, or hear it? Did he think he could beat it? Did he try to stop and fail?

Or did he see the train and just keep riding? Did he push and pump his pedals even faster? Roy shakes his head, rubs his eyes. *We've one way of coming into the world*, he thinks, *and so many ways of going out of it.* Above him, the driver slumps down to sit against the wall of his cabin, cradling his head in his hands.

"What'll I tell the wife?" the man asks. "What do I say when she asks about my day?"

Who drove the train that killed Mac Lachlan? Roy thinks suddenly. *Who was the driver—did Ani ever ask?*

Maybe she didn't, and maybe she'd been right not to. Maybe it was better not to know.

He looks down at the mess at his feet, the blood, the skin, the shredded clothes. *Is this how he looked, the minute he died? Is this how Mac Lachlan went out of the world?* He balks at the way his pulse quickens, but there's a perverse intimacy in seeing this body, in imagining it belongs to Ani's husband. This thing she would probably die rather than see. *But I can take this on—I can see this for her.*

As if this is anything to do with her at all.

The currawongs call, and Roy turns in the instant they rise off the ground—a motorcycle is coming around the corner, its noise and movement startling them to flight. He brushes his hands together, straightens himself to attention as a young policeman gets off the bike.

"Take it from here, sir," the younger man says, touching his forehead in half a salute. "What was your name?"

"Draper, Dr. Frank Draper," says Roy in that borrowed, stentorian voice. "He was dead straightaway, I should think." And he stands a moment, watching as the younger man lifts the corner of the coat up and away from the body. Then he turns and strides away from the train, towards the main road of this unknown suburb, glad to be back on the move.

He should have said something over the man, he thinks, something soothing or benedictory—in case he did have any sense of where he was, of what had just happened, or what was coming next. In case he had known it was the end and hadn't wanted to be alone.

What else is there, after all?

But the only words Roy can think of, in this belated instant of concern, are from the Yeats poem he'd sent to Frank all those years before:

> I think it better that in times like these
> A poet's mouth be silent . . .

Death has its own rituals, funerals and burials and prayers said and memorials written. Frank has told him of a German woman who killed all her children just before the war's end—*to spare them their denazified future*, he thinks now, paraphrasing the newspaper—and then sat playing Patience, working the cards again and again, trying to get them into four neat piles of suits. Ani Lachlan has told him of a widow for whom she'd made food, arriving with a saucepan of soup and half a cake. As she reached the doorstep, she said, she was pulled up by a low and guttural howl that sounded like it belonged to some wild and cornered animal. She'd frozen, she said, hardly daring to breathe, and the sound had dropped away.

"And then it began," she said, "a low, slow song like a lullaby, over and over. The woman was singing her husband out of being, singing her husband into the longest sleep he would have."

Ani had left the food and gone quietly away. And at the end of the day, she said, watching Isabel sleep, she had stood with her hand on her daughter's blankets, singing the same lullaby and hoping that this newly dead man would hear it somehow, no matter where he was, and no matter who was singing.

Roy wonders, now, if the story was about Ani herself—that terrible sound he had heard the night Mac died, as he raced along her street. And he wonders what song he should sing for this cyclist.

He closes his eyes, sees the body on the tracks, the body of the little boy who'd been dashed down against concrete, the bodies of the first 555 people Frank saw die in a world where war had ended. And as he takes the next step, he stumbles down the edge of a culvert—the shock of putting your foot out and finding nothing there.

Shuffling cards, dealing cards, sorting cards, aces at the top. *And your children dead in the next room.* He brushes his eyes. *This bloody world.*

His hands fumble in his pockets for his handkerchief and find instead the dead man's glasses. He takes them out, looks at them a moment, wondering if he should return them to the body—or the policeman. Then he rubs one lens clean, and the other, and holds them in front of his own eyes.

The world blurs.

If they could show what they had seen—if they could show you the last day of this man's life, show what happened to him, and why. He squeezes the glasses, their wire frames cutting into his palm. If he's honest, there was something glorious in the shock of the accident; he squeezes the glasses harder, hoping the pain of their wire against his flesh will transform his reaction to proper abhorrence.

Then he wraps them again and puts them back in his pocket, aware of their shape and their weight, like a talisman, or a warning.

34

PULLING THE heavy book box towards her across the library's smooth floor, Ani is back in their first night in Surfers Parade, unpacking Mac's box of books. She'd pulled *Jane Eyre* out of the box—he must have packed it last, because it sat on the top by itself, pristine and secure in a nest of recent news. It was 1936: people on the move—the Germans in Rhineland; the Italians in Abyssinia; the beginning of the war in Spain; and the British king abdicating for his love. She'd fallen in love with Mac himself, she suspected, when he told her *Jane Eyre* was his favorite book.

Digging deeper into the box, she'd found Agatha Christie and Dashiell Hammett, adventures and westerns, and Arthur Conan Doyle's *The Lost World*. And she'd laughed. Some were books she'd read; some she'd always wanted to read. And below that, a handful of magazines—*Smith's Weekly*, some exotic *National Geographics*, and a few *Harper's*. She'd flicked to their contents pages, hungry for the stories inside, and laughed again.

He'd come in at the sound, his face quizzical.

"I didn't know the extent of your dowry," she said.

"It's where my money goes," he said, as if he were confessing to horses or the dogs. He'd smiled then, and she felt entirely happy. What more did you need to share a life with someone but a stock of new stories to tell?

"*Samanlaiset linnut lentävät yhdessä*," her father had written in her daybook on the morning of her wedding. "The same kind of birds fly together."

Now, as Ani takes the last consignment of books from its trunk, a gust of wind catches the door, making it slam. And in the silence after its surprising noise, Ani realizes she's hearing a greater silence, a greater quiet, and has been hearing it for ten minutes, fifteen, half an hour, maybe more.

There has been no train.

She stands slowly, smoothing her skirt as she crosses to the window. There are passengers waiting on the two platforms—waiting. Waiting. She sees Luddy talking to this one, to another.

"Sounds like there's a problem with the trains coming through." That's what he'd said to her. "An accident along the line and they're not letting anything pass." She could still hear the exact pitch of his voice, the easiness of it. Just passing the information on, and offering to let Mac know that they were held up, and they'd decided not to wait, that they'd see him at home at the end of the day.

And we went to the beach and found a shell that shimmered like an evening gown. And we went home. And I started dinner. And Bella sat and waited. And then they came.

There was life before; there'll be life after—sometimes, now, she thinks she can almost see what it might look like. That moment, that news—the dinner cooking, and the men, and the story of Mac's death—that's the dividing line. That's all.

She crosses the gravel, waving to the stationmaster.

"An accident, a bicycle, they said." He grimaces. "Nasty." Grimacing again. "They say the track'll be right again soon."

Ani looks along the empty line, thinking about Roy heading

north earlier in the day. It can be nothing to do with him, she thinks, safe in the size of the carriages. But still; but still.

"It rings, the silence, doesn't it?" she says. And, "I still can't hear the ocean—how is it such a big sound can disappear when it comes from something so close by?"

Luddy shakes his head. "You'd notice the waves if they stopped too, I reckon."

To the north, the roundhouse windows glisten and sparkle. Ani blinks at their semaphore. "Did you know, that afternoon when Bella and I were waiting, and the trains were stopped? Did you know it was something to do with Mac even then? I know you said you didn't, but . . ."

He stares at her, his mouth open and his eyes blinking fast. "Of course not; of course not. Oh, Mrs. Lachlan, of course not."

She brushes his words away. "I'm sorry, Luddy, I don't even know why I asked you. I've never thought such a thing before." Maybe she'll ask one day to read the coroner's report; maybe she'll fill in the excruciating details of a story she's recast as a random disappearance.

Luddy shakes his head, and the movement breaks her reverie as a bus rattles by. "I'll just tell these people they're better off with a bus," he says, waving towards the other platform.

Ani nods, waving her own hand towards the library. "Could you come and tell me when they're starting again? I think I'd like some warning of the noise—today."

And he nods, smiling again. "You don't want them sneaking up on you." He blushes, but she's laughing as she walks across the gravel.

"Exactly," she calls. "Unless you can do me a big D57. Those things are magic."

Early one morning, just after the war, she'd walked to the station through a dawn thick with sea mist. It had softened hard lines, made edges disappear, and transformed the streetscapes Ani knew so well into surreal shadows, dubious connections, hovering impossibilities. The wall of one house blurred towards its neighbor; a bathtub of water for horses hovered above the ground; a jacaranda tree transmogrified into something from the northern fairy tales of her childhood.

Something had happened to sound as well, magnifying it. The scrape of a kettle on a stove; the slam of a screen door; someone singing in a round baritone; someone else suggesting jam or marmalade for breakfast.

Climbing the main road towards the railway bridge, Ani felt she was walking through one of her father's memories of winter. That's what she'd ask for for her birthday, she thought suddenly. She'd ask to be taken to see snow. She laughed. *Let Mackenzie Lachlan solve that on the east coast of Australia in 1945.*

It was only when she stepped onto the platform that she realized it was there—a great steam engine, a D57 class locomotive, puffing and blowing, its front end sawn off with a stubby funnel above. She couldn't imagine how she hadn't heard it, but there it sat, its steam indistinguishable from the morning's fog, and its big wheels waiting to spring forward, on and up the coast.

It was like walking around a corner and finding a dragon.

She looked for the driver but the cabin was empty, so she walked on, running her hand along the strong, smooth metal. "Two-fifty tons she weighs, with sixty-five square feet of fire grate, and two hundred pounds per square inch of boiler pressure." Mac could recite these figures like poetry—he loved these engines, their brawn, their sheer heft. "Get them going straight enough and I reckon they might fly," he said.

She reached its nose, patted as close to the big round headlight as she could, and turned back along the platform.

"Morning, Mrs. Lachlan." The driver, a mate of Mac's, swung

himself into his compartment. "Early for you this morning—give us five minutes or so and we'll have you under way."

And she'd smiled, following the engine's line past its truckload of coal to the passenger compartments beyond. This great, powerful thoroughbred, just sitting there, breathing, and waiting for her.

It was magnificent, and there wasn't another soul in that morning to see it.

Now, inside the library, the sun touches the cedar shelves, the polished floor, finding oranges, golds, like harbingers for spring. Pressing her hands to the warm wood, Ani wonders whose wife, whose mother, will open her door this afternoon to the insupportable news of a train, a collision. She's still there, she knows, standing spotlit in her own hallway, hearing the news again and again. She'll always be standing there, listening. And as she thinks this, she feels it, a sharp splinter wedged hard into her skin. How many times has she stroked this shelf, and why, just this time, did it harm her?

If you cannot sit in a quiet room of words and pages and unravel the idea of random or accidental harm, or the illogical and unpredictable ways of protection, how much harder to walk through war asking why that bullet found that person, why that mine was there, and why do I keep walking clear?

"I want to know," she says at last, surprised by the strength of her voice. "I want to know how to understand."

But all she can hear is the sound of her own pulse pounding in her ears.

35

THEY CATCH her unawares this year, these profusions of color—purple first, when the jacarandas begin to bloom, and then the deep red of Illawarra flame trees, *Brachychiton acerifolius*, Isabel's favorite proper name for a plant, because she thinks it sounds like a dinosaur.

They follow each other into being, bursting out along the coast and up the escarpment. The jacaranda comes with the spring; the flame, a little later, lasting a little longer. They mark Ani's months; they mark her year. And now they mark Mac's anniversary.

"Did you want to do something, Ani, to remember him, these twelve months?" Mrs. May delivers the question directly, having arrived at the front door with an invalid's food of soft butter cake and some soup.

"I'll ask Isabel," Ani says, not wanting to have to answer. "I'll see if there's anything she wants to do." And she reaches out to hug her neighbor's arm. "You take such good care of us."

This long and slow year. Wars have ended in Israel, in China, in India, and in Greece, although there are bound to be new ones before long. There are planes that can fly around the world without stopping, and Russia has made a great bomb like those that were dropped on Japan; Ani still cannot think about these without shaking—paralyzed by the idea of such noise, such heat, such silence.

Now, as she waves to her neighbor, she sees the first purple blossoms: a jacaranda can cover itself with color in a week, and then the red of the flame trees will come.

Scooping potatoes, carrots onto her daughter's plate that night, she says: "Mrs. May was wondering if there was anything you'd like to do, you know, for the anniversary of Dad's . . ." To say "death" still feels impolite, or somehow embarrassing.

Isabel looks up from the schoolbook she's packing away. "Are we supposed to?" she asks.

Ani shakes her head. "No, no, love, I don't think that's what Mrs. May meant—I think some people . . . you know, they like to mark the moment. We could walk round to the cemetery again or ask them to do a special reading in church. We could have a special meal, ask Mrs. May to come in. I don't know." She smiles, her hand resting on her daughter's shoulder. "I told her I'd ask you if there was anything you particularly wanted to do."

Frowning a little, Isabel pulls her plate towards her. "Should we do something? Like it was a birthday? Is that what you mean, Mum, what you want . . ."

Ani watches as Isabel pushes the rounds of carrots into a line, the largest disks on the left-hand side, and ranging down, perfectly graded, to the smallest on the right. It's been happening most mealtimes they've eaten together, she realizes, and she's not sure for how long. "Isabel," she asks now, "what are you doing with your dinner?" She wonders why she's let it pass before.

"I'm not really hungry," says her daughter, shrugging as she molds the dollop of potato into a perfectly right-angled triangle.

Anikka sits opposite with her own dinner; she's not that hungry either, if she thinks about it—can't remember the last time she was, the last time she actually tasted something she ate. "Maybe I should have warmed up a bowl of Mrs. May's soup—that's never let us down when we've needed nourishing."

Her daughter's smile flares, and Ani smiles wider: there she is, her bonny little girl, as Mac would have said.

"Maybe we could take Mrs. May for a picnic—down to the beach." Isabel spikes one carrot from the middle of the row with her fork, makes a great show of putting it into her mouth, chewing it twenty times. "Or we could go just the two of us; I wouldn't mind that either. But you decide, Mum; I don't mind."

Another single round of carrot disappears. When Ani looks down at her own plate, she sees she's started to make the same orange line of vegetables through its middle. She mixes the mashed potato across it, destroying the symmetry.

"Let's think about it tomorrow," she says peaceably, "and concentrate on dinner now." Pushing the problem away.

It was never a struggle to make conversation when there were three of them. It was never a struggle to eat. Ani scoops up the mashed potato: she's never thought such a thing before about dinnertime, about any time with her daughter.

And what did Mac's voice sound like?

Washing the dishes later while Isabel dries, Ani stares through their reflection in the kitchen window and into the darkness beyond. "Do you still hear him?" she asks as her daughter stacks the plates. "Do you still hear your dad say things sometimes?"

Isabel aligns the stack carefully. "Sometimes I think I do," she says after a long pause. "But there are lots of things I know I don't remember now, so I don't know if the things I think I can still remember are real or not. I think I remember him wishing me happy birthday that last time. But maybe I just remember the day and maybe it's someone else's voice. I think he sounds like my teacher at school, and I never thought that before. If people's fathers have to die, someone should make a camera for their voices."

Her hands warm in the soapy water, Ani laughs. "Something like that. I thought your kaleidoscope might have caught a piece of him for us—I haven't checked for a while, but I know he wasn't there back at the beginning."

"I guess that's because he was down under the water, and it's hard to look all the way down to a bathysphere."

"You still think he's there?"

Isabel nods. "It's better than thinking about ashes," she says—too pragmatic, Ani thinks, for someone who's not yet eleven.

She squeezes the dishcloth and hangs it on the front of the stove, as she's done every night she's lived in this house. She likes the predictability of it, that she can trust that the wet things will dry, always, and in a certain amount of time; that she can trust that process, that progression.

"Anyway," she says, drying her hands, "there's your birthday for us to celebrate first of all—I'm looking forward to our bushwalk and our picnic lunch with pasties." She stokes the fire, smiling at its flames. "I'm still anxious about keeping the meat end separate from the jam, but Mrs. May assures me it's all in the pastry."

Her homework spread out again on the red laminate table, Isabel props her chin on her hand, her pencil poised. "Where do you want to go for *your* birthday, Mum? You haven't said anything yet, about your excursion, or your dinner, or your heart's desire."

The house creaks a little as the wind rattles its gutters and eaves. Ani reaches for the tea canister, the pot, wondering how to answer.

"For my excursion," she says at last, "I'd like to take the train into Wollongong and look at the shopwindows and have a milkshake, like we used to." The ritual never again attempted after that last aborted attempt. "For my dinner, I'd like you to cook me blancmange, with the peach leaf, like they taught you at school.

That was beautiful, Bella, the night I came home and found that little dish waiting for me." She takes another long, slow breath. "And for my present," she says quietly, "my present . . ." Her fingers turn the coral brooch her daughter gave her at Christmas; she wears it almost every day. "I don't think there's anything I need, my love."

Isabel contemplates her mother awhile, sucking at the end of her pencil. "I think I found the thing Dad was making you last year," she says at last. "The thing he'd always wanted to make—I think I found it, under the house. I didn't know what to do about it, how to tell you." And she's out of her seat now and through the back door before Ani can say a word.

The house creaks and settles again, the wind puffing a little smoke back down the chimney and out through the stove. Ani swirls the tea, wondering what her daughter is about to bring into the room.

A scrape across the doorstep and Isabel appears, walking backwards and dragging something across the newly washed linoleum. Ani frowns—at the shape, rather than the mark its movement might be making—and tilts her head, as if the adjustment might transform the shape and being of the thing itself. But there's no question: it's the frame of a box, with brackets, shelves fitted to some of them, and it's fixed on a round base, like a plinth, so that it can spin and turn.

"It was under the house, behind a trunk full of clothes—I found it when I was putting away those shoes of Dad's you wanted to keep." Isabel rocks it from one side to the other. "I've never seen it before, and there are tools down there as well. I thought it must be . . . whatever it was he was making."

"A bookcase, it's a revolving bookcase—a spinner, they call them, although my dad used to call them *bibliothèques*," says Ani, stroking the smooth, dense-colored wood. There's a delicate calligraphy of whorls and patterns in its markings. *Perhaps it's silky oak,* she thinks, tracing its complexity. Her father would approve of the choice. *That's a fine grain, Mackenzie,* he'd have said, admiring his son-in-law's efforts and checking that the mechanism that turned the shelves didn't jar—just as Ani is checking now.

"I didn't know your dad was such a handyman. It took him two years to put up a shelf in the kitchen when we came here."

She presses her finger onto the wood's lines: it's like a fingerprint itself, or a piece of marbled paper. "Maybe the book was meant to go on the bookshelf," she says then. "A set, maybe, to start a new library." She laughs. "Which is funny, isn't it, because a new library is exactly what I got for my last birthday, in a roundabout way."

"What book?" Isabel parks the cabinet by the end of the kitchen table. "Did you find another present?"

Fetching the book from beside her bed, Ani passes it to her daughter without a word, watching carefully as Isabel takes it and lets its spine rest on her hand. The book opens automatically to the last poem, "Lost World."

"He said he wanted to write a poem, your dad," she says as her daughter begins to read. "I didn't find the book until months after he'd died. But I've been reading it at the end of every day. And it seemed"—she hesitates—"it seemed a private kind of thing." She laughs at Isabel's anxious blush, at her hurried closing of the page. "Nothing like that, Bella. Read it, it's lovely. I'm not sure why I didn't tell you. I found it on the mantelpiece on Anzac Day—remember, the night we went for a swim with the phosphorescence? Like you said, like you said about the green, it must have been there all the time." She smiles. "Perhaps he slipped it in while he was working on this." And she lifts the spinning shelves up onto the kitchen table, closer to the light that makes their wood glow.

"Lucky we didn't give you the spinner, though," says Isabel, concentrating on the poem again. "The piece of wrapping paper I'd painted would never have been big enough." Her fingers follow the lines down the page, tapping the rhythm of the final words:

> All this in her,
> All things, all places furled
> And folded in her, the bright messenger
> Who comes for a lost world.

From the other side of the table, Ani scans the poem upside down—not that she needs to look at it; she knows it by heart, reading it twice, three times a night, every night, before she turns out the light. Some nights, it conjures an angel for her, someone soft and light who watches as she sleeps. Some nights, it's herself she sees, dressed in white and her hair pale in some spotlit glow. But never Mac, no matter what she does or thinks or hopes. Whether he's asleep in that high room she imagines for him, or down fathoms with the stargazers of Isabel's imagination, his poem is all there is of him now at the end of her day.

"Oh, Mum," says Isabel, caressing the book. "It's like a proper poem, like they make us read at school. I knew he wanted to make you something special but I never knew he could make anything like this." She moves her hands to pin the book open on the table, her reading so concentrated that Ani half expects to see the words sucked right off the page. "And it *feels* so nice, doesn't it?" Isabel goes on. "The way the rhymes work, the way the lines lilt. Dad really knew what he was doing."

My daughter the critic, thinks Ani, coming around the table to read Mac's words again herself. Below her, Isabel's shoulders pull back and her little-girl chest puffs out. *And she's proud of him*, thinks Ani, proud.

Pulling one of her schoolbooks across the table, Isabel opens a clean page and begins to transcribe her father's "Lost World"—

from above, Ani watches, mesmerized by the reenactment of these sentences coming into being. It's like ventriloquism, through her daughter's hand. She watches as Isabel's pencil loops high on the capital letters and low, with a flourish, on the *g*'s, the *y* of "mayhem." Her pencil slows as she comes up to the need for an *s*, and on the fourth or fifth time, Ani sees why: she's pausing to replicate the precise way Mac would have written that letter.

"I've never noticed before that you write like your dad," says Ani, tracing her daughter's script with her own finger.

"I've been concentrating," says Isabel, following her mother's finger with her own. "I can always remember what his writing looks like even if I lose his voice sometimes. And I try to make my letters as close to his as I can." She holds up her schoolbook for her mother's approval. "I think the *f*'s are pretty good, and the *g*'s. But I can never get that kink in the top of the *s*'s, and you need the letter *S* for lots of words, you know." She blushes. "Like 'Isabel,' and 'authoress.'"

Ani smiles. She can see the size of the revelation her daughter has made, the courage it takes to say this aloud, and she appreciates its distraction. "An authoress." She strokes her daughter's hair. "That's a lovely word, Bell, and a lovely idea." And she watches a raspberry blush flush Isabel's face.

"I mean," says Isabel, "it's just a daydream, just an idea. I wouldn't really know what to do. But if Dad could do this"—she taps the velvety page, her fingers settling below the poem's last full stop—"well, maybe, as Mrs. May would say, it's in the blood."

Laughing at Isabel's impersonation of their neighbor's turn of phrase, Ani pushes a blank sheet of paper towards her, uncaps a Biro for her too. "I think the way you start is that you simply start," she says, straightening the rectangle of whiteness as she hears herself go on, unplanned and unexpected. "Or you could ask Mr. McKinnon. I don't know the difference between writing poems and writing stories, but they must all begin somehow. And I'm sure he'd be happy to know that someone else wanted to make new sets of words around here." The image of the two of them, sitting with their pencils, the air around them thick with sentences never before thought of—she likes it, and that thought makes her own face bright.

Turning sharply, she knocks the teapot, gasping as the hot liquid scalds her hand and floods onto her daughter's books. "Oh, Bella, Bella, the mess I've made—" which touches the thought of her daughter and the poet as much as the sudden puddle of staining tea.

"It's all right, Mum." Isabel has the books tilted high in the air, tipping the liquid down into her saucer. "It doesn't matter; I can fix it."

"I'm sorry, love; I got distracted"—she tries for a joke—"thinking of the day I'd have your books to shelve in my library." And Isabel blushes again.

"Don't even talk about it," she says softly. "Don't even pretend it might be real."

She was never a very childish child, thinks Ani, *and whatever else Mac's death has done, it's pushed the last of that out of her. Or perhaps that was me, the way I was—the way I am.* She digs her fingernails into the soft skin of her arms. *I should have done better with this; it's all I should have done.*

But she wipes at the spillage with her dishcloth, patting the table dry before she lets Isabel rearrange her books. And then she sits, very still, and very quiet, and watches her daughter's busyness, watches her hand fly across the pages, filling their lines, watches her stop and pause, thinking of a word, working at a sum, before the writing starts again.

If she thinks of Mac writing, he's signing the register on the day they were married; she can still see the way his hand moved to shape his own name on the page. It was a looping, gentle gesture, like a caress. She'd never seen anyone write anything that way before. But it's there in Isabel's writing; it's there in the way she does even this ordinary set of homework.

As her mind settles into her wedding day, Ani looks at her daughter without seeing her, a fond, middle-distance stare as she reaches out and tucks a strand of Isabel's hair behind her ear. Her fingers touch something unusual and she leans forward, back in the room, back with her little girl, worrying at whatever it is as she focuses, frowning. She frees the thing and holds it carefully between two fingers—a bit of a dandelion's puffball; the kind you might blow on to wish.

Ani smiles, opens the kitchen window, and blows it gently into the night. Beyond, in the shadows, she has the sense of something good, something still and calm, nearby, and getting closer.

"There," she says softly, tucking Isabel's hair back again. "There. That's better."

36

IT'S THE children's voices that wake him, laughter and shouting and the kind of singsong banter he remembers from so many playgrounds. Roy stretches, yawns, and looks at his watch—almost four, and he's slept since lunchtime. It's long enough to feel miraculous.

Out in the kitchen, Iris is clattering saucepans and their lids. Inching out of sleep, Roy can find no other explanation for the cacophony of sound, and he rubs his eyes and pulls on a sweater, intending on going out to help her.

The kitchen, though, is empty, except for Iris's three chickens, inside somehow and making their way around the shelves and the cupboards. A baking dish tumbles, another in its wake, and the chickens step on, unimpressed or unaffected by the racket.

"Out, out." Roy runs at them, his arms flailing as he herds them towards the open door. "Iris? Are you here? Your chooks have broken in." But there's no answer—he can't imagine she'd have left them pecking in the garden, or left the door open, for that matter. "Off you *go*!" Shouting the last word, as if the hens might move if he matches them noise for noise.

They regard him with their sideways eyes, and set their heads down to peck at the pattern on the lino. One of them drops a wet brown poo, and Roy yells again, imagining his fastidious sister's horror.

Amazingly, the chickens respond, bobbing their way across to the back door and on out into the garden. He closes them into their coop and looks around for Iris's ever-present mop. "Our little secret," he whispers darkly at the birds. "But do it again, and I'll have you in one of those pans." He's never killed a chicken, and suspects he wouldn't be able to. He wonders if the birds know this—they pay no attention to his words.

Splashing eucalyptus oil liberally into the bucket of water he's boiled, he takes a deep breath of its aroma and sways with the movement of the mop. If this is cleaning, he thinks, he can see why Iris likes it—there's a rhythm and a grace to it, and something seductive about seeing the difference you've made. *Perhaps I've found my calling at last*, he thinks, twirling the mop as if he were Fred Astaire. But he stows it again as soon as the single soiling is dealt with, rinsing it carelessly and knowing his sister will find fault with its treatment.

Hat in hand, then, he makes for the beach, pausing on the esplanade to mark the snake of children heading north along the sand, the snake of children heading south. *The beach at the end of your each day at school*, he thinks. *It must not get better than that.*

In the shadow of the pump house, a knot of girls has gathered, their bags piled haphazardly in the soft grass that fringes the sand, and their voices high in the afternoon's air. Roy heads towards them, aiming for the jetty beyond, but slows as he hears the words they're calling—"Nut!" "Jerk!"—and sees them trying to start a fire with a small pile of books. Enclosed in the mess is Isabel Lachlan, so still and quiet that it takes Roy a moment to realize she's the butt, the center, of whatever's going on.

"Hullo!" he calls, watching the gang's immediate reaction. "You should take care with those books on the beach—sand in the binding; it ruins the glue." Ignoring the insults, ignoring the matches.

The girls step back, wary, watching for what he'll do next. They've probably been warned about him, he thinks, the crazy man who walks around all day and night, calling out words to himself.

"Are they your books?" He turns now to Isabel, stepping towards her and smiling. "Would you like some help getting them home?"

Her smile beams as the other girls scuff their way through the sand, trying to look casual as they pick up their bags and disperse.

"Thank you," she says. "Thank you, Mr. McKinnon. It's the reading they hate, and I know big words too. Like 'floccinaucinihilipilification'—I just learned that one; or 'honorificabilitudinitatibus'—that's in Shakespeare, you know. They think I'm saying I'm smarter than them."

"You probably are—smarter, I mean, not saying so." He squares the books into a single pile and slides them into her bag. "What were you doing down here?"

Isabel takes the satchel from him, fastening its clips and placing it carefully onto the grass. "I come down after school sometimes—I've been practicing tunneling, and cartwheels. Mum's at the library, you know, and Mrs. May doesn't have tea on till later. So I like to come down here and play. They usually leave me alone when we're not at school."

"I suppose the daughter of a librarian couldn't help but be a big reader," says Roy, squatting down in the sand beside her and looking out across the water. "Your mum must be very proud."

"I think she still misses Dad," says Isabel, and Roy blinks. He's forgotten the leaps a child's mind might make, and of course, for Ani, and perhaps her daughter too, everything must still come back to Mac.

"She used to read all sorts of things," Isabel goes on, "and now it's all romance and happy endings." She screws up her pretty face.

"I suppose that's okay, but it's not what I'd want to write—" And she blushes across the size of saying this, and to this man, of all people, who must know about these things.

"Not another one." He feigns horror. "I don't know if this village has room for the both of us—so you're lucky I don't do much writing these days. The stage is clear for you, Isabel Lachlan. You should give it a try."

Her blush deepens. "It feels dangerous to make jokes about it," she says quietly. "Did you make jokes about it? When you were little?"

"Constantly," says Roy. "I still do." He's forgotten the fake bonhomie of distracting a child—he loves it; he's missed it; he could sit here for days. "Now these tunnels," he says, switching her attention again. "What's their purpose? What are we making? Is it transportation you're thinking, or defense?" And before he knows it, he's bent down and is following her instructions for an intricate series of ramparts around her latest sand city, shoveling sand through his legs with the stance of a busy cartoon puppy.

"I told Mum I was thinking about writing," says Isabel after a while, "but I didn't know quite how to start. She said I might ask you about it. Would that be okay, if I did?"

Roy straightens up, pulling his shoulders back and pushing his stomach forward. "I'm probably the worst person to ask," he says, serious. "I was almost five years between poems, can you believe it, and you know what got me started again in the end?" She shakes her head and he pushes himself forward on the serendipity of the meeting, the bravery of seeing off her foes. "Your mother, Isabel, it was your mother. The first poem I wrote after the war, I wrote about her." His voice is quiet now, as if he's forgotten he's talking to anyone but himself.

"Did you publish it?"

"The pragmatic questions of youth." Roy smiles. "Not yet, but

I'm going to, I hope. I did leave a copy for her—but she mustn't have found it. She never mentioned it, did she? A small present? A tribute from a poetic admirer?" You can say anything to children—he's forgotten that too—and they'll sift out the gold from the dross.

Isabel shakes her head. "She found a poem my dad wrote—he must've written it before he died. It's so beautiful—maybe she'd let you read it. I guess all her attention for poetry has been taken up with that at the moment. That's how it is," she says, stretching her shoulders, her stomach, in imitation of him, "with things to do with Dad."

The exquisite torture of infatuation: standing tall next to this young girl, Roy registers how foolish he must look with his shoulders back and his gut out, how foolish, when he's no reason to be proud or sure. There's a burning taste at the back of his throat and his stomach knots around unknowns—if Ani has mistaken his poem for one by Mac, and the gall of thinking a railwayman might make such a thing. *It wants elegance, and talent, and craft to make a thing like that,* he wants to shout, like a man discovering he's been double-crossed.

And beneath the bile and the spasms, there's something else, the memory of Mac charging down a football field, powerful, broad, and alive. Roy can see him as clearly as if he were bearing along the sand right now—*she's mine, McKinnon, mine to dream of, mine to know.* He steps aside as if to dodge the apparition, surprised by the real, wet feel of the ocean's water against his feet.

He would run me down in a heartbeat, Roy thinks as the outer edges of Isabel's metropolis is saturated by the sea, and weakens, and falls. *Why not throw down a poem from the other side of death?*

But I'm alive, he wants to shout at Anikka Lachlan, or perhaps even at her daughter. *I'm alive, I'm here, look at me.*

And then I could stamp, the way a ten-year-old girl might stamp. He laughs at himself, shaking his head. *They taught me well, those kids I used to teach.*

The next wave surges across the sand, washing out one section of Roy's ramparts, and he leaps to repair it as if it were the most pressing problem in his world. Well, either Mac did write a poem and Ani's not found his, or she's found it and taken it as a gift from someone else. Either way, she'll know who made it soon enough. He'd balked only twice before handing it over at the post office and seeing it off on the next mail train, bounding home with a palpable sense of relief as its vans disappeared from view. *It's beyond me now*, and his editor would read it soon enough, Roy was sure, and print it after that; he was sure of that too. He knew its worth.

The magazine would come; Ani would read its words. And then—well, and then.

He scoops the sand and packs it hard, drizzling wetness like mortar along the top to hold it firm. "This is how you can reinforce buildings," he says. "But I'm sure you know this already, a practiced sand architect like yourself."

Because her citadel has reached the base of the pump house, she pokes the triumphant banner of a Norfolk pine's needle into its last edifice before turning three cartwheels to get back to Roy.

"Did you teach your mum to cartwheel, or did she teach you?" he asks, applauding.

"Cartwheel? My mum can't cartwheel."

Roy smiles, tries a cartwheel himself, and lands in a heap on the sand. "I saw her—I saw you both one morning. I have to say, you made it look quite easy." He tries again, and fails, laughing.

"I think that's the only time she tried—it was a rare sighting, Mr. McKinnon, of a rare species: the cartwheeling Anikka Lachlan." Her hands curled like the twin tubes of binoculars, she's scouting the landscape for this beast when another wave comes, washing at her feet and demolishing another section of her city wall. She lets out the wail of a much younger child.

"Come on," says Roy, "we can triumph over this. We just have to make it bigger and stronger," ignoring the logistics of an incoming tide.

He watches her from the corner of his eye, the way she scoops the sand up so quickly, marking out ramparts and skyscrapers while he beavers away at small things—reinforcements, buttresses—and makes much less progress. She's set on the task, he can see that, while his own attention wanders now and then, registering the yellow flowers that have bloomed among the grasses that fold down towards the sand, and the satisfying crunch this undergrowth makes under the pressure of his feet as he climbs in among the greenery, picks some of the pretty blossoms, and carries them back to fashion a garden along the inside of one of the citadel's smooth, sandy walls.

Down at the waterline, he retrieves tiny shells and tendrils of seaweed, planting them here and there across Isabel's expanding complex. He picks at the edge of the cliff face itself, astonished at how easily the fine pink sandstone becomes its original grains. Up above him, towards the top of the headland, he can see narrow bands of siltstone, and coal above that, striping the cliff like a licorice allsort. He's never noticed the delicacy of all these colors and their transitions before, and he wonders how he might thank Isabel for making him pause here this afternoon and look more closely at this place.

"Look how much you've built up," he calls then, astonished at how far her work stretches north along the beach. "What happens at the end of the day? Do you leave it for the tide or jump it down yourself?" He'd do that, he thinks, with the satisfaction of destroying something you'd labored so hard to make.

She's working in the fold where the beach meets the rest of the continent as he speaks, and Roy watches as she turns towards his voice, glancing west towards the setting sun and out, hasty, towards the encroaching tide. *Her hair*, he thinks, *lights up just like her mother's.*

"What was it about, your dad's poem?" he says, not wanting to let go of the girl or this sweetly cross-purposed conversation. "Did you read it, did you say?"

"It said Mum was like an angel," says Isabel softly, "and it was lovely, really lovely." She sits back, digging her hands in her pockets. "What about yours? What did yours say?"

"Well, it's funny, you know," says Roy as the sun dips down behind the edge of the scarp, "but I think mine was about that too." Watching her closely, as if he might see Ani's own reaction through her child's.

"Wowee," says Isabel, softer still. "I wonder if someone'll write me a poem like that one day."

"If you're a writer, you can write your own," says Roy, matter-of-fact. "Takes all the bother out of having to rely on another person."

She considers this, considers him, considers the rim of light where the sun has disappeared behind the mountain—and suddenly looks at her watch.

"I have to go, Mr. McKinnon," she says, twisting the face of her watch towards him—although whether she means for him to admire it or read its time, he's not sure. "My teatime in ten minutes. Oh, do you like this watch? It was my dad's, you know. But I can wear it now, to be in charge of wherever I have to be."

He catches her wrist and does good work admiring the time-piece. "Your dad would be proud you're in charge," he says, brushing the sand from the watch's webbed band. "It was nice to see you, Isabel Lachlan, and don't worry about those girls. They'll grow out of their jealousy and you'll leave them far behind." He hopes she can wait that long.

"Thanks for the help with my sand work," she says, shouldering her bag and turning to go.

"And listen," Roy calls after her, casual and diminishing. "Can you ask your mother if she did find my poem? It's no trouble if she didn't—it's bound to be published pretty soon. She can see what she thinks of it then." Buoyed by the unexpected afternoon.

Isabel nods, settles her satchel, and heads up the hill. But halfway home, she sees a small brown rabbit ambling along the verge, stopping and nibbling, its ears and paws as winning as a picture-book drawing. She crouches for a while—the time, the message, the dinner all forgotten—picking nasturtium leaves and bright-green grass stems, and holding them out to it as snacks.

When she finally reaches Mrs. May's table, the rabbit is all she talks about, wondering where it came from and whether it needs a home. And by the time she sees her mother, later that night and home late from the library, Isabel is almost asleep and even the rabbit is almost lost.

"Mum? Do you think we could get a bunny?" Her words slur towards each other, their consonants blurring. "There was one near the beach, and Mr. McKinnon . . ."

"Shhh now, Bella, we can talk about it in the morning."

"But Mr. McKinnon said, he said . . ."

"I didn't know Mr. McKinnon was anything to do with rabbits," says Ani gently, smoothing her daughter's hair, soothing her into sleep, and wiping the thought of the poet from anything that might be remembered in the next, new tomorrow.

While Roy, heading home, finds Iris sitting on her own front doorstep, her cheeks flushed and her smile wide.

"Hullo, dear. Did you leave your key? I was just over at the beach—you could have found me. . . ."

"I've just proposed to Dr. Frank Draper," she says, leaning back on her hands and looking triumphant. "I was so sick of it, I just asked him. The silly bugger, of course he said yes."

37

ROUNDING THE street, Mac looked up and saw the tail of a shooting star—extraordinary—and stopped. If Ani were with him, she'd make him make a wish. He slung his bag over his shoulder and breathed in the crisp night air. He loved these nocturnal starts, loved walking through the village as everyone else lay inside, warm and sleeping—it was like being able to walk through their dreams. Occasionally he'd hear a dog bark or a baby cry; occasionally a light would come on as he passed by a house, and he'd wonder if it was his footfall its inhabitant had heard.

Tread softly, he thinks now as he passes along a street of darkened windows, *because you tread on my dreams*. That's Yeats, that is—Ani had read it to him in the evening—*and you couldn't get better than that*. His steps lengthened, crunching the gravel as he ran through Yeats's words:

> Had I the heavens' embroidered cloths,
> Enwrought with golden and silver light,
> The blue and the dim and the dark cloths

Of night and light and half-light,
I would spread the cloths under your feet:
But I, being poor, have only my dreams;
I have spread my dreams beneath your feet;
Tread softly because you tread on my dreams. . . .

Then came another crunch, and another, out of time, and Mac peered into the darkness to see the young doctor—Draper—and Iris McKinnon's brother, Roy.

"Good evening, to you, gentlemen—or is it good morning? I'm never quite sure at this time." He enjoyed their start; Roy McKinnon almost jumped. "And where might you be bound at such an hour?" As if he had the perfect right to interrogate anyone he encountered on his way.

"Good morning to you." It was the doctor who spoke. "A fine morning for a walk. A fine morning to feel the air around you." His voice was tight, his face flushed—Mac wondered if the two of them had been up somewhere drinking.

Roy McKinnon patted his friend's arm, and then held out his hand to shake Mac's. "Don't mind Frank," he said. "We've just been listening to the latest news from Spain—some terrible bombing raid—they're saying there might be thousands dead, and thousands of children orphaned too." He shook his head. "It's no news to greet a man with on a fine night like this; I'm sorry."

"A marketplace, man, they bombed a marketplace. Are they safe in their beds"—the doctor grabbed at Mac's arm, clutching it tight—"the people you love? Do you have a wife? Or children?"

Mac stepped away from the man's fingers, let his own hand rest on the doctor's shoulder. The flush, the tight breathing: he was just like Ani when she tried to take in too much of the world's news. "I've been following the stories, Doctor. It doesn't bode well for the world, not at all." And he watched how the doctor's hands shook as he took a cigarette from the packet in his pocket, how the flame of the match quivered in the darkness.

Silence then, and then a long breath made of smoke. The doctor held the packet out to Mac, to Roy McKinnon, shaking his own head as each of them refused. "And what can you do, then, what can you do?"

Mac tipped his head back, looking up at the stars and the wisps of cloud that obscured slices of the constellations here and there. There was the Southern Cross; there was the Milky Way running up from the south towards the high dark line the mountain made to the west. "My wife is at home, asleep, yes, and we're not yet lucky enough to have a child." He shrugged. "That world is a long way away, and I hope if it comes close, I can keep my wife safe from it—and any children too."

"As every father in Europe has thought before you."

The tip of the doctor's cigarette flared bright as he inhaled; Mac stared as its color flickered. There was something hypnotic about these wee licks of fire people carried around with them, but then, he was like that with any flame, always drifting a little closer than he should. It scared the life out of Ani when he had to work a spell near the engines' fireboxes, he knew, as if she feared he'd be sucked in and immolated in one random rush.

"Every father everywhere, I suppose." Frank Draper threw the cigarette down on the ground, stamping at it impatiently. "I want a train that goes far enough and fast enough to take me away from stories like this—and I know that there'll only be more and more of them to come. A pessimist, my friend here calls me a pessimist. But I'm a doctor, a man of rationality and investigation. And I say this is what we men do best—we fight, we kill, and we use our best imagination to find newer ways of doing it."

"Come away, Frank," said Roy McKinnon. "We're keeping this man from his business—come away."

But they stood there, the three of them, like the fixed points of some perpetual triangle. An owl called, and another answered, and in the next lull Mac heard the turn of the waves, sneaking along streets in which they usually kept their silence. "The oceans and the skies," he said, "and the sun coming up each new day. That's all there is, I think. That's what it matters to think on, not the news and the wars and the dying and the loss. It's not a bad sort of insurance."

The doctor laughed, and clapped Mac's shoulder hard. "And I thought Roy here was the poet—didn't know this place had managed to infect two of you." He pulled his coat around him, fastening another of its buttons. "All right then, let's get on. I could use a drink to settle me down—a dram of whisky." He tried to mimic Mac's accent, and laughed again. "You'd go, wouldn't you, if there was some mad call to fight?"

And Mac, without thinking, found he was shaking his head. "No," he said slowly. "I've never thought of it before, but no. It's not my war, not my world. I'd stay here, you're right. I'd stay here and keep my wife safe, and my children." He could feel his shoulders straightening with resolve.

"White feathers this time? I wonder if people will do that again." But Dr. Draper smiled. "I'm with you. It's not to do with us and ours, you're right. But I've a sense we'll all be pulled into it, with some nasty inexorability." He fumbled in his coat pocket, drew out his cigarettes, and then put them away again with a sigh. "So when you do go, sir, as we all will, you make sure you leave someone here to take care of your people. That's a better insurance than your waves and your stars."

Hitching his bag higher onto his shoulder, Mac tipped his hat. "Perhaps I'll see you gents for that whisky sometime—I shoot billiards now and then, if a run gets in early. We can unravel the ways of the world some more. You can tell me your plans for this war you say is coming."

Roy McKinnon coughed, rubbing his hands for warmth. "I suppose we'll all end up in it, no matter what we think. Frank here will stop doctoring. I'll stop teaching—and dreaming my silly poetical dreams. And maybe someone else will see your trains through the stops of their timetables." He pointed at the guard's lamp that swung from Mac's bag. "Hang on to your happiness if you can. We should none of us let them make us change what we do in the world."

Mac watched Roy's mouth as it spoke its words. This man was the one who dreamed of becoming a poet: what a weightless thing to do. No momentum, no material, just a blind gaze out in the direction of the future. "So you're the one who wants poetry," he said. "My wife's a reader—read me Yeats this very night." His chest expanded a little with the story: *Bet you'd not expected that.*

But from farther along the road, he heard the sounds of an engine coming up to steam—he could hear clanking and grating and puffed exhalations, and he knew how every particular sound was being made. That was his world; he was a railwayman. The engine bellowed again, and Mac stepped back a little more.

"An odd pleasure, to find you on my way to work—an odd pleasure to talk of this much in so short a time, and just here on the road I happened to be walking along. All the best to you both." But he nodded to the doctor. "You should meet my wife, Doctor. I think you and she could terrify each other with the ways you take on the world." He tilted his hat again and headed towards the shunting yards, leaving Roy McKinnon and Frank Draper to head on to their whisky and their beds.

And as he walked in and out of the puddles of streetlight, he thought about Ani, perhaps still awake, and waiting to hear his train. If she could see him now, as she waited to sleep again, she would see him walking fast, and free, and strangely exhilarated. If she could see him now, as the night crept towards sunrise, she would see him fly on to the yards and up into the guards' van, his light bright with its beacons of red and green.

Maybe a bairn next year, he thought, swinging himself into his carriage. *Or mebbe a war.* Who, apart from those old Scots' women with second sight, who could ever know what would happen next in a story?

A nice couple of chaps; he was glad to have met them—not that there'd been any proper introduction; he wished suddenly that he'd told them his name. But then it was such an odd meeting, he almost wondered if he'd dreamed it, if they'd both walk right past him if they met again somewhere in the village streets in the brightness of a day.

Who knew which characters ended up in which story. *Another question for that second sight*, thought Mac. And as he jumped down to wait for the signal from his driver, another engine came surging along the tracks beside him, leaving Mac to leap clear, and fast, out of its path.

His heart beating, he climbed into his box again, and sat, his breathing rapid. *You're all right, you're all right.* He pressed his finger against his pulse, could feel his blood racing through his wrist. *You always check, mate, you always check.*

He closed his eyes and slowed his breath. Suppose there were so many accidents you didn't have in a day, a week. Suppose there were near misses, close calls, some of which you didn't even notice. One of them would find you sooner or later.

He took Ani's packet of sandwiches out of his bag, unwrapping the carefully folded paper. Egg. And two slices of ham with a slice of tomato carefully between the two to try to stop it from making the bread soggy. She made them with love, she said. On a morning like this, he could almost taste it.

Yes, he would spread the universe beneath her feet, if it were his to spread—the thousands of stars, the stretch of the sky, and the vast deep of the oceans it held and everything in them. If he were a different man, he would write her a poem. He would write her a poem about this place, its colors, its sounds, its shapes. The mountain, the water, the sky, and this nest of a village held safe by all three—she'd love that; it would make her smile from the deepest part of herself, the part that was his. He wondered about how he might start—but nothing came except the signal from the driver that the train was ready to go.

Mac finished his sandwich, flicked his light around to green, and leaned out of the window to taste the steamy air of the train as it pushed north.

Out along the horizon, a smudge of red cut through the darkness, a bright and glowing start to the next day. He thought of the two men he'd just met, the horror they had been carrying with them. He tried to imagine the sounds of war—of bombs and burning, of loss, of dying—and shook his head at it. The world couldn't come to that.

But the sun on the water reflected the stories of the doctor, of the poet: the sun on the water that morning looked like blood smeared on steel.

38

WHEN HE opens his eyes, the room quivers with a sharp green light. Roy blinks and blinks again. After the first blink, the green light fades down to darkness; after the second, he realizes he's in Iris's spare room, in Iris's house.

He blinks again. That green light: it must have leached out of his dream. His terrible dream. The guard's light green; the train coming on; and Roy himself riding fast towards the engine on a flimsy bike, trying to beat it, trying to best it, trying to fly across the tracks. He's dreamed this dream every night, every night for the three, four, five months now since the accident. He reaches for a glass of water, coughing as he takes too big a mouthful. From the hallway outside, he hears a clock's chime—three times—and he lies still a moment, wishing for the power to advance the time closer to dawn, before he lets himself confirm it with the glowing green numbers on his watch.

Just gone three. The cold, quiet time. The left side of his body feels pummeled and bruised as if it had been buffeted by something with the force of a train.

Easing himself out of bed, Roy finishes the glass of water and gazes at the street. Three o'clock; he's slept just over four hours, but it's the longest stretch of sleep he's managed yet. And he's exhausted by the dream, the night, the waking.

He creeps through the dark house, out to the kitchen, refilling the glass and draining it again and again. *I am forty years old*, he thinks. *I may live another forty.* The idea is somehow untenable.

Back in his room, he feels around for clothes, boots, his coat and hat, in the darkness. His thumbs brush against his legs as he pulls on his trousers; his palms brush against his body as he pulls on his shirt. And in each touch, he feels papery skin against papery skin, as if the warmth, the blood, had already evaporated from his being.

Navigating the desk for his notebook, his pen, his hand finds the rectangle of the magazine that came with the previous day's post—his poem, his "Lost World," so distinct and incontrovertible in its regular type. He should take it up to Ani now, he thinks; leave it in her mailbox for her to find in the morning.

It's breathtaking, the addictive powerlessness of unequal love, and the myriad explanations his mind can generate for Ani's ongoing silence. *Maybe Isabel didn't want another man in the way of her father's memory; maybe Ani didn't want to know.* The permutations of whether the girl even told her mother or not branch and multiply like the complex math problems he used to set, *when all you have to do is ask her yourself.* Easy to say at three in the morning, yet whenever he's seen Ani, he's stepped up to the precipice of this conversation, gulped, said nothing, and stepped back down, making his peace with himself with some line about her being his muse.

Bollocks: you don't dream of taking a muse by the hand, of holding her, of tasting her kiss—he makes himself stop, batting at his forehead like the dunderhead he is until his mind is blank again. And calm.

Later, he will take it to her later. No secrets this time; no sneaking around; no anonymity. Just him, Roy McKinnon, offering up this thing he has made. He lets his hand rest on the magazine, wondering what Anikka Lachlan will think of her mistake. Well, his poem is beyond her now and out in the world. And he feels lighter for it.

He slips through the front door and across the road, tracing the waterline as he heads south along the sand and over the rocks. A single light from a ship pulses briefly on the line of the horizon and he watches it awhile, trying to remember the dots and dashes of Morse code. Perhaps it's a message for him, he thinks, trying to count a pattern of dots and dashes until he rubs his eyes and the light transforms into a regular pulse of flashes.

What are you thinking, mate? Why are you here?

He crouches down on the rocks, away from the onshore wind, and watches as the light disappears. As if there was a message; as if there was a sign. His back stiff against the hardness of the cliff's face, he flexes and tenses each of the muscles in his legs, trying to sit still a little longer. Some nights, he's fallen asleep down here, waking up with the gulls as the dawn rolls around. That bloke who gave his address as Thirroul Beach when he joined up for the war; maybe this was his very spot. Maybe this was the place that he thought of as home. *Guess he didn't get back,* Roy thinks out of nowhere, *or I'd've run into him by now.* He only realizes he's crying when the tears penetrate his trousers' heavy fabric. He should build a cairn, he thinks then, and starts immediately, taking up the curved flutes of purple barnacle shells and smooth grey elliptical pebbles from the ground around him.

This do in remembrance of me.

Something moves along the sand, and Roy turns to see a fisherman casting out beyond the breakers. Balancing the last two pebbles on the mound, he gives it a salute. *There you are, mate,* he thinks, *home at last.* But before he turns to make his way along the beach, he crouches down again and scoops up handfuls of the stones, stuffing them into his pockets like candy or coins.

"Much biting?" he calls to the fisherman as he nears him, his fingers working the stones like a rosary.

"Bit of bream, bit of tailor," the man replies, indicating a bucket with his foot. "Where's your gear, mate?"

"Couldn't sleep," Roy says. "Just came out to stop myself staring at the ceiling." He loves these nocturnal meetings, their accidental connections and random conversations. He crouches again as the man's line tenses with a bite. "And another?"

"Bit of power in him," the angler agrees, reeling in the line and dropping this next fish into his bucket. "Take one if you like; I've enough here to keep the wife busy awhile."

But Roy shakes his head. "Thanks though, I've got some walking to do before I head in." Tipping his hat to the fisherman, falling back into his stride. Ahead of him, the old jetty's pylons and crossbeams stand like a luminous forest of trunks and their branches, and as he nears them, he picks up speed, remembering his climb, his salty jump, when he first came home.

All right, he thinks, *come on*—springing along the sand as fast as he can, and up. *Do your St. Simeon again.* Thirty-nine years St. Simeon stayed up his pillar—*my whole life again, more or less.* It still feels an unconscionable time.

From the top, he counts the rhythm of the breakers, timing his breathing with their ebb and flow. Beyond their surge, something pale shimmers against the water, like a miniature iceberg, he thinks, although he knows that's as daft an analogy as looking for Morse messages from a passing ship. He squints, blinks, and squints again. *It's a bloody albatross,* and he wishes he was still standing with the other man, to have someone with whom he might share the sighting.

"Hey," he calls back along the beach, pointing to the bird. "Hey look." But the fellow is too far away.

He watches as the albatross rises and falls on the ocean's tiny crests: wherever it's flown from, or is flying to, it's resting here, off the south coast of New South Wales. The distances it might have traveled; the expanses it might have seen. It would be something, thinks Roy, to be able to glide around and around and around the world, so rarely stationary, so rarely stuck on land. *That'd be the life*, he thinks, suddenly tempted to pack up his gear and move on. Whatever respite he had from coming here, from stopping awhile—he shivers in the cold air, and his torso keeps shaking, impossible to still.

But of course, to keep moving would be to move away from Ani Lachlan—*or your ideas of her, you yellowbelly*, he thinks, rubbing at his arms to try to stop their trembling. No, now that day is coming on, in no part of his imagination can he see himself approaching her, declaring himself—even managing to present her with the blessed magazine.

Damn it, man, you never even asked her on a day trip. Cross-legged up the pillar, he pulls the stones from his pockets one by one, flicking them down into the water below. *She loves me; she loves me not; she loves me; she loves me not.* It's a fool's game of desire, but maybe there's as much joy in the act of loving as there is in being loved.

He pulls one last stone from his pocket, a perfectly fluted purple cone, and studies it awhile in the dim light. Out on the water, the albatross bobs gently and Roy remembers how once, on one of the worst days of his war, he'd happened to look up from his gun's sights at precisely the right instant to see a huge white ball of floss—feathers, he supposed, or some other sort of fluff—soft and gentle and floating above the mud. The impossibility of its purity, its fragility, its perfection. Now, with the purple shell balanced like a coronet on the plinth of his fingers, he pushes himself to his feet and stands on the pylon's top, holding the barnacle high and then tossing it higher again into the darkness. And as the little thing soars and tumbles through its arc, he sees its edges catch the light here and there, watches it rise up and drop all the way down, into the wide, dark ocean. He can see the albatross out there too, waiting just beyond the upright of the jetty's deepest stanchion, and he walks forward towards it, jumping between what's left of the jetty's girders, its beams, its old tracks and sleepers.

Here I am, a railwayman at last, he thinks, and he laughs out loud at the idea of it. *A man of spectacular movement and action.*

The next pylon, he reckons, is a few feet away, and so on by regular gaps out into the water. He'd be tall enough, lithe enough surely, to spring out along this causeway—he balances, carefully, his arms out like a crucifix. And then he starts to run, out towards the horizon.

That phrase Frank had remembered—*a solid man; I was a solid man*. Roy laughs again as he feels himself surrounded by air. *There's nothing solid about me now.* In the water ahead of him, he sees a dark shadow like a right angle, and he remembers his hunt for the signs of hidden letters, remembers walking through the village as it slept, calling out rich words.

"*L*," he shouts, for the fun of it. "Levity, luminous, lampyridine."

Leap.

On and on, faster and faster, his feet as light as Fred Astaire's. In the end, he couldn't have said if he jumped or fell. In the end, the fisherman said, it looked like he was flying.

39

ON THE last day of his life, Mackenzie Lachlan kissed his wife at the top of the steps, waved back to her from the corner of the street, and kept going without another thought. He walked most of the way to the railway with his daughter, telling her nothing stories about a tree here, a cloud there, the routes and runs his day would take. "And then your milkshake at the end, love: what'll you have, chocolate malted?" Her favorite; her automatic choice.

He did not hug her harder than usual when they parted. He did not kiss her one extra time, or call some message after her. He did not stand and watch her go, did not think about her future or her past. He simply hitched his bag onto his shoulder and walked down to the yards.

"Morning, Mac," his driver called. "A great day." And it was. It was. The sun was high and bright, the sky cerulean, and he knew the ocean would be glittering when the train reached Scarborough, Clifton, Coalcliff.

"Great day," he agreed, checking his lamp, swinging up into the van.

"Thought of you this morning when I was coming in," the

driver said. "In fact I almost came by and fetched you—they were out there again, a whole line of albatrosses as far as you could see. Reckon they stretched for a good three or four miles, just bobbing along on the water. A grand sight, Mac, magnificent."

And Mac laughed; let Ani have her phosphorescence. Let Isabel have her dolphins. What Mac wanted, more than anything else, was an albatross out on the ocean, or turning and gliding in flight.

"Reckon they'll be there when we get up the line?" he called and the driver shook his head. "Third time lucky, maybe." It was getting to be a joke between them—the birds coming, and settling, and Mac never quite in the right place at the right time to see them.

"Well, let's get on then, and fetch me next time, will you?" Mac added. "I'd get away early for that any day."

A harbinger of good fortune; a bright omen at sea. *Let's face it,* he thought, *a man needs all the luck he can come by.*

So that later, when it happened, he saw this, the omen of the bird. He saw his wife, her hair shining, stepping out of the sunrise; he saw her eyes closed and dreaming on the night of their wedding. He saw her dancing through pools of light at the end of the war, and twirling on the ice, around and around. He saw himself talking about writing a poem—maybe he'd meant to; maybe he would. He saw himself running for a football, running with his daughter, running across a wide, green field, and then he was running along the uneven surface of the line's ballast. Running from this, whatever this was. Running from every accident he'd dodged and missed on every other day of his life. He saw all the things he wouldn't know about the future—Ani alone in a quiet room of books; Isabel practicing words on a page. He saw a man running along a railway line, running towards the sunrise. And then he was running along his own silver line of track, etched here between the ocean on one hand and the scarp high on the other.

Running through this place.

He saw all this in the blink of an eye, like fragments dislodged from his daughter's kaleidoscope.

After that, there was nothing but light, from white, through blue, and beyond.

40

ON THE first day of her first vacation, Ani is on the beach before the sunrise, watching its colors come up through gentle purples and silvers, and then a wide clear sky of perfect pale blue. She walks south along the sand, following the line of the tide so that her feet are brushed with the thinnest edge of the water's foam as each wave flows and ebbs. The ocean's still cold, although the year is touching summer, and she loves the slight shock of each ripple against her skin, the way her footprints disappear with each salty surge. Looking up from her feet a moment, she sees an albatross rise from the ocean—the power of it, and the majesty. The one bird Mac had always wanted to see on the coast. The one sight he'd always somehow missed.

She stands facing the brightness: she loves this moment, when the sun appears, loves the feel of the earth's ball rolling forward, rolling on, turning itself in space.

Coming out of the grocer's the day before, Ani had met Mrs. Padman, one of the ladies from the church, and they'd stopped and talked awhile, of this and that, a baby born two streets down and someone's mother taken ill. There was a new roster being planned for the church's flowers, Mrs. Padman said, and she hoped she might be able to include Ani's name on it—no mention of why Ani had stopped doing this, of how long it had been, of whether Ani was ready to return. And Ani had smiled and nodded and said there were so many flowers in her garden at the moment—it seemed a shame that only she and Isabel were enjoying them.

Walking home with her flour and her sugar, a little bag of sweets for her daughter and her half a pound of tea, she realized it was the first meeting she'd had in the village streets where the weight of Mac, and what had happened, hadn't hung over the moment—where his story hadn't been there in the conversation, said or unsaid. Where she hadn't been spotlit by its circumstance, and raised up somehow, like someone famous—or infamous.

Now, under the first warmth of the sun, she feels light, and smiles. She thinks: *How dare you die.* But the force has gone out of the phrase, and the words lie across the top of her imagination, thought, registered, but powerless beyond that.

In the pocket of her cardigan, she fiddles with an old library card on which she's jotted a shopping list, the soft pads of her fingers pushing against the sharp prick of the card's corners. *Imagine me, a librarian*, she thinks. *Imagine me, in charge.* All the things she'd never had to manage when there was Mac—bills and time and having coal delivered or the roof fixed and remembering which night the pan man came; all the things she'd never wanted to have to think about. And here she was, doing it all, and doing fine. She wants to feel proud of it, but the thought feels too close to being grateful for its circumstances—*Mac or a library; Mac or capability*—which is always an unthinkable thing.

Heading south along the beach, she scans the empty sand and then, before she can change her mind, runs forward and springs into a cartwheel. Another and another and another, although the last leaves her tumbled on the ground, gritty and laughing.

She looks around again, not for any unwanted witnesses, but for wanted ones—Roy McKinnon is down here some mornings, and it's always lovely to talk with him about the world. Even Frank Draper might have laughed at the silliness of it, if he'd been there. There's some kind of busyness a way away, at the foot of the headland beyond the jetty; Ani peers across the distance and turns back for home, too far away to pick out either the doctor or the poet among the fray.

Who'd have thought, she wonders, *what those two would be in my year?* Almost twelve months ago, they were newcomers in her world, slightly awkward at her Christmas lunch. This year, there was no question that they'd eat anywhere else. *And I will show him my poem*, she thinks, the first time she hasn't tagged it as Mac's. *It's such a beautiful thing.*

Walking on, Ani's foot scuffs something hard beneath the sand, and she leans down to work free a strange white shape, curled and twisted, turning it one way and then another until she realizes what it is—teeth! a little set of jaws!—and throws it away from herself, far out and into the ocean. Her hands rub furiously against her trousers, trying to erase the texture of the skeletal bone. There's a horrid taste in her mouth too, and she bends forward, spitting and spitting again to try to clear whatever it is.

Teeth; jaws: she can't begin to imagine what kind of creature they've come from—an animal? A fish? Some strange, snapping reptile? She shivers, wringing her hands in the sharp, salty water. That's why she hates Isabel's idea of Mac stuck under the water. There are too many things that can bite down there—bite him, tear at his body, and sever that lifeline that runs between them. Even the pretty-sounding stargazer her daughter mentioned turned out to have a horrible mouthful of teeth.

She washes her hands once more, rubbing them dry in her pockets. Her lightness has evaporated with the morning's haze: she's Ani

Lachlan again, a widow, fixed and alone. It's never-ending, after all. She should go home and make her daughter her breakfast.

Climbing the cliff near the famous writer's house, she pauses, staring in at its deep, shaded veranda. If he hadn't happened on this village, if he hadn't happened on this house, what story would he have invented in those winter months instead—and would it have had anything to do with her?

A curtain flicks open at one of the house's windows and Ani turns hurriedly to give the appearance of looking out to sea. A man comes onto the veranda, and she thinks, for an instant, that it's Lawrence himself, come back to life and come back to see what other story has been going on in this place in the space after his novel's last page.

A seagull shrieks, startling Ani as she comes on up the stairs. The man leans out towards the vastness of the sea, waving at Ani as she passes.

"A beautiful morning—we've got some view."

Ani waves back, nodding. "Perfect, isn't it? Bound to be a perfect day." She takes the last steps at close to a run, her lightness recovered again and flooding through her limbs.

She runs to the end of the street, around the corner, and back along to her own gate, bounding over its low fence and up the front stairs two at a time. She unlocks the front door and steps inside, closing it quietly and standing a moment in the reflected rose and blue of its two glass panels.

It's quiet in Isabel's bedroom, and dark, the blinds still drawn. Ani rests her hands on the high frame of the bedstead. Isabel is sleeping on her stomach, as she always has, her head turned slightly, and her hands up on her pillow.

Eleven years, thinks Ani. *I have stood and watched this baby sleep eleven years.* Isabel stirs a little, and Ani creeps away, listening as her daughter coughs once, and settles. She opens the French doors onto the front veranda, letting in the first of the morning's sun. She'll make tea; she'll take it outside—it's the first day of her first vacation, and there's no rush. No rush. The sun sneaks across the boards of the veranda's floor; by the time she boils the kettle and soaks the leaves, it will have warmed the place where she can sit and gaze out at the ocean.

Which is where she is and what she's doing when the car turns into the street and draws up near her gate. When Frank Draper comes into her yard, and climbs her stairs, his hands held out towards her.

"Anikka," he says—he's never used her first name before—"I'm so sorry to be coming like this on such a gorgeous morning." And he sits down on the floor, before she can stand; sits down, cross-legged, facing her.

She wonders about the dust marking his nice suit. And she wonders, the question looping inside her head, what news he can possibly have brought, *because Isabel is safe inside; Isabel is asleep.*

As if nothing else mattered in the world.

"I've just come from Iris McKinnon's," he says at last. "I thought you'd want to know. There was an accident, and Roy McKinnon . . ." He ducks, his face working silently. "Roy McKinnon has been drowned."

Watching him closely, watching the way his mouth twists at the end of the sentence, the way tears come into his eyes, Ani feels like some part of her is standing up, tall, looking down at him and looking down at herself as well. She's leaning towards Frank Draper, patting his hand, saying "there" and "shh" and "it's all right," like she used to say to Isabel when she was tiny and woke herself with the unknown trembling of a dark, bad dream. She sees herself doing this; she sees Frank Draper grab onto her hand and hold it, tight. She sees their heads close, his dark, and hers bright.

She sees them sit like this as the cicadas begin to sing.

The first man's hand I've held, she thinks from somewhere far away. She has never imagined it would be his. *I don't know what to think; I don't know what to do.*

But as she sits and grips the doctor's hand with hers, she remembers the minister, the hot, sweet, sugary drink he made her. And, "I'll get you some tea," she says, easing her fingers away. And she makes it hot and strong and sweet—makes it in the chipped cup the minister had given her, as if that might be some important part of the ritual.

He drinks it in four or five scalding mouthfuls, blowing his breath out and wiping his hand across his eyes. "I thought you'd want to know," he says again, looking at her properly for the first time.

And she nods—*of course*—and says, "Poor Iris. I'll go down later. I'll take her some food." The commotion on the beach, she thinks suddenly, but doesn't want to ask. It feels discourteous somehow, or even cowardly, to have turned and walked away.

"No," says the doctor, "I don't think—no . . ." He's holding a large envelope out towards her; she opens it and sees a magazine, a strip of paper marking one page, and *"Lost World"—a new poem by Roy McKinnon.*

"I don't understand," says Ani slowly, her fingers rubbing at the page. "I mean, I knew he was writing again—he seemed pleased with what he was doing—and how awful to be stopped—" She strokes the paper awhile. "Such a curious title; I wonder how he came by it."

And then she looks at the poem's lines:

Let this be her.
A fold of light . . .

"I don't understand," she says again, her face pale and her fingers unsteady.

"He wrote it after Christmas." Frank Draper's voice is distant, somehow muffled. "I read it then—I told him it was good. He said he would show it to you. I mean, it's obviously about you."

"No." Ani closes the magazine, shaking her head. "No, my husband wrote this poem. Mac wrote this poem for my birthday before he died—he left it in a book for me; I found it on my shelf months later. Mr. McKinnon must have taken it; he must have copied it. Because they can't both have written the same poem, can they?"

There's a sudden movement in the yard, and Ani and the doctor both turn to see a magpie swoop in and settle. Ani holds fast to the magazine and its shockingly familiar verse, her eyes fixed on the bird, while Frank Draper worries at the skin around his thumbnail, pushing and chipping until the quick begins to bleed.

"Roy wrote it after Christmas," he says again. "He was anxious about showing you, but he said he thought he might leave it somewhere where you'd find it. I thought he'd probably slip it into one of his library books, see if you happened on it when you were packing them up. But he must have brought it up here—maybe one night after the pictures, I don't know." He pauses, touches her hand. "Roy McKinnon wrote it, Ani, you know that. Your husband was a railwayman; he wasn't a poet."

Opening the magazine again, Ani follows the familiar words, a little less familiar, somehow, among the precise reportage of other articles, other words. "Mac told me once he wanted to write a poem," she says defensively. "And so I thought maybe he'd tried. It was beautiful, so beautiful." She watches a single tear—which must be hers—splash down onto the paper, darkening its color. "And it was mine."

The doctor leans forward, takes her hands again. "It's still yours, Ani. It's just from someone else—that's all."

"But I thought it was from Mac—I thought it was from him.

What business does Roy McKinnon have thinking I look like an angel in a white dress and the sunshine?"

"Well, none, now, does he, but he thought the world of you—you must have known that." She can hear the impatience in his voice as he stands and raises his empty cup. "My turn to make the tea then?" And he disappears inside, leaving Ani and this newly dense idea alone in the morning.

She shifts the magazine, leafing through it at random. And when she finds the poem again, and reads it, it's Roy McKinnon's voice she hears, not some far-off trace of Mac's. *Of course my name wasn't in Mac's writing*, she thinks at last. *How could it be, when he didn't write it?* She pushes her nails into the palm of her hand like a run of sharp pins. "And the brooch," she says under her breath. "My Christmas brooch." The simple words stick in her throat.

Inside, through the open door, she can see the luminous wood of her little *bibliothèque*—no question he made that. She glances down at the page again and sees in tiny letters beneath its title, *For A.L.* A new and big thing that she was too afraid to see.

No question, no question at all.

She looks up as Frank comes out with the tea—"No milk or sugar in yours; I think I remembered it right?"—and wraps her hands around the cup's warmth as if it were the coldest winter's day.

"Thank you," she says—for the tea, for the poem, for whatever. The warmth burrows deep into her. The magpie begins to chortle, and she lets it finish before she speaks: "And Roy? What happened? Did he see this before he—before—"

There are dark smudges on the skin below the doctor's eyes, and his eyes are red and rheumy. He leans into Ani's pause, taking a mouthful of his own tea and holding it in his cheeks awhile before he swallows and answers. "The magazine came yesterday, Iris thinks, and Roy went out last night. Hard to know what happened, except he drowned, fully clothed, with a few pebbles in his pockets—a fisherman saw him trying to run along what's left of the old jetty."

A great blast comes up from one of the railway's engines, and Ani starts, as surprised by its noise as if the train were in her very yard. "The first time I saw him, when he came home," she says as its sound fades away, "the first time I saw him, he was perched on one of those poles. I always wondered how he'd gotten down." Only later will she remember that Mac was there too; only later will she realize she's excluded him from the story.

The doctor sighs and wipes his eyes. "I was hoping for a happy ending," he says. "If I could manage it, surely anyone could." He frowns at her frowning, at her blank incomprehension. "You must have known, Ani. Every second gossip in this village has been talking about it for months. How long you'd wait. And what you'd wear." He laughs, but the laugh makes a cold and empty sound. "You know how they are, how they all like to dream."

Ani picks up her teacup and is tempted for a moment to throw what's left of its liquid in his face. Then she moves her hand to throw it past him and away over the veranda's rail and onto the garden down below. "The year I've had, Dr. Draper, here, with my daughter, making sense of this strange new world. I've lost my husband. I have this job. I wake up in my own room, in my own house. And yet everything, everything is different. Meeting Mr. McKinnon, even meeting you; you were new people in my new world. And I appreciated that very much. I didn't think about much more than that. I paid no mind to what the village was plotting might happen next. I've just been trying to get us through the days, just me and Isabel, that's all." There are truths and untruths in this, she knows, but it feels too late to worry about any of them. And as she says her daughter's name, Isabel appears, lovely and smiling and half full of dreams.

"Bella." Ani reaches up to her girl. "You've had the loveliest long sleep. Dr. Draper's been here drinking tea with me. And now he's just on his way."

And she holds on fast to her daughter's warm hands.

"Ani," says the doctor, standing now and fumbling with his hat. "It's all right—I only meant . . ." And he sighs, pointing to the magazine. "I'll leave you this, then, and I'll leave you to your morning, Mrs. Lachlan."

From across the village comes the hard pull of an engine's brakes, and they both react, the doctor and the railwayman's wife. Frank Draper turns and walks away, still shaking his head as his car purrs and he pulls out onto the empty road.

Up on the porch, Ani keeps her eyes on the nothing of middle distance until the car has gone. She feels Isabel crouch beside her, sees her reach for the journal, and hears her gasp as she starts to read.

"The poem, Mr. McKinnon's poem, oh, and I—oh, Mum."

While Ani, leaning in, reads along, wondering what she might feel about any of this—not now, when everything seems pushed away and at arm's length, like trying to bring a line of type into focus, but some other time, on some other day. Then a sentence leaps at her from the facing page, its words wrapping around her, and she disappears into their world, enveloped and contained, lost to anything in this here or now, its chances, its hazards, its missed opportunities.

Overhead, the sun is still climbing, and as it catches the edge of a shiny tin roof across the street, Ani looks up from the page, staring straight at the bright disk until she's blinded by its glare. She reaches for her daughter's hand again, hanging on, holding on.

Somewhere in the world, the sun is always rising. Somewhere in the world, the day is getting light.

Acknowledgments

The earliest drafts of this novel were completed under the auspices of a doctorate of creative arts at the University of Technology, Sydney. Thanks to Catherine Cole, Paula Hamilton, and Paul Ashton for their encouragement, guidance, and supervision both ahead of the project's beginnings and throughout its span.

The epigraph from Stephen Edgar comes from his poem "Nocturnal," originally published in *History of the Day* (2009), and is reproduced here with his permission.

The poem "Lost World"—written specifically for this novel— also came from the talented agency of Stephen Edgar, without whom Roy would never have found such an elegant and appropriate voice. I cannot thank him enough for his enthusiasm and generosity in this.

The research for this novel drew on a large number of written sources, and quotes several—most crucially D. H. Lawrence's *Kangaroo* and Charlotte Brontë's *Jane Eyre*. The text also refers to articles from *Smith's Weekly,* 18 March 1944 (the story of the engine driver and his blackberries); the *National Geographic* of November 1947 (the northern lights); and *The Sydney Morning*

Herald, 14 June 1949 (the newspaper Roy reads on the train). The other poems referred to in the text are Siegfried Sassoon's "Everyone Sang," Elizabeth Barrett Browning's "How Do I Love Thee?," and two by William Butler Yeats—"On Being Asked for a War Poem" and "Aedh Wishes for the Cloths of Heaven."

The description of Ani Lachlan as "an angel from a lost world" was inspired by "Angel," a poem by Justin Moon; the librarian who wonders to Ani if paradise might be a library paraphrases Jorge Luis Borges's words from his *"Poema de los Dones"* [Poem of the Gifts]; Roy borrows Heinrich Heine's words from his 1821 play *Almansor* when he talks about burning books; and the extracts on bathysphere diving are taken from William Beebe's 1934 memoir *Half Mile Down*. Joseph Davis's *D. H. Lawrence at Thirroul* was an invaluable reference and the source of the inspirational information that Yeats's doctor, too, had found himself in this part of the world.

The idea for Frank Draper came originally from a conversation with Les Murray—for which many belated thanks.

Thanks to Julianne Schultz at *Griffith Review* for publishing an extract from the novel-in-progress in *GR30: The Annual Fiction Edition* (2010). Thanks to Caroline Baum, Sue Beebe, Tegan Bennett Daylight, Lilia Bernede, Ruth Blair, Ilithyia Bone, Leah Burns, Michelle de Kretser, Stuart Glover, Gail Jones, Richard Neylon, Daniel Perez-Bello, Mark Tredinnick, Brenda Walker, Geordie Williamson, and Charlotte Wood, and to Gail MacCallum, as always, for all their encouraging and helpful conversation and other things along the way.

Thanks to Allen & Unwin: to Jane Palfreyman, Clara Finlay, Ali Lavau, Kathryn Knight, and Louise Cornege in Sydney; to Clare Drysdale and Sam Redman in London. Thanks to Hannah Westland, Jenny Hewson, and Federica Leonardis at Rogers, Coleridge and White. And new thanks to Sarah Branham at Atria Books.

Thanks to the whole family—Hays and Beebes, but particularly

ACKNOWLEDGMENTS

Nigel Beebe and Huxley Beebe—for the time and space to complete this.

And thanks to Les Hay for not minding my imagining this story. It is for him.

This story is a work of fiction. Some of its locations do exist, as did the inspiration for some of its moments. But these events and their characters are the stuff of my imagination.

About the Author

Ashley Hay is the author of six books including the nonfiction narratives *The Secret: The Strange Marriage of Annabelle Milbanke and Lord Byron* (2000), *Gum: The Story of Eucalypts and Their Champions* (2002), and *Museum* (2007; a collaboration with the visual artist Robyn Stacey).

The Body in the Clouds—her first novel—was shortlisted for a number of prizes including categories in the Commonwealth Writers' Prize and the New South Wales and Western Australian Premier's Awards. It was also longlisted for the 2011 International IMPAC Dublin Literary Award. *The Railwayman's Wife*—her second—was awarded the Colin Roderick Award by the Foundation for Australian Literary Studies, and won the People's Choice category in the New South Wales' Premier's Literary Awards. It was also longlisted for the Miles Franklin award.

A former literary editor of *The Bulletin*, she contributes to a number of Australian publications including *The Monthly*, *Australian Geographic*, and *The Australian*. Her essays and short stories have received various prizes and listings, and have appeared in volumes including *Brothers and Sisters* (2009), *Griffith Review*, *The Best Australian Essays* (2003 and 2015), *The Best Australian Short Stories* (2012 and 2013), and *The Best Australian Science Writing* (2012). In 2014, she edited *The Best Australian Science Writing* anthology for that year, and in 2015 she was awarded the Australian Book Review/ Dahl Trust Fellowship.

She lives in Brisbane.